"I mustn't let you think that I can court you," **Barrett said. "It's not possible."**

"I don't care about your affliction." Annie shrugged, the gentleness in her gaze almost taking him out at the knees. "I really don't."

He took in a breath. "I can't court you. I can take you out of your prison today, but you must find a different jailer, and a different path. I have my work. My father. The things that have kept my attention my whole life. You have been a bit of a respite, but we live in two different worlds."

"Only because I haven't been allowed out in society. I've always been a wallflower, even in my own home. But I'm willing to learn to be a part of your world. I would like to. I have already told my parents that I want to go to soirees."

Soirees. This was not about a simple dance or two. No, she would never wish to be a part of his world. It would destroy her, and the only thing that could destroy him would be to see such a thing happen to her.

Author Note

This book started with the glimmer of an idea of a man returning home at night, tripping over his father's whiskey bottle. A man trapped by holding his duty to his father close, and a man disinterested in anything resembling a family.

I wanted my character to grow and be able to feel something. I remembered the story of Helen Keller, who couldn't see or hear, and how one word, *water*, opened her to language and life—and it was through the efforts of one person. One word and one person.

And how much more valuable the effort is when the odds are against success...

Liz Tyner lives with her husband on an Oklahoma acreage she imagines is similar to the ones in the children's book *Where the Wild Things Are*. Her lifestyle is a blend of old and new, and is sometimes comparable to the way people lived long ago. Liz is a member of various writing groups and has been writing since childhood. For more about her, visit liztyner.com.

Books by Liz Tyner

Harlequin Historical

The Notorious Countess
The Wallflower Duchess
Redeeming the Roguish Rake
Saying I Do to the Scoundrel
To Win a Wallflower

The Governess Tales

The Runaway Governess

English Rogues and Grecian Goddesses

Safe in the Earl's Arms
A Captain and a Rogue
Forbidden to the Duke

Visit the Author Profile page at Harlequin.com.

Dedicato a Ornella. Grazie per l'arte che crei.

Chapter One

Falling in love with a shadow, a whisper of husky voice or laughter softer than silk, was impossible.

But when he saw the flash of wrist move in the hallway beyond the door, saw the bracelet slide and heard the innocence, he didn't care that he hadn't believed in love until that moment.

He stilled, only aware of the movements and sounds outside his vision.

Then she was gone. Footsteps pattered away.

He took in a breath, trying to hold the moment close, trying not to let the drone of her father's voice cover the memory of the laughter.

He shook those thoughts away. Love was for people who didn't know how to make money. They needed something to hold on to. But Gavin kept saying that Annie would change Barrett's mind on marriage and love.

Barrett had wagered to let Gavin out of the obligation incurred from sending him to university and Gavin had put up taking care of their father one day a week. Gavin insisted that Barrett had to spend several days in the Carson household before he could declare himself a winner.

'So tell me, Carson…' Barrett forced his lips into the closest resemblance to a smile he could manage and leaned closer to the older man. He knew the power of his gaze. Knew the broadness of his shoulders and knew his voice could put more force behind his words than a fist. 'Tell me more about this flying balloon business you started.'

'It's the wave of the future.' Carson hesitated, moving sideways in his chair, fumbling with the cuff of one sleeve that enveloped his wrist, a tremble to his fingers. 'A wondrous method of transportation.' He glanced down. 'But I believe I've told you all I know about it.'

'Nonsense.' Barrett's trouser legs strained against muscle momentarily when he stood. 'I'd like to return tomorrow and spend a few days with you. Discussing business, of course. Very important. Your words help shape my decisions. You've a wealth of experience, Carson.' And a wealth of hot air. Carson didn't understand that he needed to put his efforts into his chandlery shop and bring it up to snuff before starting any new venture, particularly one so nonsensical as flying balloons.

Carson touched his sleeve in an attempt to straighten a fold of the cloth, but he missed his goal. 'Do…do you really think that's necessary?'

Oh, it had become very necessary the moment Barrett had heard that laugh. He'd not been sure his brother told the truth. But apparently he had. Carson had a daughter who hardly ever attended society events and, Barrett's brother claimed, was more beautiful than either of her sisters. An impossibility—and if his brother hadn't had an insistent gleam in his eyes, Barrett wouldn't have given the words a second thought. Curiosity had propelled Barrett forward and the wager had only cemented his intentions.

The laughter he'd heard lingered in his head, tantalising him. In that second he'd realised he wanted to see the woman, Annie, and hear her voice again.

He bowed to Carson. 'I must thank you for the invitation. I'm quite honoured. I shall arrive tomorrow and I hope seven days is not too short a time for us to become better acquainted.'

'Seven—' Carson's voice squeaked at the end.

'I agree wholeheartedly.' Barrett's strides could never be considered long, but they were stealth and power in one.

'Until tomorrow, then...' He turned. 'And I am almost embarrassed to say this—' he tapped his thigh '—but I've a difficulty walking stairs. If you've a room on the first storey, that would suffice. Perhaps one with a ray of morning sunlight to brighten my spirits.'

The woman's room was on the first storey. He'd see her face.

Then, to the sound of the man's gasp, Barrett stepped into the hallway. His brother stood not far from the door. The barest glance was all the acknowledgement Barrett gave to the smug blink as he walked down the stairs.

'Mr Barrett, a moment...?' His brother's voice.

Barrett didn't stop and Gavin strode behind him, keeping pace.

At the entryway, Barrett kept walking and he hoped Gavin would take the hint.

Outside the door, Barrett paused enough to let his brother step beside him. 'Go away.' Aware of the many windows around them, he kept his voice soft. 'I would prefer people not know we are acquainted.'

'I knew you could not resist—the challenge, or seeing her.' That swagger of Gavin's head—the same Barrett had seen on his father—sent a sizzle of irritation down Barrett's spine.

'I still haven't seen her face,' Barrett said. 'I'm curious. Get me a meeting with her. I just want to see what she looks like. That's all.'

Gavin held two fingers extended and made a walking movement with his right hand, then he reached out with his left and snapped his hand closed over the fingers. 'Last words of the unmarried man.'

'My last words are *go away.*'

Gavin turned on his heel. 'Good day, Mr Barrett. Please take a care with those poultices I mentioned.' His voice rose in volume. 'They'll do you well, but be sure you stop with a single one. Otherwise, before you know it, you'll be trussed up like a big goose waiting for the stewing pot.'

Gavin bounded back into the house.

Barrett unclenched his hand, wondering why he'd ever thought it good to have a brother—except Gavin had told him about this woman, Annie.

His town coach was waiting and Barrett gave a nod to the man in the perch, eyes telling him to keep his seat. Barrett strode to the vehicle door, pulled it open and slid inside with one lunge.

The awe in his brother's voice had caught Barrett's attention when his brother had first spoken of the Carson sisters.

If it weren't for the bracelet sliding on her wrist, he might have been able to put her from his mind and wait out the seven-day wager unhindered. But he wondered what kind of face went with such a gentle laugh and what Annabelle Carson looked like.

He could usually turn his thoughts away from any direction he didn't want them to go, but he couldn't close away the question of the appearance of the woman who had such delicate laughter.

The sound of purity. Unblemished laughter.

If only she'd stepped into the opening so he could have seen her. He drew a fist up and put his elbow against the side of the carriage, feeling cramped in the close quarters, but still unable to put her from his mind.

At the soirées and society events he attended, he never paused to look at the innocent ones sheltered by the chaperons. Work did not stop because the sun set and the music started.

A smile might be halfway on his face, but he put it on much like he did his cravat. He preferred building an empire over having a nice bit of fluff hanging on his arm. The fluff was a weakness for a man who needed adoring eyes gazing up at him in order to build his image of himself.

Barrett closed his mind to the woman, moving his focus to how he would renovate Carson's shop, thinking of the light fixtures, and updates to bring the business out of the seventeen hundreds.

As the carriage slowed at his home, he opened the door before the vehicle came to a complete stop, then jumped free in the last seconds of movement, letting the door swing behind him, knowing the driver would shut it if needed.

He bounded up the stairs to his chamber, forcing his mind to the world around him. In his room, he tossed his coat and upper garments on to the chair he used when donning his boots. The woman's laughter returned to his memory. His trousers landed on the table that framed the foot of the bed. He stretched, head back, eyes closed, arms at his side, fists clenched, reliving each second of the moments she had stood outside the door.

A thump and crash switched his movements into action. He grabbed his dressing gown, throwing it on, the collar on one side folding under at his shoulder. He tied the sash as he rushed from the doorway and up the stairs to his father's room.

Even in the darkness, the shape lying on the floor didn't surprise him.

He reached down, fisted one hand on his father's shirt, the other on the back of the loose trousers, and lifted the wiry shape almost without effort. He only stumbled when he put his bare foot down on a bottle.

In a few strides, he stood at the bedside, and tossed his father on to the bed.

Without turning, he acknowledged the footsteps he'd heard behind him. 'Summers—somehow see he is bathed tomorrow. And air out this room, if possible.'

'Yes.' Summers sauntered to Barrett's side. Neither man moved for a moment.

Barrett thought of the morning's antics. He tilted his head up so he could watch the servant's eyes. 'Has the maid recovered?'

'She's fine. Just a fright. She understands.'

Summers, who only had two speeds—slow and blink-fast—was the only man who'd ever been close to besting Barrett in a brawl and it had taken Barrett longer to recover than he'd wished.

'We can't leave him alone any time at all. He'll burn down the house or attack one of the smaller servants.' Absently, Barrett clasped his left hand over his right fist, tracing the scars.

'He was asleep when I left him with the maid.' Summers had no emotion in his voice.

'Or pretending…' Barrett stopped. 'If you absolutely must leave him in the future, make sure he has at least two people with him. You and I are the only ones to be allowed alone here. He's stronger than he looks. Always has been.'

'He's begun to get loud. Shout out the window. The neighbours…'

'Do the best you can. And don't turn your back on him. Ever.' Barrett felt the weight of his decision. The sensible thing would be to have his father confined. And he couldn't understand why he didn't do it. It wasn't as if he particularly cared for the man.

'For now, just let him be and keep the women away from him.' He paused. 'Go back to bed. I'll sit with him for the rest of the night, but I doubt he'll as much as roll over. He'll be having pleasant dreams.' Dreams of taking food from the mouths of others, perhaps. Or using a lit candle, planning to catch a dog's fur on fire. He'd only tried that once, though. Barrett looked at the scar that ran along the side of his forefinger to his thumb and covered his first knuckle.

What other people considered nightmares, his father considered fairy tales.

'A brandy before you retire, sir?' Summers asked.

Barrett shook his head and ran one hand through his locks. Then he pulled out the collar bunched at his neck, straightening it. 'Not if this is what it might do to me. If one of the maids is about, you might send her up with tea.'

He heard Summers leave, then Barrett turned, walked to the overstuffed chair, righted it and sat. He'd almost asked Summers to put a pillow over his father's face. But he couldn't say for certain Summers wouldn't do it.

His thoughts drifted to the innocent laughter he'd heard earlier in the day. His brother would jest at him if Gavin knew he thought of the woman. Gavin had been right. The Carson daughter did pique Barrett's interest. But no matter.

He closed his eyes, rested his head against the upholstery of the chair and imagined a world filled with the gentle laughter that he'd heard.

Annie raised her head at the sound of the knock. 'Come in,' she said, holding her place in the book.

Her father peered around the door. 'Dearest, we're going to have a guest and you'll need to stay in the floor above this one.'

She wrinkled her nose. 'Is my aunt bringing friends?'

'No. This is a visitor. A man. I do business with him.' Her father stood, feet planted, his voice persuasion soft.

'A visitor? One?' She stared at his face. 'And I'm to move?'

Her father nodded, his jaw working sideways.

The rose room was empty. In fact, both of her sisters' rooms were vacant. Honour was in Scotland and Laura had married a man who'd courted her through letters.

'Besides, you are getting older now and it will be comfortable for you to have your own storey.'

'I'm to stay above?' She glanced at her book, not really seeing it, and then looked again at his face. 'Are you sure?'

'Very.' He nodded, his lips thinning. 'Our guest is a man. His father, the Viscount, is ill and our guest handles the duties for the family. I want you to stay from underfoot, Annie. While he's here at least. We'll be discussing important matters. You must not be a distraction for me.' His face relaxed. 'Please, dearest. He and I will be busy. He wants to change the chandlery shops. He thinks the improvements I planned are not the right ones.'

She paused, studying her father's face. 'He's a viscount's son?'

Her father kept his mouth closed while he gave a quick nod. 'Yes. But not an important one.'

'Not an important one?' She leaned forward, trying to figure out what her father was thinking.

'No. A title is not everything.' He checked his pocket watch. 'It's a lot. But not everything.'

Annie opened her mouth. 'I'm glad to hear you say that.'

'Well, it's not that I didn't want your sisters to marry well. I admit it. I admit it freely. And I do want you to have the opportunity they squandered. But this man, well, he is not marriage minded.'

'I'm not either.'

'Bite your tongue.' He put the watch back in his pocket, the chain dangling. 'Marriage is everything. The right marriage is everything. And your sisters did not understand. You will do us all proud and wed someone who will bring respect to the family.'

He lowered his chin and looked at her as if looking down the sights of a gun. 'You'll marry well. You'll be happy. Just like your mother and I. And your children will thank you.'

She bit the inside of her cheek, waiting.

'This is enough of this talk,' he said. 'You'll be going to the upstairs room and you will be staying there until you come to your senses.' He bent his head down. 'I did not appreciate how you stayed off to yourself at Lady Cruise's birthday celebration. You hardly spoke one word during your dance with Lord Richard. His father is a duke, and even if the lad is only the fourth son that's still a duke's son.' He raised his hand in tandem with his face. 'You hardly looked at him during the whole dance.'

'Father. Have you ever listened to him? Yes, he's a duke's son and he can say that in five languages.'

His jaw shuddered when he shook his head. 'Enough. I will not allow you to throw away such opportunities like your sisters did. We will do right by you.'

'By sending me to the *attic*? Where the maid sleeps?' When a viscount's son visited? That was so unlike her father. She would have expected him to have pulled her by both arms into the room with the man.

'In this case, yes.'

'What's wrong with him?'

'Nothing,' her father said. 'But he's spent his life…

not like the Duke's son. Lord Richard is admirable. Respectable. And I know he thinks highly of you.'

Before she could stop herself, her eyes flicked to the ceiling.

'You will stay out of the way for the next few days.' Her father's brows met in the centre.

She tucked a finger into the book. 'I have no wish to interfere. I just don't wish to move to the upper floor. Although perhaps it will seem more lively with Myrtle about. I never know what she might say when I ask her for something. She once returned three times to ask me what I sent her for. It was easier to get it myself.'

'She's a good servant.' Her father moved his head so that he looked into her eyes. 'Myrtle has served my family her whole life. Loyal to the last heartbeat.'

'But both my sisters' rooms are empty now. The guest will have a place to stay there.'

He shook his head. 'No. He is here to discuss business. We cannot risk you disrupting it. And it would not be proper for you to be near. Besides, he is not interested in a marriage. Lord Richard is. End of subject.'

She closed the book and watched her hand as she ran her fingers over the spine. 'Do you not think I am wise enough to make my own decisions?'

'Of course you are.'

'I would sometimes like to… Perhaps I should go stay with my cousin while the visitor is here? I would like that. You always insist she visit me and never allow me to take the coach to their home. I hardly ever leave the house and, if I do, it is always with you and Mother.'

'I do not want you, my only sensible daughter, to risk becoming ill like your mother. Your mother has

never been the same since your birth.' His bottom lip
quivered. 'But, of course, we are ever thankful for you
and we would not change a thing.'

She could not answer. She hated her mother's frailty
as well, but she would risk her own health to step outside the doors.

'It is only because I care for you.' His chest heaved.
'If you do not wish to wed, I can accept that. But if
you do wed, then you will marry a man of standing.
It is for your benefit to marry well.'

'I know.'

'Promise me you'll keep out of sight while my guest
is here. And not forget like you did last time. I heard
you in the hallway.'

'I won't forget.'

It would be no use arguing with him. He only cared
for her safety and happiness. She smiled at him. He
nodded, glanced at the book in her hands and left.

She turned back to the novel although she wasn't
fond of Swift. She didn't feel like reading.

Twisting the bracelet on her arm, she stared at
it. The circle of sapphire stones in the silver setting
swallowed her arm. But what good did it do to have
jewellery if no one ever saw it?

If she had mentioned a wish for a dozen horses, her
parents would have put them at her fingertips, but not
at her disposal.

She knew the man had been in the sitting room the
day before. Had heard the deep rumble of his voice
and had followed it. Then the physician had almost
caught her eavesdropping, but she'd managed a laugh
and told him he had a smudge of jam on his face. That
smudge of jam had diverted his attention.

The only person besides relatives and servants to visit was the physician. She didn't particularly like him, but he did have a rather pleasant voice when he talked to her mother. A strong voice. Almost the same as the man she'd heard speaking with her father.

Only the Viscount's son's voice rumbled a bit more. Didn't sound so friendly. Almost a growl.

She wondered what he looked like.

She stood, went to the drawn shades, and moved one aside enough to see out. She couldn't even see the street. Just another house across the way. Now she would be one storey higher above the road. One level further from the rest of the world. And fewer windows.

She wanted be with her sister. Knew in her heart that her sister, Honour, needed her. It would hurt her mother if Annie left, but Annie couldn't help worrying about Honour. Laura was fine, she was certain. She'd run off to be with the man she loved.

Without them, life was one day after another. Everything the same. She knew she could find a way to bring Honour home and to reconcile her parents to it. Yes, there would be tears. Disgrace, perhaps. But the family could rebuild itself, or just accept things as they would be.

Chapter Two

Barrett nodded at Carson's recounting of stitching used in the air balloons as he and Carson returned to the house. The man's notion of a rousing evening left a little to be desired. It didn't improve with the tenth telling. Barrett had had to insist they return home early as he couldn't bear another moment of the camaraderie.

Barrett gave the servant his hat, letting Carson ramble on. Three days. He could not take another balloon story and he had yet to see the daughter. Several times he'd caught a whiff of perfume in the air or heard skittering noises above his head, and just a hint of a voice that he'd heard only once before. He remained in the house, surprised that he was willing to stay, but aware he'd always had a persistence inside him that he couldn't quite understand.

Carson remained at the doorway, giving the butler instructions to pass along to the housekeeper to pass along to the cook. Barrett continued up the stairs.

As he ascended the stairs, he realised she stood at the top, watching him.

A slender woman, with little of her face left over

if you subtracted her eyes and lips and hair. She was seemingly frozen at the sight of him.

It would not have been out of place for her to be bathed in sunbeams and yet she hardly seemed the incomparable that his brother had spoken of. More like a whisper of a woman than the temptress his brother described.

He walked into her presence, unable to look away in those moments, trying to discern what was different and yet not staring. 'You must be Miss Carson.'

She nodded, dipping her head to him.

'Annabelle,' her father called out behind Barrett, 'you are supposed to be in your room.' His voice intensified so much that Barrett turned to him.

'I thought you were to be out all evening,' she responded.

The man moved up the stairs with more speed than Barrett would have thought him capable of.

Barrett stepped aside.

'You are not to be bothering our guests.' Carson's face had reddened and Barrett didn't think it all from the exertion of running up the stairs.

'It's no bother,' Barrett reassured Carson.

'She's not to be about,' Carson said, shooing her away with his hand. 'I've told her many times that she is not to interfere with business.'

The smile left her face. 'Yes, Father. I was just going to see how Myrtle is doing. Her feet were hurting her so, as she has been running up and down the stairs to make sure I am fine.'

'You are not to be traipsing after the servants. It is their duty to care for you. I would not want Mr Barrett to get the wrong impression of you.'

She looked down, but Barrett wasn't sure if it was submissive or to hide her eyes. He'd seen the set of her jaw.

'Go to your room,' Carson instructed.

'Wait.' Barrett held out a palm in Carson's direction. 'It's her house. I wouldn't want to displace her. And my only impression seems to be that she understands someone else's discomfort.'

'She doesn't mind staying in her room,' Carson said. 'Annie is used to it. Prefers it most of the time.' He spoke the last words almost as an accusation.

'I'm sure she wishes to keep out of the way. And I would imagine she does quite well at it.' Barrett could attest to that. He'd tried for three days to see her in the family quarters and apparently the only time she would be there was when no one was around.

'You don't realise what it is like to have a daughter,' Carson eyed Barrett. 'Annie is the sunshine of our days. She tried to keep her older sisters from upsetting us. She's the youngest and above all else I want her protected from business and the strife life can bring.'

'My sisters—I have two,' Annie said, lifting her eyes. 'Father is concerned that I don't follow in their footsteps. They've both recently…moved away.'

'Laura married and Honour is visiting family because she could not be content at home. Annie is all we have left. And we don't want anyone getting any wrong ideas.' He glanced at Barrett. 'She's half-betrothed, but I must beg your confidence in the matter.'

'Of course you have it,' Barrett said.

Annie took in a breath and stared at her father. Barrett caught the apologetic glance her father gave her.

'I'm sure there are few men who are good enough

for a woman who might be concerned for a staff member's feet,' Barrett said.

She turned to him. A glimmer of appreciation flashed across her face.

Carson nodded. 'It is indeed difficult to find someone suitable. I'd thought the man her sister Laura married half-good enough for her and—' he shook his head so that his chin wiggled '—he sorely disappointed me.'

'Perhaps Miss Annie and your wife could join us for a cup of tea,' Barrett said.

Now Carson turned to him, suspicion in his eyes. 'The women would not be interested in the things we men like.' He clasped his hands behind his back and frowned at Barrett.

Annie smiled, but it dimmed her eyes. 'I would not.' She turned and walked down the hallway, head proud as any peer, and disappeared around a corner. The servants' stair.

'I don't remember ever seeing your other daughters about London,' Barrett said.

'No,' Carson said. 'They chose to leave. I expect them both to return eventually, sadder but wiser.' Carson stared at the path Annie had taken to leave. 'Sons would have been so much easier to raise…'

The older man walked to the door of the sitting room, went through the doorway and then, within seconds, returned for Barrett, seemingly forgetting about his daughters. 'Oh, and I've some balloon drawings to show you. I sent for them and they arrived while we were out.'

'Certainly,' Barrett said. He didn't need drawings of balloons. He had something else entirely to visualise. In fact, based on the exterior of the house, the rooms he'd seen and Annie's departure up the stairway, he knew the house as well as the one he lived in. Annie's movement up the stairs had filled in the last question in his mind.

'Dearest.' Her mother stopped at the doorway, head down, her hand shielding her eyes. 'Please close the curtain. I fear my head is going to start hurting. I see the little waves of pain prancing in front of my eyes.'

Annie turned, noticing the green beads sparkling on her mother's slippers.

'Of course.' The curtain fluttered back into place.

'Would you please read to me until the physician arrives?' Her mother's voice wavered.

She held an arm out and Annie guided her to the darkened sitting room, helping her sit. Annie picked up the footstool. Raising her feet, her mother waited for Annie to put the stool directly under the slippers. The older woman settled in place, fidgeting into a comfortable position.

'I could fetch you something from the apothecary. I'd take Myrtle for a chaperon,' Annie offered.

'Nonsense, dear,' her mother muttered, waving a hand but still keeping her eyes closed. 'The housekeeper can send someone else. You have a weak constitution. I won't have you catching your death from that tainted air. And please hand me the cinnamon biscuits.' She waved an arm. 'The physician has had them made to his instructions. I can see why he has been physician to so many families of the *ton*. He is so knowledgeable and so caring.'

Annie stepped away from her mother and lifted the tray of confections, the scent of them trailing behind her as she walked. She put them on the table at the side of her mother. Her mother took the nearest one, leaned back in her chair, shut her eyes and crunched at the edges of the biscuit, tasting more than eating.

Annie looked over her shoulder at the flowing velvet covering the windows. Some days she didn't care if the air was unhealthy or the people all carried the plague and vermin crawled about. Some days she would just like to go to the shops without having to fill the carriage with people who must go with her.

Then her mother peered over Annie's shoulder, and the older woman's face brightened. 'The physician can verify that you need to take care and stay inside.'

Annie moved, her eyes following her mother's gaze.

'Your mother is right.' The physician stood in the doorway, perfectly dressed, perfectly perfect and very perfectly annoying.

Now she was sure she didn't like the man. If he wished to keep her locked away, too, then she had no use for him. The house was bigger than a crypt, but just as closed. Well, no. The people in the crypt had more freedom.

He walked in, placing his bag on the floor, next to the pedestal with the bust of King George.

'Oh…my…' The physician stared at her. His eyes widened. Then he put a hand to his coat pocket and pulled out a monocle.

Annie leaned backwards as she pulled in her breath. Her mother straightened, as if waiting for a life-or-death pronouncement in a trial.

The doctor paused. He turned to her mother. 'How long has your daughter been this way?'

'What?' her mother gasped.

In one stride he stood in front of Annie. He held the glass against his eye and peered at her. The scent of dried weeds tainted the air. The man smelled like a poultice. 'Her skin. It's too thin.'

Annie didn't move. Her stomach knotted. She would be a near-invalid like her mother. She would be trapped forever. Her breath caught. She put her hand over her heart.

His head darted around, vermin-like, and he did all but wiggle his whiskers. 'I can't see straight through to the bones exactly. But I'm sure they have the texture of sawdust now.'

He lowered the glass to his side and bowed his head. 'I would hate to see one so young forever… Well, forever not with us.'

Annie took a step back. She had to get away from his words. And if she was going to die anyway, she'd rather do it away from the house.

'I can save your life. Should it be necessary.' He raised his face. Then he saw the look in her eyes. 'Don't worry, Miss Annabelle. I have a cure.' He held out a hand in a calming gesture. 'A very reliable cure.'

Her mother tensed. 'What's wrong with her?'

'She has epidemeosis.' He patted a hand to his chest. 'That term is my own as I am the first to be aware of it. In the rest of the world it's unknown—for now.'

'What does that mean?'

'Well. Nothing really.' He blinked his words away. 'The cure is so simple as to be…simple, for lack of a better word.'

'But her illness?'

'It's merely a lack of bile. A serious bile blockage.'

'The humours again,' her mother whispered, eyes

widening. 'Those devilish humours. They never stay in order.'

'Yes. But she's young. She'll recover fast. I just would not want it to hurt her spleen. If it reaches the stage where it damages the spleen...' He shook his head, and expelled a lingering breath, seeming to paint the room with his concern.

'I will recover?' Annie asked. She clutched the back of the chair, using it to keep herself upright.

'Of course.' The physician turned in her direction, but he glanced briefly at the ceiling, as if he'd heard the words before and perhaps did not even believe himself.

Annie sensed something wrong, but she wasn't sure if he lied about her recovery or something else.

Then he took the manner of a tutor. 'It seems the night air right before dawn can build strength. By exposing a person to a small amount of some poisons, they can build a resistance. Edward Jenner discovered this with his cowpox theory when he created a way to save us from smallpox.' He puffed at the glass of the monocle, blowing away a bit of fuzz. 'But we mustn't be overzealous. Give me a few moments and I'll search out the room which has the highest chance of filtering the air in the right amounts.'

'Are you sure it will help?' Annie asked.

'It's very simple. You'll have to sit alone, awake, in the room between four and five in the morning—breathing. Those are the best hours for the air. You can read, or sew or whatever suits your fancy.'

He tapped the monocle against his leg and stared at her mother. 'I would certainly pass the word throughout the staff and family that they are definitely not to disturb her at this time. It seems the humours are most likely to be put askew by the people who are closest to her the most often. I—' He put his monocle away. 'I could speak with her for hours and it wouldn't bother her as I've hardly been near her. But there's something shared, a miasma of sorts, in people who have been closest to her... She needs to be away from them for a bit.'

'Are you certain it will cure her?'

'Oh, yes. I have studied this extensively. For years. I wrote a paper on it.'

'Well, let me know which room and I will tell the maid to wake her in time for her recovery regime.'

'I don't want to do that,' Annie said. She didn't trust the man.

The doctor looked at her as if her spleen had just spoken back to him.

'Miss Annabelle. You must. You have no choice. I have my reputation to keep.'

'You've not been able to cure Mother's headaches.'

Her mother leaned towards Annabelle, reached out a hand and swatted at Annie's arm. 'They are so much better, though. And the lavender oils he has the maids rub into my feet... It always eases my pain.'

The doctor raised a brow in one of those *I told you so* gestures.

'Very well.' She stood and looked at her mother. 'But only if you promise to let me go somewhere the next week.'

Her mother's eyes narrowed. 'Where do you wish to go?'

'Anywhere. Anywhere but a soirée or a gathering. I would just like to not feel I am being coddled every moment.'

'Your father will forbid it.' Her mother's lids lowered. Her eyes drooped closed and she pinched the bridge of her nose. 'My pain just increased tenfold.'

'We will get that corrected right away.' The doctor stepped forward, but glanced at Annie. 'I will discuss which room for you will be best and I expect you to be there from four to five in the morning.'

'Yes, Annie.' Her mother opened one eye. 'Do as the physician says.'

Annie left. She would do as the big miasma of a physician said, but if it became too tedious, she would walk in the gardens, darkness or not. She was tired of being a puppet.

Chapter Three

Annie bundled her dressing gown tight and took the lamp from the servant and waved the woman away. She twisted her hair up, unwilling to have the wisps tickling her face. After pinning it, she added the jewelled one—the pin her grandmother had given her.

The physician had told her mother to send her to the portrait room. Annie hated the Granny Gallery. It had apparently become a tradition for every woman of her heritage to have a portrait painted and, if the woman didn't like the portrait, she would commission another and another until one finally pleased her—and then the artist would soon be asked to paint a miniature, or two, or ten.

Annie walked into the room, past the two shelves of miniatures her mother had insisted Annie and her sisters pose for. She held watercolours in her hand and a sketchbook under her arm. The barest flutter of air puffed the closed curtains. The doctor had insisted the window be opened the width of a finger. No more. No less.

Eyes from musty portraits almost overlapping stared at her. The ancestors. They'd probably all died in the house.

She put the lamp on the table between the chairs, which faced away from the window. They were the only two chairs in the room. Both squat, flat, and with clawed feet. The chairs were heirlooms and probably looked the same as the day they were made because no one willingly sat on something so uncomfortable.

This was the room where her mother put the furnishings that one had to keep because they'd been in the family forever, but that she would never have purchased.

And now Annie sat in the middle of it, thinking of which road would be best to take her from the house.

She rose, prepared her watercolours and stepped over to one of the portraits of her great-great-aunt. Very carefully, she took the wetted brush and added a beauty mark just outside the eye. It hardly showed against the oils. She sighed. She wasn't even allowed the true paints of an artist.

She put the brush away, crossed her arms and paced back and forth in front of the trapped eyes.

If she went to find her sister, her mother and father would be desolate. She was the good daughter. The Carson sister who wasn't wild. The one that took after the Catmull side of the family. And now she was inheriting her mother's afflictions and she was standing in a room of discarded furniture. She jerked her arms open, her hands fisted, and grunted her displeasure. Making a jab at the world which had trapped her. She punched again.

'Keep your thumb on the outside of the fist, don't swing the arm and thrust forward with the motion. It works better.' A masculine rumble of words hit her ears.

She jerked around and backwards at the same time.

A man stood in the doorway. Although it wasn't that he really stood in the doorway. More like he let it surround him. A dark shape with an even darker frame. The man she'd seen earlier.

He took one step closer to her and she took in a quick bit of air so she could remain standing.

He wore a coat and cravat and could have been stepping out to attend a soirée, except no one would think him in a social mood with the straight line of his lips and the hair hanging rough around his face. He needed a shave—really needed a shave.

His eyes looked as if he'd just woken, but not the softened look of someone gently waking from slumber—more the studied look of a predatory animal ready to swing out a paw at the little morsel who'd dared disturb the beast.

She moved back.

He extended his arm in one controlled move, but she didn't feel threatened.

He made a fist, held his elbow at his side, and moved the hand straight forward, but angled away from her. 'This way. You don't want to swing wide. Gives someone an easier chance to block.'

Her eyes travelled down the length of his arm, past his elbow, and lodged at his fist. Four curled fingers and then a thumb. The scarred thumb alone could have flattened her.

'Yes.' She nodded her head and moved her eyes to his elbow, his shoulder, past the chin, right to his eyes and then one dart back to his chin. She didn't know what she'd said yes to, but at that moment, it was the best she could do.

She forced herself to look into his eyes and felt she could see the solid wall behind them.

'It would not matter if I kept my thumb in or out if I should hit you,' she said.

'I would think not.' He shrugged. 'But, I'm sturdier than most.'

She nodded. 'Especially stepping out of the shadows. You're rather...daunting.'

'I try to be. It helps.' No smile to soften the words. He meant them.

He walked forward, picked up the light and held it high. It flickered on her face. She stepped backwards into the curtains and her fingers clasped them tight.

'I did not believe it possible,' he said. 'I thought my eyes lied and my memory as well.'

Now *he* examined her.

With splayed fingers, she touched her cheek. 'I've been ill.'

He choked out a laugh, lowering the lamp to the table. The side of his mouth curled. A smile that turned into a private chuckle before it reached his eyes. He looked away, seeming to discount her, and his own words. 'Then I can hardly wait to see what you look like when you recover.'

'Sir.' She cleared her throat, because it hardly seemed to work. 'I believe that is improper for you to say.'

'Of all my choices, it was the most proper,' he said. 'But I do beg your pardon.' A pause. 'As I should.' Words exactly perfect. Emotionless.

Now he stood so close the light flickered on his face. He had more ragged edges than smooth. She could not believe her father would invite this man into their home.

But this man would understand others defending themselves.

And if she were to go out without a true chaperon, she might need to take care.

Presently all she needed protecting from was her embroidery needle and that she might tumble out of the chair when she fell asleep stitching. But by Tuesday morning, that might change. She was ready to take her chances with the outside world. 'So how does one hit someone effectively?'

A muscle in his jaw tightened. 'Punch straight. Keep your elbow as close to the side as possible. Don't swing out. Move like a lever. Not like a windmill. A windmill...' he demonstrated, holding his arm straight from the shoulder and moving his fist forward '...is too easy to block.'

'I will never be able to punch someone,' she said, feeling helpless. She would never be able to go after her sister. 'I'm always surrounded by chaperons,' she said, concluding her thoughts out loud. 'You would think I am gold, the way my parents guard me.'

True lightness touched his eyes. 'Perhaps you are.'

Then darkness moved into his face. 'You are standing alone in a room with a man you know nothing of. The world is full of evil and evil enjoys waiting for just the right moment.' He stared at her. 'Evil is patient. It only needs one moment of opportunity.' His eyes narrowed and he leaned in. 'One moment.'

'You were invited by my father. He makes no decisions rashly.'

His slow intake of breath through his nose raised his body enough to show a muted dismissal of any disagreement she made to his statement.

'I can scream.'

'You would be surprised,' his voice thundered, 'how little noise can carry—even on the most silent night.' He waited and cocked his head. Listening.

Then his voice took on an innocence. 'Well, perhaps my words were not loud enough to summon help for you. Scream,' he said. 'See who comes running.'

'It would be embarrassing for you.'

'Just say I startled you in the shadows. You thought me an intruder. A ghost. A raging bear. You were sleepwalking. Whatever.'

'I could say you accosted me. Do you not realise the danger in that for you?'

'I'll take that risk.' The muscles at the side of his face moved. 'I've taken many worse.'

He gave a twitch of his shoulders and blandness settled in his eyes. He took two steps to the door. When he touched the door, he moved with liquid stealth and turned back to her. 'And how truly unsettling for me to be thought a rogue.'

Instead of leaving, he shut the door. He leaned against it, arms relaxed, hands behind his back, trapped by his body against the wood. 'Now. Embarrass me. Scream. And not just once.'

Her stomach thudded, but she wasn't truly afraid. He'd put his hands behind him and he had one of the *I told you so* looks in his eyes.

Silence engulfed them. 'I'm not trying to scare you, nor am I jesting.' He spoke in measured tones. 'Your voice cannot carry through wood and stop dreams of dancing angels. By the time the first shout was out of your mouth, my hand could be over it and, if someone awakened, they would think it an imagination.

They might lie awake for a moment to listen, then sleep would grab them again, telling them that they heard nothing.'

She rubbed her arms, trying to soothe away the chill. 'If you're trying to make me uncomfortable, you are succeeding.'

He opened the door and stood aside. 'You can leave at any time you wish.'

He paused a second. 'Did you hear my last words? Really hear them? *You can leave any time you wish.* Why would I even think it necessary to say such a thing to you? Is this not your house? Where you are safest in the entire world? I take it for granted that I am stronger than you and can control you because you are smaller.'

She couldn't untangle his words. They just didn't make sense to her.

'Make a fist properly and use it properly.' His chin lowered. 'You can leave after punching me. Fair enough?'

'Not fair at all.' She stared at the beast in front of her.

'A fist,' he commanded.

She did.

'Thumb out.' He stepped forward.

She did.

'Not like that. Your thumb is in a straight line.'

With two steps and keeping his body to the side so he did not block her exit, he moved closer. His eyes locked on hers for a moment, no threat, and a softer question behind them. 'May I?' He raised his hand level with her side as he spoke.

With one fingertip reaching out, he rested it at the

base of her fist. Then with his other hand, he slid her thumb down until it rested against the outside space after the second knuckle of her hand, making sure her fingertips folded in, and her hand had a square shape to it.

This beast of a man touched her as lightly as if she were made of silk. His fingers, so tender against her hand, shot bolts of awareness into her. She couldn't move her hand.

'It might save your life some day.' His voice rolled over her, reaching deeper into her than the touch had.

'I doubt that.' She took a step back, causing his hands to fall to his side. 'I am careful. To have you in my house is an aberration.'

'True.' His eyes registered the jab and lightened. 'But aberrations happen and sometimes more than once. You may still shout if you wish. As many times as you like.' He shrugged. 'Perhaps someone would come instantly to your rescue. Perhaps you would see how much longer it takes for someone to rescue you than you realise, or perhaps I would truly see how safe you are. Convince me of how well you are watched.'

'What kind of game are you playing?'

'I want you to see how much your survival could depend on you and how much fighting back is the best, or even only, friend you may have at hand.'

'I am coddled. Every moment of my life.'

'Which makes you a perfect victim.'

His gaze lingered on hers. He held up his hand, fingers splayed, but curved inwards. 'Hit me. Hard.' His voice softened. 'Just don't hurt your hand.'

'No.'

He brought his hand closer. 'Hit me.'

'I can't.'

'Why not?'

'I hardly know you. And though I don't like you at all, I don't have any wish to hurt—*much* wish to hurt you.'

He shrugged. 'I've hit men I didn't know at all. And men I knew quite well.'

'I will not hit you. It'll only hurt my hand.'

The tension in his face relaxed. 'You're right.' He moved to the sofa and pulled a pillow into his hands and raised it. 'Hit gently, then. Just to feel the movement. Not the windmill, but the direct hit.'

'I said no.' She looked at him. 'It's as if you like to fight.'

'I do.'

He shook his hand sideways, emphasising the location for her punch. 'I've never *not* hit anyone who asked me to.' His lips curved. 'Chaperoned Miss who cannot even scream.' His face moved closer. His breath burned at her cheek. 'You may hit me any time you wish, buttercup.'

His face not moving away, chin so close she could almost feel the bristles.

'A woman designed to do nothing but wed well.'

The words jabbed her skin.

'You're a sweet confection only to look at, a well-designed form to display jewellery. If you've a thought in your head, you bat it away with your eyelashes so it will not confuse you.'

He moved around her, circling. 'You're dandelion fluff. The feathers in this pillow have more of a brain than you.'

She swung, straight to the chin.

His left hand moved up, his fingers trapping her wrist before it touched him. With a soft clasp, he moved her hand away from his face.

Then his eyes flinched and he tensed. He snapped his fingers back from her.

She touched her skin, to cover the heat his grasp had left behind. 'If you only did that to show you're stronger than I, you proved it. To yourself, I suppose. But I already knew it.'

He threw down the pillow. Again he raised his hand, palm to her and fingers open to clasp her punch. 'Hit it.' His voice now had the raggedness of anger. He shook the right hand again. 'Don't be scared, Miss Fluff. Don't be afraid.'

Again she refused.

He leaned in. His eyelids dropped, humour and venom mixed, even as his voice softened. 'Pretend I took your favourite doll.'

She punched out, force behind her arm. He didn't clasp his fingers around hers, but moved back with the hit. 'Better.'

All movement of the room stilled while their eyes locked.

'Again,' he commanded. 'And don't look at where your fist is going. Your eyes tell me your plans. Before you tried to hit my face, you looked at my chin. I saw your movements before they were made. Watch my face. *Read* my actions. Lie to me with your eyes.'

'Why?' She let the word flow with her breathing. 'Why are you doing this?'

After gazing at her for a second, he dropped his arm. 'Because everyone should know how to protect themselves. I was taught it by my father.'

Thoughts raced. Yes. A father might teach his son to box. But why was he doing this to her?

'Apparently you did not hear that my mother died from falling down the stairs. Breaking her neck.'

She nodded. 'Well, yes—I think.' Perhaps she'd heard it. But it was a very long time ago. 'My condolences on her passing, but what has that to do with—?'

The glare from his face would have stopped a horse from rushing ahead.

She said nothing, stepping back.

'I was in the house that night.'

His sigh was silent. He waited long enough to blink. He frowned, shrugging away the words. 'Servants carried her upstairs and put her on her bed. My grandmother instructed everyone exactly how Mother's hair should be prepared and what clothes she should wear and told them to be quick about it. For the first time, she seemed to want my mother to be beautiful.'

Annie tightened her arms around her midsection, imagining Barrett watching his mother's death. His eyes showed no reflection of the memories. In fact, he seemed more interested in how she would respond.

Annie remained stationary, hiding in herself as best she could.

Annie's father had told her when her grandmother had passed on. That afternoon, her parents had asked her sisters if they wished to say goodbye. She and her sisters had held hands and walked into her grandmother's room. Her grandmother had seemed to be sleeping with her prayer book in her hands and her favourite miniature of her husband placed against the book.

'My mother was gone,' he continued. 'Grandmother

was dancing around her and saying what a shame one so beautiful died so young. I didn't realise Grandmother considered my mother beautiful.' He touched his upper lip. 'Mother had a broken tooth and all my grandmother had ever called her was Snaggletooth.'

'That is a cruel name.'

'She had her own version of endearments.' He moved his fingers from his lip, twitched a shoulder and held out his palm for a half-second before his hand fell to his side.

'At least she realised at the end that your mother was beautiful.'

'I suspect she realised it all along.' He stepped away, touching the lamp, and turned the wick higher, as if trying to get more light on Annie. 'I often had a lot of time in my childhood to do nothing but think and listen. I don't think the servants realised how their voices could carry or that I might be nearby.'

His head tilted a bit and he gauged Annie's reaction, and she didn't know exactly how she was supposed to react. Or what he watched for. She didn't know what he expected from her. She didn't think he wanted sympathy, or platitudes. But she had nothing else to offer and she didn't know what he was looking for.

She couldn't really take in what Barrett had said to her. He was talking about seeing his mother's *death*. Every word had the resonance of truth in it, but it sounded cold. Unfeeling. As if he talked about a Drury Lane performance that bored him.

She truly didn't know how to respond. She grasped for words that seemed right to say in a situation where someone talked about death. Nothing seemed to fit, but she had to say something.

'I am so sorry. To lose a loved one in such a way… But you couldn't have saved her from an accident.'

'I might have—helped her. Somehow. I pacify myself with the thought that I was only six.' He parted his lips slightly. 'The last thing—'

She'd already started her next words and they rushed out of her mouth. 'That is much too young to lose a mother.'

Then she realised she'd interrupted him. She'd spoken a moment too soon. His shoulders relaxed. Whatever he'd been going to say next was lost to her. She wanted to hear it and she didn't think he'd known whether he should say it or not.

'My mother told me that I had been a gift that she claimed had been found inside a big heart-shaped pie served to her for breakfast. She said she'd been quite surprised to poke her fork inside and hear a baby cry. She said the fork is how I got my navel.' He touched the buttons of his waistcoat over his stomach. 'She repeated the story several times. A strange thing to remember of her.'

Now his words moved in a different direction and she couldn't pull back time to find out what he'd meant to say earlier. But she wanted to know. She wanted to ask, but it was his mother. She couldn't interrogate him. 'A mother's loss would hurt anyone.'

'I did not shed a tear then or in the year afterward. I was six. I had to be a man.'

She moved back. Her heels touched the wall, she gripped the curtain, but she looked him in the eye. 'You didn't shed a tear. For your *mother*?'

He looked at her. Just looked. 'Fine, then. Years later, on the thirteenth of June, I cried buckets and buckets.' His voice held no emotion. His head tilted a bit. 'Feel better now?'

'Her birthday?'

'No.' His eyes narrowed in thought and he took a second before answering. 'I just realised I have no idea when her birthday was, or even the day she died. I wonder if the man of affairs knows. Not that it matters.'

'What of her parents? Her family? Couldn't you ask them?'

'I have no connection to them. I met her brother when he arrived a few months later to give condolences, but Father saw that the visit was short. Neither she nor her family were a match for the world.'

'I don't live in the same world you do.'

'You think that. You think it now. Even your father with all his nonsense knows—'

Her mouth opened and she rushed her words again.

'Do not insult my father. You are a guest in his house.' She'd thought him respectful, but now she wasn't sure. She knew her father's stories carried on and wandered, but she hoped her father had not joined his business with a viper.

'My pardon.' He moved, a bow of dismissal, and turned. 'I made an error and I know I will not change a path a person is determined to take. You do as you wish and so do I. Parents can only delay or detour. Pity.'

His shoulders relaxed and he stepped to the door.

'I wish you well.' Now he said the platitude, but mixed it with a condescending air.

'Wait,' she said. Temper pushed her voice.

He stopped and, without wasted effort, rotated to

see her face. She wasn't used to someone dismissing her so easily. She *could* ask him questions.

'Why didn't you cry for your mother?'

He didn't answer. He studied her face. His eyes didn't criticise, they just waited for his thoughts to form or for him to choose his words. She didn't know which.

His voice held the gravel of someone who might be ready to doze off. 'I may have been only six, but I understood the world around me even then. Mother and I lived in the same house, but just as your parents seclude you from strangers, I was secluded as well. Mother played with me for half an hour a day before the governess took me away. Before I had the first solid bite of food in my mouth, I was slated to learn the family business, in all ways.'

She could see past the orbs of his eyes. Her chest tightened. He meant it.

'Mother was a gentle spirit. Tirelessly in over her head at the choice of whether to ask for a peach or apple tart.' He laughed, but the sound had a darkness mixed in that she'd never heard before.

'Father probably chose her for what he saw as a lack of spirit.' He put his head back, looking towards the ceiling, and a jesting rumble came from his lips as he moved his eyes back to hers. 'Just as you are protected by your parents and aware of only the sugar plums in life, I was in a world not of sugar plums and I knew no other existed. Innocents were merely easier to move about as one wished.'

'So you have...changed?'

'Oh, yes,' he said and then his eyes locked on to hers in a way that let her know she'd be daft to believe him. 'I now even believe in good-hearted pirates and that one can stop droughts by putting a nail under a pillow. It just has to be the right pillow. A pirate's pillow. On the right day. Which is the day before a rain.'

'If your mother had lived, perhaps you would not be so cynical. Six is hardly an age to be without a mother.'

'I was an old soul in a child's body. I just had to wait to grow. It just took a bit more time to fill out and for my arms to gain strength. Now, that—that was a considerable wait.'

'Did you have brothers, sisters, your grandmother?' She could not imagine herself in his world.

He turned his head, staring at the wall. 'My grandmother was an addled witch who kept a fire poker at her side to gouge people with. My father was her shining star.'

No wonder he spoke so coldly of his mother's death. The one person who'd been gentle in his life had been taken from him and an uncaring person had been put in her place. From childhood, he'd been forced to live without compassion.

She loosened her grasp on the cloth of the curtain. 'At bedtime, who told you goodnight?'

She imagined a little boy in a huge bed and a grandmother whispering an evil cackle of goodnight from the shadows in the darkened room.

He turned his head sideways but kept his gaze on her. 'I didn't need anyone to tell me goodnight in my own home. That was for innocents.'

After speaking those words, he walked through the doorway.

She took a step sideways and dropped into the chair. No wonder her parents did not want her around others.

A tap on the door frame caused her to raise her head. Instantly, she fell back into her way of dealing with and soothing her parents and sisters. She smiled.

Surprise flickered on his face. His knuckles fell away from the wood. 'Goodnight.'

She thought of the six-year-old boy he had once been. With all the softness she could put into a whisper, she spoke. 'Goodnight.' She looked at him. 'See. It is a rather pleasant way to end a conversation among friends.'

'I wanted to see your face again. The words were an excuse.'

The eyes. Tortured.

The barrier had fallen away from him.

'Don't let yourself be moved by easy words, Miss Carson.' He lowered his chin. 'All words are easy. Friendships can be more dangerous than blades.'

She shook her head. 'The most important words aren't easy.'

Her heart thumped louder in her chest and it took all her strength to keep it inside.

He nodded to her. 'Pleasant dreams.' He waited a moment. 'Don't let your guard down.' And then he walked away without making another sound.

Chapter Four

Annie's mother took the last sip of her tea and placed the pink rose teacup on the saucer. The pink rose meant it was Tuesday. Wednesday would have had the gilt-rimmed ones. Thursdays were for the silver vines. One could always tell the day of the week by the teacups.

'I hate that your father didn't have tea with us this afternoon, but he has had to lie down. This is our only time as a family. Even though it's not quite the same since your sisters left.' The grey curls bobbed as she spoke. 'He has been touring the shops with the man who has all these ridiculous ideas about updating them and it has exhausted him. I think it may have tired Mr Barrett, too, as he is with the physician. But Mr Barrett will be on his way tomorrow. He upsets your father— all that talk about commerce.'

Mr Barrett did not seem someone who might be exhausted about talk of commerce. Not if he roamed around in the night and could speak so easily about fighting.

'Are you sure you are not feeling distressed from the

air last night?' her mother asked, patting the strands at her forehead. 'You look pale.'

'Not at all.'

'I will call the physician to look at you again.'

'I don't need a physician, Mother. And why is he here so often?'

'It's my bile again. You know how it is… He is so thoughtful. Not at all like Mr Barrett.'

Annie's cup rattled when she placed it on the saucer. 'I don't quite understand why Father invited him.'

'Mr Barrett does have a good man of affairs and seems quite interested in helping your father manage the shops your grandfather left him. But stay far away from your father's guest. His eyes. Something about them. It's as if he's thinking all the time.' She moved her hand, waving a napkin as she spoke. 'He stares. I don't like people who stare. It's just not polite to look at people and think. It distresses the head so. The physician said it causes wrinkles as well.' She patted her cheek. 'I suppose that is why I look so youthful.' She looked at Annie. 'He says he can hardly tell we are not sisters.'

Annie smiled. 'While you are quite the beauty of the family, Mother, I think the physician is full of his own miasmas and spreading things a bit thick.'

'Nonsense.' Her mother's eyes darted to Annie's face. 'He's a true scholar. He studied at Oxford and the Royal College of Physicians.'

'Who are his people so that he could pay for his education?'

'I believe he had a benefactor. When our last physician left after receiving the post with one of the

Prince's brothers, he recommended Gavin. He is well respected.'

'Then I suppose he is qualified.' She dismissed him from her thoughts, but she couldn't keep Barrett from her mind.

It was so unlike her father to invite anyone like Barrett into their house. But he was a viscount's son and her father knew how important that could be. Her father spent more time befriending people from the aristocracy than he spent doing anything else.

The memory of the Granny Gallery flitted through her mind. The man had tried to teach her to hit someone. She didn't doubt he pulled his punches.

She would like to see him in the daylight hours. She touched her cheek again. 'I do want to check with the physician to see if he can note an improvement,' she said.

Her mother's gaze wavered. 'But not if he is with that man. You should wait. I'll summon him. Ring for a servant to collect him.'

Annie stood. 'But, Mother, the physician is close. It will only take a moment.'

Her mother shut her eyes and put a hand to her forehead. 'Well, just be quick about it. And don't let your father know if you see Mr Barrett.' She whispered to Annie, 'Your father says the man was seen about at a b-r-o-t-h-e-l when he was young. It's said he visited every day. Not even waiting until the proper night hours.'

'Oh.' Annie went to the door. She stopped, looking back at her mother. 'Do you think he thought it safer during the day?'

Her mother fanned her face. 'Men do not go to a b-r-o-t-h-e-l to fight.'

'Just a thought.'

Her mother shut her eyes and shook her head.

Annie wasn't really looking for the physician. Walking down the hallway, she moved to the library, but Gavin wasn't there, and then she tiptoed to the Granny Gallery. No one.

She would have thought the physician would have consulted with Barrett in the main rooms.

Then she moved to the room across from her old one. She could hear male voices.

She stopped, listening. The physician and Barrett talked. A rumbling sound. She wondered if Barrett had an ailment.

A few minutes later, the door opened, but the physician still looked back into the room as he spoke and stepped forward. 'I cannot be in three places at once, but I'll see what I can do.'

'You'd best.' Barrett said.

Annie stood, her mouth open.

'Oh. Miss Annie,' Gavin said, seeing her, then he smiled. 'What can I do for you?'

'My mother requested you.'

Gavin nodded, head turned to the side. 'I'll see to her.' He walked away.

Annie didn't follow him. Barrett stepped into the doorway, eyes dark.

'Were you teaching him to fight?' she asked.

He shook his head. 'He looks like a soft flannel, but I'd say he can hold his own.'

'I heard that,' Gavin called over his shoulder, but didn't stop walking.

'Are you ill?' she asked Barrett.

The creases at his eyes deepened, but his lips didn't really smile and he seemed to be waiting until Gavin got out of earshot. 'Miss Annie, might you be concerned for my health?'

'No. You don't seem to need any sympathy.'

'I don't.'

'Or even someone to tell you simple pleasantries.'

He paused, watching her face, his own headshake nearly imperceptible.

'You may know how to fight,' she added, 'but you could learn a thing or two about being pleasant.'

'For me, pleasantries—' his chin lowered '—were much more difficult to master than a simple punch. But I think I do rather well.'

'Is it all a pretence?' she asked.

'Most of it.' His eyes challenged her to make what she would of his words.

Her gaze mirrored his. 'For most people their pleasantries are real.'

He gave one quick head shake. 'It's all a game. *Quid pro quo.*'

She raised her brows in question.

'You do this for me and I'll do that for you because some day I may need something else or you may and then we'll work together because we are both working separately for our own interests.'

'It's a shame your mother died when you were so young. You might have believed in goodness otherwise.'

'I suggest you do not leave your chaperon's sight for one heartbeat.' Then he stepped back, nodded to her, said a goodbye and gently shut the door.

Somehow she felt she'd been thrown under the wheels of a carriage.

She turned and walked back to her mother's room.

'Oh, my dear, we were just going to send for you.' Her mother looked up, her pale dress flowing softly and pooling around her slippers. 'The physician wishes to examine you so he can see how the treatment is going.'

He stood, the look of a schooled professional in his face and the monocle in his hand.

She waited, her demeanour that of a perfect patient, yet not looking at his face. She couldn't get Barrett from her mind. Ever so politely, he'd shut the door in her face. The beast had shut the door in her face. No wonder he did not believe in kindness. He had none in him.

The physician touched the monocle to her skin. She didn't move at the brush of the cold glass. Barrett's eyes had chilled her more.

'Oh. This is amazing. Amazing.' He peered. 'Her skin is perfect. After only one night of treatment. She's cured.' He stepped back.

'After one night?' she squeaked out the words. Relief. Disbelief and relief again. And then a memory of their guest, who seemed to know the physician, and then that Barrett had found her alone in the room the physician had sent her to.

Her mother clasped her hands in front of her. 'How wonderful. Wondrous. Gavin, you are a physician without compare.'

'Odd.' She dotted her hand over her cheek. 'I still feel the epidemeosis.'

'Well, you may have a lingering trace I can't detect.' Gavin put the monocle back in his coat pocket. 'If you wish to sit alone in the night air a few more times, I see no harm in it.'

'I will consider it,' she said. 'And I do wish to thank you for saving my life.' She put a little too much smile into the words and he glanced away.

'Well. I wouldn't go that far.' He turned to her mother. 'But miracles do seem to follow me around.' His back was to her. He waved his arm out, his movements so close to the same gesture she'd seen on Barrett the night before.

She shut her eyes, listening, trying to gauge a resemblance between the men.

'Do you think there is any chance she will develop it again?' Her mother spoke.

'No. Not at all. Miss Annabelle is recovered. We are fortunate to say the least.'

Annie excused herself and left them as they each congratulated each other on having done such a perfect job with her.

She'd only seen Barrett in the dim lighting but still, she'd looked at him with her whole being. She'd not paid as much attention to the physician before, but now she had. They were related. She would wager a month of her epidemeosis on that.

The physician had arranged a meeting and she'd attended just as planned. And Barrett had seen, or not seen, whatever he wished and now he was satisfied not to see her again if her miraculous recovery was anything to go by.

She remembered when the physician had first visited. He'd been so genial with her parents. So caring. He'd even enquired after her father's business and they'd talked long into the night. She'd thought it odd that the physician had been willing to stay and listen to the tedious details of her father's different holdings.

Then, later, her father had mentioned selling one of the shops at a ridiculously low amount, but how happy he'd been to get the money just when he needed it and he'd mentioned the Viscount's son for the first time. Her father had been happy Barrett wasn't the viper his father was and she'd felt reassured—freed from worrying about how her father would survive after she left home.

She reached up, took a pin from her hair and put a lock back in place, then walked to the window of her room. No carriages moved along the street. Each house as perfect as the other.

Barrett must live in a house much the same, yet the house had the memory of losing his mother.

A curtain fluttered in one of the windows across the street, and she wondered if a child had been looking out at her. And she wondered if Barrett's grandmother still lived. If she'd passed on, Annie hoped he'd not danced on that day, though she wouldn't have blamed him if he had.

Her eyes opened into the darkness and she wasn't sure what time it was because she could no longer hear the clock's chimes. The lamp still burned because she'd turned the knob low instead of putting it out.

Washing her face with cool water from the pitcher woke her completely and confirmed her determination.

She worked herself into her corset, putting it on backwards, lacing it, turning it and then pulling it up a bit more. It wasn't easy, but it sufficed.

She wound her hair into a knot quickly and the pins went in place.

Creeping downstairs, she moved to the library to look at the clock. Two thirty. Well, let the soirée begin. A man's room. She did have her sisters' blood in her.

But not the ghastly, simpering, hug, hug, kiss, kiss, *can't live without you* sop they'd inherited.

She couldn't bear to be a victim to such nonsense. Barrett might think her an innocent and he was right. She had no reason to lose her innocence where love was concerned. She'd seen women about the *ton* carrying on with tales of broken hearts and husbands gone astray and being locked in a marriage with a lout.

A bad marriage led to misery and a good marriage led to brain rot.

Her own parents truly cared for each other and sighed over each other's perfection. Their hours of conversation about what to ask Cook to prepare could destroy an appetite.

'Whatever you would like, dearest.'

'No, whatever you *would like, dearest.'*

'Oh, no, whatever you *would like.'*

'Dearest...'

'Dearest...'

'Dearest...'

But her mother wasn't a mindless fluff when her father wasn't around. True, she was a bit of a hypochondriac because she loved being fussed over, particularly by her husband. But, separate them and her mother could tally a balance sheet and organise the staff, all while twirling a knitting needle or playing pianoforte.

But Annie could not stay in *ton* and become one of

the pretty posies doomed to decorate a man's arm and his house and his children. She shuddered.

Barrett had a good thought when he told her she should learn to defend herself. She was destined, not doomed, but destined to become a spinster with a mind of her own. She'd almost perfected the spinster part, but having a mind of her own was giving her some trouble. She'd never be able to do that around her parents. They cried too easily.

She knocked on the oak door, hoping Barrett was right and that sound didn't carry well.

She rapped again. He was certainly right about not being able to wake people easily in the night.

Then she considered kicking the door.

She couldn't wait in the hallway forever.

Then she turned the latch and eased inside. The four-poster did look to have a shape in it, but she turned her head slightly aside because she shouldn't look at a man in bed.

'Pardon me,' she whispered.

He didn't move.

She slid back against the door and knocked on it from the inside.

'Mr Barrett,' she began on a whisper, but ended on a high note.

The form rolled over. Long arms. A muttered oath. 'What—do you want?' A wakening growl.

'I thought about what you said.'

He sat up. Covers fell away. She closed her eyes and swallowed, forcing her courage to remain with her. Even in the dark, the man was a tower of strength. She opened her eyes and looked over his head.

He exhaled and his teeth were clenched. He finally

spoke. 'Couldn't you have thought about it—tomorrow, after breakfast? Before dinner.' He raised his hand and ran his fingers through his hair. She'd seen that movement before. On a pedlar when his cart of apples had been overturned.

'You know I'm watched closely. I'm not even allowed to sleep on the same floor as you.'

'For good reason, apparently.'

'Did you have the physician arrange for me to be in the room?'

He didn't answer.

'Why?' she asked.

'You are said to be one of the beautiful Carson sisters. He said I would fall slavering at your feet. I was curious. That's all.'

Her stomach gave the oddest flutter when Barrett mentioned falling slavering at her feet.

'And the physician has kept you informed of my father's business dealings?'

'Not particularly. Not considerably. Your father has kept me informed. He talks when he's nervous.'

She ignored his words and instead focused on her purpose. 'I want you to help me learn to defend myself. In case it's needed.' And it might be once she left home. She wouldn't be living in a large house with servants.

His eyes shut. 'Practise your punching. Learn to scream out and shout *No*! If in doubt, bring a knee to the private parts. Goodnight.'

She didn't move. She'd knocked on his door in the early morning. He should appreciate what an effort it had taken.

'That was a mannered way of telling you to go

away.' He lay back down, rolled away from her and pulled the covers over his shoulders.

Barrett could feel her eyes on his back. He should never have spoken with her. Never have convinced his brother to arrange a meeting—wager or no. The damn little innocent was standing in his room in the middle of the night. And he was naked and the bed was warm and big and cosy. Way too comfortable for one. A perfect bed.

But not for him and this naive miss. She was little more than a pretty piece of pottery. Much too young. Younger than he'd been at birth. She was too naive for her own good. And she wasn't doing him any favours.

'I…I would prefer to hit you.' Her voice moved like music along the air. 'Hitting a pillow alone is not as intimidating. It doesn't have eyes.'

'Hire a footman.' If he rolled towards her, he would not be able to go back to sleep. Well, that didn't matter. He was unlikely to fall back asleep this night.

'My parents would never let me punch a footman.' She sounded shocked.

Heaven save him from an artless miss shocked at the thought of hitting a footman.

'Go away.' He put force into the words. No man would dare ignore such a command.

'I don't think it's polite to keep your back to me as you talk.'

Much better than telling you to get the hell out of my room. A thread of civility remained in him. 'Said the woman holding a lamp near the man's bed.'

'I'm across the room and you wouldn't answer the door.'

He slung his body into a sitting position, using both hands to comb back the hair that had moved to cover his face. 'Because knocks in the middle of the night never bring peace.' He bit out the words.

Now she flattened her back against the wood, but her feet remained still.

'Reach down. A little to the left. Open the latch. And go to your room and practise hitting the pillow. I will speak with your father about sending a maid to you so you can practise dodging punches.'

'Oh, that would never do. If you make him think I am in any kind of danger, he will have me sleeping in my mother's room the rest of my life.' She took in a quavering breath. 'I would have thought you would want me to be safe. After what you said about shouts in the night not waking anyone…and then we have the physician in our house.'

'You have no need to worry about the physician,' he grumbled. 'The man has a strict code of honour. He only lies on weekdays and is careful not to speak on Sunday.'

'How do you know him?' she asked.

He shook his head, causing his hair to move over his vision. 'Everyone knows Gavin.'

'Well, that doesn't mean he's trustworthy.'

'He's a whole damn lot more trustworthy than I am.'

He threw back the covers and she dived for the doorknob. She scurried.

'Portrait gallery.' He bit out the words before the door shut.

He would teach the wench to fight. And he was not in the mood to take pity on her. A woman who woke a man in the middle of the night needed to learn that was the number one thing *not* to do for safety.

He stopped. And a man who woke in the middle of the night should not be following along after a chaste woman like a puppy on a string. He was going to need that knee in the bollocks.

Chapter Five

Annie waited. And waited. She crossed her arms, sitting straight on the chair. Tapping her foot. He was taking his time. But she wasn't going to go back and knock again. She would let him know just what she thought of him for keeping her waiting. She could tie a corset faster than he could manage a few waistcoat buttons.

She would tell him that surely combing a bit of hair didn't take nearly as long as putting it in a knot on top of the head.

Guilt grew in her, but she brushed it away. He thought she wanted to learn to defend herself in case something happened in her own household, but she wanted to be stronger in case a highwayman or a cut-purse might be in her path.

Punching out at a pillow was like punching a pillow. And poor Myrtle tried, but no matter how she rushed at Annie it was a little like swatting a gnat.

When he stood close, trembles of fear started inside her. Or something. It was not the same as Myrtle, who Annie feared she'd injure, or the pillow, which slept through the attack.

Goodness, he took his time.

Her mind stopped thinking of how long he'd taken when he strode into the room.

He hadn't put on a waistcoat. He hadn't tied a cravat at the neck of his shirt. He was bare—naked under his clothing—just like he'd been in the bedchamber.

It hadn't seemed so wrong when she'd been the one trespassing. But for him to walk about in an area where anyone might see him… That little triangle at the top of his shirt, for instance, where the shadow made a V. That was frightful—frightfully fascinating.

She stood, the movement making her feel bigger and not quite so overpowered as she was in the chair.

She put her hands behind her back and clenched them into the fists he'd been talking about before, but she didn't care whether the thumbs were on the inside or outside, just that her hands were secured.

He kept getting taller and broader in her eyes and that wasn't possible. Her eyes told her his head didn't touch the ceiling and he walked through the door frame easily enough, but still, he did seem bigger. Perhaps it was the darkness in his eyes.

She really should search out an undernourished footman to help practise her defence. That might be much—less daunting.

'You took a bit of time to get here,' she said, covering the lump in her throat with strength in her words.

'I was hoping you'd tire of waiting and leave.' His voice reverberated into the room. He looked past her and then at the floor, a small negative movement in his head. He had two pillows clasped in one hand. She didn't know how she'd missed seeing those before.

He tossed the pillows on to the chair and one tumbled to the rug.

Whip-fast, he stood in front of her, hardly giving her legs any room between the chair and him.

He leaned closer, bringing the scent of a rosewater shaving soap so close she would never think of roses as delicate again. She could almost see the reflection of the thorns in his eyes. He moved closer and she had to tilt her head all the way back.

'The first rule. The rule that is hard and fast—'

She'd read about pirates, but they'd all been worlds away. This man was in front of her and she didn't quite know which direction to step. He surrounded her. And she couldn't even see the V in his shirt and he wasn't touching her, but her body didn't know that. When she breathed in it seemed to pull him closer and closer, but he couldn't actually be moving against her. His eyes held her in a vice.

The strength left her body, but she couldn't fall back into the chair. His hand snaked around her and rested against the small of her back, trapping her upright. Lightning moved through her body and the sensations of his hand seared into her back.

'The rule is to never, ever, put yourself in a position without thinking about whether it could be dangerous to you. Such as this one.'

'This shouldn't be dangerous.' She croaked out the words. 'You're in my father's house.'

'You cannot depend on a father, a husband or a brother to protect you.' His words were so close they no longer fanned against her cheek, but the air moved from his lips to hers. 'They may avenge you, but by then, you can't undo anything. You can only learn to live with it.'

'If you wish to scare me, you are.' But no matter how scared she was, she was going to make her own way.

'I wish to terrify you.' His voice scraped into the air. 'You need to remember. You need to keep this inside you any time you hear a little warning voice and not let the fluffy curls your maid took hours perfecting swab that thought away. That little voice is there to keep you alive.'

Her heart pounded in her chest.

'That warning voice you hear is the only voice in the world that can see to your interests. That warning voice is the heart telling you what the brain cannot fathom. It responds to a movement the corner of your eye caught, but the brain didn't decipher. A smile that is fake. An arm with too much tension in it. Listen. To. It.'

She touched her neck. 'I don't understand.'

'When your eyes are looking at fashion plates, the brain still functions. If someone walked into the room behind you and disturbed the air, the nose may get a whiff of the shaving soap—a scent that is too small for the brain to grasp. Instinct picks up on it. We are nothing more than animals that have formed better shelters. When you suddenly feel something is wrong, don't brush away that thought. What if you act on it all the time and it is wrong half that? That's still *half* that it helped you in a way nothing else could. What if it is right only one time out of a hundred and that is the time your life is saved?'

She shuddered. 'You make the world sound so evil.'

'Oh, dear me.' He put a finger to the side of his lips. 'I do believe it is.' He cocked his head to the side.

'You are a hideous man.'

'I had a pint with a bodysnatcher once and I decided I'm not the only one who is. *That* is the problem. He told me if I'd pay him he'd prove it and deliver a body to my door—but I couldn't keep it because he had a customer waiting for one. From the amount of dirt packed under his nails, I suspected he could do it.'

She didn't move.

He swept a bow to her and then moved forward. 'Prove to me that you can defend yourself.' He grasped both her arms, enclosing her.

Her breath stopped.

'Now fight back.'

She gulped air to be able to speak. 'You've got my arms. I can't move.'

'What can you move?' he asked.

'Nothing.'

He stood, perfectly still. 'Think about it.'

'My legs. But they'll tangle in my skirt. I can't even kick.'

'Then take your slipper and scrape down my leg. You'll be able to stomp my foot that way.'

She moved, raising her leg, but he jumped back, pulling her off balance and towards him. 'But not today, sweet. I may need to walk tomorrow.'

'You need to let me go.' She pulled at her arms, but he didn't release her.

He lowered his voice. 'I will.' He shook his head and his voice softened. 'But don't you *ever* wake me again.'

'I will never wake you again. Just let me go.' She shook her arms, but he didn't loosen.

'One last thing. You have another weapon you've not used. And please take care. I plan to eat tomorrow and teeth are handy for that.'

She looked at him. He dropped her arms and stepped back.

'Your head. That block of wood can do damage rising up to crash into my chin.' He reached up and tapped at the side of his head. 'And don't forget about the weight of your body. You can drop your knee a bit and twist with your hip and turn towards me, taking some of the weight from your legs to pull me off balance if you can.'

He bent his knee and twisted, moving his shoulder down and around.

'And you can surprise me. If I'm pulling you into me, then lunge against me, perhaps, to get me off balance. But whatever you do, try to stay off the ground. You can't fight back well there. It's possible, but you're going to have to get up to escape and that takes time.' His voice became a wisp. 'You need to do everything you can to run to safety.'

She put her hand over his touch, regaining her own skin. 'Were you just born knowing this?'

He laughed. 'I've spent my fair share of time at Gentleman Jackson's.' He looked away, reminiscing about something. He put his hand to his neck, rubbing just under the collar, kneading the muscle. 'And I don't seem to feel pain like others.' He chuckled. 'A handy skill to have.'

'Not feeling pain?'

'Well, I'm aware of it. I know if someone twists my arm behind my back that it doesn't feel well.'

'Oh.'

'It just doesn't matter at the time. Or later. What

matters is that I let someone get that close. They should be on the floor with my boot on their chest.'

'Oh.' She looked down at his toes. The first one was big and on the bony side. The others were thin, longish, though not well defined in the shadows. 'It must take a lot of effort to get those into boots.' She looked up. 'I guess that's why you didn't wear them.'

'It seemed a waste to put them on just to take them off again in a few moments.'

'Of course.' She raised her eyes, moving up the length of him.

'Has anyone ever twisted your arm behind your back? Your sisters in play?' His voice was flat.

She didn't move, afraid to commit. 'I should think it doesn't hurt very much.'

'Turn around.'

'I think that might be breaking your first rule.'

'Turn around.' His eyes darkened and his voice roughened.

She studied his face and nothing inside her warned her about him. She turned around.

He put a light touch on her shoulder, only touching her with two fingertips. No other part of him neared her. His hand slid forward and down an inch. Sensations jumped inside her, tightening her stomach. Heat. Warmth. And a shiver from his breath on her neck. 'Now, let me—' His left hand touched her wrist, slowly clasping to hold her in a gentle vice.

She swallowed.

'Relax.' He shook her wrist a bit. 'I'm not going to hurt you.'

She gasped.

'Tell me when it hurts and I'll stop.'

Gently he began pulling her arm behind her back. She tiptoed with the pressure. Then words rushed out. 'Stop.'

He released her. She stumbled forward and then turned. He watched her.

She rubbed her arm. 'You must have been around a lot of toughs in your youth.' She spoke softly, slapping down the inner warning voice. The one her mother had instilled. 'At the brothel?'

His head turned, as if he'd not heard her correctly. And his jaw relaxed. He seemed to have a moment finding words, but his eyes reflected humour.

'Those were the good people.' He laughed, his head falling back, and his eyes locked on the ceiling for a moment. The rumble of his voice stirred into her insides, causing a flutter.

'Yes, I was around a lot of toughs. On a daily basis.'

He pushed up one sleeve and moved to the light. A scar ran the inside of his arm. She turned her eyes away. The man had a lot of skin.

'It's just a small one. Grandmama's poker got me.'

She steeled herself and looked. A small indention. 'Your *grandmother* cannot have been as bad as you claim.'

He chuckled, softer, yet more lethal to her insides. 'Perhaps, but she didn't like to be disturbed at tea time.' He leaned forward. His breath tickling her skin. 'I would not have dared to wake her in the night.'

'Oh.'

He'd unbalanced her and she didn't quite know how he'd done it. She reached out, clasping his arm, and the skin of his forearm was soft. So much softer than she'd imagined, except she could feel—she could feel his muscles underneath. Almost to the blood pulsing in his veins and the very life of him.

She pretended to examine the mark about the width of a thumbnail, yet longer—but all she could think of was how alive he was. A tower of strength and thoughts and so much more and she didn't understand any of it. How could one person have so much energy inside himself that she could feel it rushing into her body? So much strength inside him. Surely it was an accident. Surely.

He said something.

Her eyes moved upwards. 'Of course.' The response seemed to satisfy him and he didn't even seem aware she touched him. She dropped his arm and moved back, but she was still thinking about skin. And one patch of it. With a scar in the middle. The scar was sad, of course—what she remembered of it. But the surrounding area just looked…warm.

'You'd be best to stay near a chaperon at all times. Sleep with a maid nearby. A sturdy one.' He raised his hand, touching the back of his forearm. 'One who looks like she could pull a tree up by the roots.'

'I've only met one person like that. A friend of my maid's.' The woman who would help Annie leave.

He raised a brow.

'A—' One did not associate with friends of the servants. Normally. And she didn't want to lie. She looked down. 'She's a woman who can help with female pains.' That was safer than telling him the crone claimed herself able to help any female with any ache, large or small, for a price.

'If you have female pains, speak with Gavin. He is a good physician. The best. No matter how he acts.'

'Oh.' She looked at his face, and caught him studying her. Usually, mentioning any female pain sent her father into the next room.

Barrett's eyes moved to half-open and he chose his words. 'Now I realise, with the physician so close, it's possible he might have diagnosed you with an ailment or two. But if he says you're cured, you're cured.'

'I don't like him.'

'I understand. He annoys me. But he's a sight more upstanding than I am. I possibly was switched at birth for a lightskirt's son.'

She studied his face. An odd thing for him to say. 'You do know him?'

'We've met. Before your mother patronised him, he took care of my father. On occasion, he takes care of him still.'

She nodded. That explained why the two men were talking. But then she felt that feeling he'd told her not to ignore. The one that told her something was different than she thought. 'And where did you meet?'

His eyes smiled again, daring her. 'At a brothel?' His brows darted up.

She examined his face and she knew he jested at her.

'Gavin and I are the same age,' he said. 'I suppose we were about eleven or twelve when we met. At the brothel.' Then he smiled again. 'Don't let me paint a wrong picture of the good physician.' He shook his head. 'The man would not touch a fallen woman if his life depended on it. He has the morals of a saint. I offered to pay for an—excursion—for him once and he declined.' He touched his cheek. 'I really should have been paying closer attention. He almost broke my jaw, but I deserved it.' He chuckled.

She just stood there, unsure of the turn of the conversation. She didn't get the jest he'd made. And he'd admitted to offering to pay for an—excursion. There was another world out there she didn't understand.

'Now let us see if you can break my jaw,' he said, turning and grabbing a pillow and holding it at his side.

'Wake up, Annie—' he leaned so close she could not have fallen asleep if her life depended on it '—then punch.'

Her eyes and brain began to work together again.

She imagined the scar. His grandmother could not have done that. He must have been lying.

He moved the pillow higher. She tossed out a fist. So the man was a liar. Wonderful. She let out a tiny huff. A liar.

He stopped movement and looked at her, shaking his head. 'Give it some pepper.'

She tried again.

'The pillow is tougher than you are.'

She swung harder. *Take that.*

He moved it around. 'Remember to look at my face when you strike out. Watch me. Not where your fist is going. Surprise. Is. Everything.' His voice softened, but gained strength. 'When you are the smaller person, surprise and wits are all you have. You have to use them.'

She dropped her shoulders. 'I could never defend myself. I can't.'

He brushed the pillow against her nose. 'You can't. Because men are so much smarter than women. No woman has ever been smarter than any man ever.'

'You're just saying that to taunt me.' She moved forward, kept her eyes on his, and, with only a bit of pressure, stomped his toe. 'Did you feel that?'

He smiled. 'Better. Now hit the pillow like you mean it.'

She punched and kept her eyes on him. Then she swung again, following the pillow from the corner of her vision.

She hit until tendrils of hair plastered to her forehead. She reached up, brushing a lock from her vision, and then she looked at her hand. 'My arm hurts.'

Strands of his hair had spiked and he heaved in a breath. 'It's work learning to defend yourself. Now all you need to do is practise.'

'Can we practise tomorrow?'

'I need to leave. I have to return to my own home.'

'Well, I suppose that I am fully prepared to defend myself.' Although she didn't feel it. She would have to work on practising in her room. Anything could happen when she went north.

'Against anyone younger than five years old,' he said. 'And don't stomp my foot again.'

He held the pillow up. 'Get a maid to help you with this.'

She shook her head. 'We tried. Myrtle is the only maid I trust, but she gets confused. I will have to convince her that I'm not angry and that it's a new soirée dance.'

He held out one finger. 'Don't forget. A man is sensitive in his private parts.'

She raised both her hands, palms up, and shook her head. 'I am not going near there.'

He grunted. 'I understand why your parents seclude you. It is for your own good.'

She clenched her jaw. 'I am not a bad person.'

'Well, so you're not. That doesn't mean there aren't

bad people out there. You can't defend yourself, even against a five-year-old, if you're afraid to muss your hair.'

'I couldn't hit a man in such a place. It's indecent.'

'Oh, my. How could anyone bear to be indecent?'

He then put his hands behind his back and bowed to her, still holding the pillow. 'I beg your pardon, but I can have you ready to knee my knots all the way to Elba within a few minutes.'

He put distance between them. 'But that's not what you need to learn. Now I want you to punch me. Straight.'

He held the pillow at his chest. 'Don't use all the strength in your punch. The movement is what you're practising. If you're prepared and something truly happens, in the moment, your body will take over and you'll hit with all you have. Your arm will ache afterwards, but you'll be safe. And look at my face.'

She punched out.

'Again,' he said.

She hit and he moved the pillow to deflect the blow. Then she stumbled on her skirt, caught her balance and swung to the side. He blocked the thrust. 'I could do better than that before I was birthed.'

She slugged again, this time for his face. Her hand brushed his hair as he pivoted to the side.

'Infant.'

Again she swung, going right for the face. She missed as he leaned back.

'Do not pause as you get close. And you're like a windmill again. Do not let your anger override your fist. Hit straight.' He made a fist and touched under his chin. 'If you go with an upward movement here, it can take less force to knock a man back.'

She looked into his eyes. They stared back.

'Don't swing and hit my head.' He thumped his forehead.

'I would not hurt you.'

He laughed. 'It is your hand we are concerned about. Heads are blocks of bone. A nose, a chin, a jaw and the temples are the places to aim for. Your hand will almost splinter if you punch my head. It's blasted hard.'

'I would imagine.'

Their eyes locked. Her breath came in rapid bursts. That lopsided smile he gave her held her close.

'Pay attention,' he said, diverting her attention. 'I will not let you knock me out. Just go for it and don't pull the punch. I'll move. But you have to be ready with a second attack.'

She moved her fist backwards and then jabbed forward, throwing her weight into the punch. He caught the punch with the pillow.

'Again. Follow up.' She lunged with her fist, her whole body pivoting into the thrust.

'Annie.' Her father's shout rang in the air. 'Mr Barrett. What is the meaning of this?'

Her father stood in the doorway, still holding playing cards. The physician stepped behind him. Her father walked into the room, his eyes goggling and his mouth still open after he spoke.

She jumped back. 'Nothing, Father. Nothing. We were just talking.'

Barrett glanced at her, gave her a half-second, exasperated stare as if to say *talking*? 'I was teaching Miss Annie how to defend herself.'

'Outrageous. Impossible. Insensible. In my own house. Under my roof.' Her father sputtered, slinging the cards to the floor. His jaw wavered before he spoke. 'I cannot believe a guest in my house would do such a thing.' His voice rose. 'Annabelle. Go to your room this instant.'

Annie took a step forward. 'Which one?'

Barrett held out an arm, blocking her path. 'She's a woman. She has no brothers. She needs to know what the world is like should she ever be on her own.'

'I...' Her father's face turned red to his ears. His shoulders tightened and he glared at Barrett. 'She is my daughter. And *you* will not be teaching her what the world is like.'

Barrett's chin went up. His stance firmed and his arm dropped, but it didn't loosen. His chin jutted and he turned his head so that he looked at her father with a sideways glare. 'The world is not all tea and biscuits.'

Her father sputtered. 'Why, it could lead to...anything.'

'Not with Mr Barrett,' Gavin inserted before Barrett could answer, having appeared from the doorway. 'He, uh, has a very delicate—improper to discuss in front of a lady—condition.' Gavin spoke softly. 'Sort of a delicate condition of the glands which causes a specific part of the male anatomy to be non-functional.'

Silence.

Her father stared at Barrett.

Barrett took a step towards her father, but he looked straight into Gavin's eyes and Gavin moved so that her father stood between him and Barrett.

Gavin peered around her father's shoulder. 'Barrett, as your physician, I assure you it's not altogether uncommon. Many men are im— Well, spared the rod, so to speak.'

Annie stared from one man's face to the other. Everyone had some affliction. She didn't see why one more added to the mix caused any irritation.

Chapter Six

Barrett shot a look at Gavin.

'Gavin. Let us not discuss this subject in front of Miss Annabelle. To my room.' Barrett bit out the words, fighting to keep from pulling Gavin outside by the neck.

Gavin dashed for the door.

Barrett looked at Mr Carson. 'If you've any problem with any occurrence in this room tonight, I suggest you take it up with me. I began this.'

'You're only half-dressed. I know what you had in mind.' Then his eyes flickered. 'Er, uh… A cure.'

'What I had in mind was to get back to my bed alone and try to get it through Miss Annie's head that should she find herself unprotected, she will have to depend on her own resources to save her. I do not need a *cure*.' His voice lowered. 'If I'd had something else in mind, the scenario would have been quite different. I assure you.'

'But you can't—'

'Never mind,' Barrett growled, jerked his head to indicate his brother precede him and stalked after the man. Gavin rushed to Barrett's room.

Barrett moved behind Gavin. He crashed into his

room, kicking the door shut behind him to prevent them from being overheard. Gavin had lodged himself behind a chair.

Barrett grabbed Gavin by the arm and pulled him past the chair, letting it fall to the side.

He had the man's coat in both his fists and they were nose to nose before he could get out the first words. His voice was guttural. 'You just told them I can't get a rise.'

Gavin sputtered, eyes large, and he gave an apologetic half-smile. 'Brilliant of me, wasn't it?'

'You lying— You're never going to have another one when I finish with you.'

'Think about it,' Gavin near-hissed, voice low, trying to dislodge Barrett's hands. 'It's truly your heart that doesn't work. They can draw their own conclusions. He'll trust you alone with her now.'

'No,' Barrett ground out the word. 'I do not wish to be alone with her.'

The door opened and Barrett kept his eyes on Gavin. 'Leave,' he commanded, not looking behind him.

'Mr Carson,' Gavin said, twisting his head against the constraints. 'Assure my patient that you don't think any less of him for the sad affliction.'

With one forward move, Barrett pushed Gavin closer to the wall.

Then he stopped. He must not behave rashly. Rash actions were mindless. They accomplished nothing. He could throttle his brother later if he wished.

He shook the coat and Gavin looked at him. And Barrett could see the resemblance of his father in Gavin's eyes. He pushed back until Gavin touched the wall, then stepped away.

Perhaps his brother would make Annie a husband—then he slammed that thought to the floor. No. His brother made ridiculous jokes about rods and bollocks.

He looked at Gavin, ignoring Annie's father. 'You touch her and I will kill you.'

His brother shrugged the words away and Barrett relaxed his arms. After all, Gavin had told Barrett about discovering how Annie's mother kept her secluded from the world. Gavin surely had no designs on Annie.

Her father would have his wish. Mr Carson would work for Barrett quietly and Annie could stay in her own home, safe from predators.

Barrett heaved in a breath.

Gavin sidled away from the wall and from Barrett. The physician pulled down his jacket, straightening it.

Barrett stood there, calming his breathing, telling himself that every path had obstacles. Gavin had made an honest mistake. His brother was good. He was, mostly.

'Now don't let it upset you.' The whispered voice of Annie's father. 'A lot of men have that problem. I never have, but I've heard of it before and I assure you that you have my discretion.'

Annie's face peered around her father's shoulder and he turned, pushing her several steps away and out of the room.

'I am quite capable—' then Barrett lowered his voice at Carson '—of doing the deed.'

'Oh, certainly,' the other man said. 'I certainly understand. But it doesn't make you less of a man, just an impaired man, and they do wonderful things with modern medicine now, don't they, Doctor?'

'Oh, yes.' Gavin took a breath, frowned and stepped sideways again. 'Although in Barrett's case…it is a lost cause.'

Barrett snapped, 'There is no case.'

Carson's eyes consoled Barrett.

'Absolutely.' Gavin stepped closer to Carson, but kept his eyes on Barrett. 'I would never discuss the specifics of any patient's care. As far as the world is concerned Barrett is quite the stallion. An active man.' He nodded, lowering his voice. 'But more of a gelding, I'd say.'

Barrett turned his head but kept one eye on his brother, his face signalling an area which his fist could connect with.

Gavin took a step aside, almost choking on the smile he tried to hide. 'Of course he is occasionally seen about with a woman.' Gavin was almost out the door. 'Older widows, usually.' One more step into the hallway, voice squeaking from his struggle to speak without laughter. 'The widows—they don't expect much.' Then he stepped outside the door and Barrett saw him bow before leaving. Annie had to be listening.

Barrett turned to Mr Carson. Compassionate eyes under burly brows stared at him.

He moved back. He feared the man might pat him on the arm.

Later, after Gavin recovered from the thrashing, he would confide a 'miraculous cure'. Not that it mattered. Barrett could get a rise. He'd proven that too well when it had taken a while to quit thinking of Annie's silkiness after she woke him. He'd never had a problem and if he had, proximity to Annie would have cured him anyway.

'It doesn't matter.' Barrett turned to Carson. 'I'm returning home tomorrow. I've business to attend to.'

'Don't rush off,' Carson said, one palm out, hand up. 'I've been far too hasty. You just warned the physician away from Annie.'

'I spoke…' Barrett paused. He'd spoken without thinking. He took in a breath. Annie's unworldliness had somehow robbed him of his lack of it. He bit back an oath.

Carson cleared his throat as Annie walked into the room. It was one of those moments when the ticking of a clock in the next country could have been heard.

Barrett looked to Annie's widened eyes. He calmed. She shouldn't be seeing such a display, although perhaps it was for the best. 'I'll leave today.' He remembered his charm. 'I should not be upsetting the household this much. And I've many business affairs to attend to.'

Carson's cheek puffed for a half-second and Barrett saw that the man studied him.

'You really must stay a bit longer.' Carson's face changed. Barrett could see the planning behind the eyes. 'I was hoping we could have a nice family dinner together, now that you've…rather… Well, it is good to know that you're a man concerned for a woman's well-being.'

The man was daft.

But perhaps not so much.

To dangle his daughter in front of the man who now owned his shops, particularly if he thought she could remain untouched and safe from the risk of childbearing, might sound appealing.

'I do need to get back.'

'Of course. Of course.' Carson interlaced his fingers. 'But please do plan on staying at least one more day. I'm still a bit uncertain as to how you plan to make the changes in the chandlery shop.'

Only a goose would misunderstand. The candles and lamps were going to be lessened and gas lamps would be slowly included. Records would be kept. To the last penny. The shopkeeper who slept all day was to be replaced.

Carson's lips went up. 'It's so rare I feel someone is worthy to be included in our family.'

Barrett would have been enraged, except, even when Carson knew he was on the brink of losing his home, he'd hidden Annie away. But now that he thought his daughter to remain innocent forever, and also protected, he was willing to bring her to the forefront.

But it wasn't a good forefront. The man didn't have a smattering of sense, but apparently he cared for his children, which was more than many parents did.

The man simply could not make a good decision, but he valued his daughter.

'I will leave.' He needed to get out of the house. Let his brother make sheep's eyes at the virtuous little babe. He had better things to do.

'Oh, please stay for breakfast,' Carson said. 'I have the new shopkeeper coming round in the morning and I think you'll be pleased with him. Annie will have breakfast with us and she can apologise for being a ruffian and beg forgiveness for making a fist at you.'

His instincts kicked in. The feeling that he was being led to a trap. He looked at Annie. She stared at her father as if he'd just tried to push her off a cliff.

'I don't eat breakfast with your guests,' Annie spoke to her father. 'I have it in my room.'

Barrett took the direct hit and she'd not even used her knee. A pretence of wanting to have breakfast with him would have been acceptable.

'We decided I would hire the new shopkeeper.' Barrett made a statement.

Carson fumbled with the button on his coat and moved back. 'My wife's cousin. He's a good lad.'

'We'll see,' Barrett said. 'Have him here right before dinner. I have to attend to other business. I'll be back later, but now I must excuse myself from breakfast.'

The night had started fine and then a woman had walked into his bedroom. Now her father was giving Barrett a smile that said he wouldn't mind having a new son-in-law. And Annie stared at her father as if he'd punched her.

'Goodnight, Mr Carson. Miss Carson.'

He walked forward and nudged Carson out with a smile.

He would not finish his sleep. It made no sense to stay in the Carson household, but it had been a holiday of sorts. Holidays were too much like false sweetness. He needed to step out of it and get back into his life.

He would have breakfast in his room, in his house. And it was a long walk and he did not look forward to it, but if a cutpurse stopped him, he pitied the results.

He finished dressing and slipped from the house. He was less than a few feet away when a rickety cart rumbled along the street. No one was ever out at this time of night for a good reason. Moving into the shadows, he watched the donkey plodding along. The cart stopped not far from Annie's house.

'This be it.' A woman's voice.

'We're too early. I told you we would be too early.' The man.

They were out of place. People did not sit in a cart unless they were waiting. They could be delivering things ordered, but they weren't.

'Be quiet,' the old woman said. 'I'll wake you at daybreak.'

The man grumbled, handed the woman the ribbons, and moved to the back of the cart and slid out of sight.

They were definitely waiting for something.

Annie had said something about an older woman, a friend of her maid.

Barrett blended into the darkness and walked to his home, certain he could trek the distance before daybreak.

When he arrived at his house, he found Summers sitting in the Viscount's room. Summers opened his eyes and nodded at Barrett.

Barrett motioned for Summers to step out of the room. Standing, he yawned and moved to the hallway.

Barrett pulled the door shut after Summers exited.

'I'll sit with Father. Have the carriage driver go to the Carson household. A few steps away, he'll see an old woman in a cart. A man asleep in the back. See what he can find out on the sly about the old woman watching the Carson house.'

'I almost miss the quiet life of the stews,' Summers said, walking away.

Barrett stepped into his father's room and took a seat in the comfortable chair.

Annie. She wanted to learn to defend herself. And a woman watched the house in the night.

Chapter Seven

Annie ran her hand along the small bedside table.

Now she had three rooms, not just a bedroom and small dressing chamber. Three rooms and all of them dark. The wood was as smooth as her old table, except at the corners, and her handkerchiefs were stacked tightly along with her books. The bedside lamp took all the space on the top and the novel had to be stored inside the drawer because it wouldn't fit alongside the lamp.

The walls had been papered long ago and she could see the lightened spaces where the maid had removed pictures from the wall.

No main stairway connected Annie's room to the others. Only the servants' stairs. She'd tried to make the best of it.

She supposed she should go sit with her mother, but she didn't wish to. She wished to have her old room back.

'Miss.' The kitchen maid slipped inside Annie's doorway without a knock and shut the door quickly behind her. Her cap hid every strand of her hair except the tightly pulled back grey at her temples. She kneaded the cloth in her hands. 'My pardon for interrupting.'

Annie nodded, dismissing the apology without comment. They both knew the woman would lose her job if caught.

Myrtle was still sleeping and Annie had worried when her father had suggested she have breakfast with him. She'd known the old woman was supposed to be at the house at daybreak.

'I contacted the woman who is waiting. She wants funds, of course.'

'I gave her funds.'

'I know, miss. But she claims it takes hiring a cart again and she wants to be paid for the risk to herself. If she's caught, your parents will have her put in gaol for taking you. She says it will be her word against theirs and you'll not have a chance to speak to the magistrate. The Old Bailey can be spiteful. It could be her very life, but she said she's willing to take that chance to help you.'

Annie moved forward, one finger touching the empty spot on the wall. 'Tell her she mustn't be caught. It's hardly worth someone's life.'

She went to her jewellery case and took all the money she'd secreted away, passing it to the maid.

The girl paused, turning the notes in her hand. She raised her eyes and then handed the funds back. 'You are making a mistake.'

Annie reached out, pressing away the hand with the funds in it. 'It will be one of the first I've ever made then, as I am too closely watched to make any others.'

The maid counted the money and handed half of it back. 'You need to keep some to give to her later.'

'True.' Annie turned, hoping no one had to find out. She didn't want to bring shame to her family. She'd have to leave a note so they would know she'd left on her own. And she'd have to be careful because she would be leaving everything behind.

She thought about how well suited everything in her room was, yet her parents had moved her one floor up to keep her from speaking to a man because they hadn't chosen him for her. Just like they tried to push her sisters into marriage with men they hadn't chosen.

And now her father had changed his mind about Barrett. She was fortunate they let her choose—her room? No. Her tea? No, her mother chose the tea. Her dresses? No, her mother and the seamstress consulted her, though.

Her parents even chose the books allowed in the house.

She looked at the maid in front of her. One of the few people she spoke with that her parents didn't know about.

The girl ran her fingers over the notes. 'Your sister, Honour. She chose to leave.'

'I know,' Annie said. 'And I want to see for myself how she is.' And when she saw Honour, and reassured herself that all was well, she would ask Honour what it felt like to pick the tea she wanted to drink.

The maid held the money against her heart. 'I miss your sisters, too. I'll give the old woman as little as I can.' She stepped away and held the door open for Annie. 'You mother will be sending someone else to find both of us if you don't hurry to her.'

Annie pressed her lips together and nodded. 'Tell

the old woman I'll be ready about a quarter-hour after the light goes out in my window.'

Annie stood in the centre of the room. She practised throwing each elbow back behind her, stamping her foot on a boot, and when she tired of that she picked up the reticule she'd filled with coals and swung it around until the ties broke.

She sighed. She would have to spend her day making a stronger reticule.

That evening, after she had made her reinforced reticule, she walked down the stairs, her palm on the side to guide her so she didn't trip over her skirts.

Inside her mother's room, Annie met a sparkling smile.

'Mr Barrett has returned to eat with us tonight. He's a little rough, but do be nice to him, dearest one.'

Annie's mother walked forward. A perfume bottle at the ready—her mother's choice of weapon. Annie held up her hand to keep her mother from spritzing another dash of jasmine perfume on her. Now that the Viscount's son was seen as an acceptable suitor, Annie felt rebellion blossoming against Barrett.

She'd liked him at first, but now she wasn't sure.

He'd definitely been quite careful to keep his distance from her when they'd been sparring. She could not imagine him delivering any of those sonnets and poems and flowery love faradiddle that her sisters found so enthralling. Instead, she could imagine him cocking a brow and giving a silent look of censure to such a thing. The same one she'd tried to hide from her sisters.

Barrett had done nothing to show that he had any fascination with her.

But then Annie paused, hearing the inner voice that Barrett had spoken of. Yes, he found her attractive. Knowledge tumbled inside her, causing her stomach to flutter. Mr Barrett watched her differently than he watched other people.

She had no idea how she knew that, but she did. Perhaps the shadows increased at the side of his eyes, or perhaps he stared at her a bit longer than usual. She didn't know what it was, but he'd spent a lot of time in the night sparring with her.

He'd not tried to steal a single kiss or touch her. He'd been quite respectable. Sensible. Not like Lord Richard, who'd tossed his hair back and expected her to admire him, causing her to line the other wallflowers up in front of her like a shield.

'Mr Barrett is only going to stay with us one more day.' The older woman raised the perfume bottle again, eyes hopeful. Annie shook her head.

'You can move back to your room. Although you can move into it any time now that we know Barrett is such a moral man. It is like your father told you, Annie, a man does not need to court a woman. But the family needs to let him know he is acceptable and the woman must not hide behind the wallflowers at the soirées. Men do not want to marry a wallflower.'

'I believe I will stay in the attic,' Annie said. 'I like the window. I can look down on the gardens and see further.'

'If you're sure…'

Annie nodded. She would be less likely to be missed as quickly from the upper storey. Her mother tended to send servants up and down stairs, but when Annie was nearby, she constantly stopped by Annie's room to chat about this or that.

Her mother put the bottle on the table. 'You know I need you close when my breathing is bad.'

'But the doctor is here now.'

'Yes. And the curatives he's given me do help tremendously.'

Her mother reached out and patted Annie on the elbow. 'Please try to like Mr Barrett, Annie. Your father says he is extremely knowledgeable about business.'

'He mentioned that he likes to fight.' Annie looked at her mother.

'Well, dear one, that's what I mean by rough, but just be pleasant to him. Your father said their business is almost finished. While he's not pleased with the ideas for the shops, he's going to go along with them. I think the beeswax candles are fine just as they are, although I don't mind the oil. He thinks it will some day be a thing of the past. He also thinks your father should visit the shop more. You would think a viscount's son would know as much as an earl's cousin. People are hired to take care of those matters.'

Annie stood, brushed her hand along the top of the dressing table and picked up the perfume bottle.

Barrett would never accept her plan to be with her sister, believing four walls were more important than bringing her sister back into the home.

But if she succeeded, then maybe Laura would somehow find them as well—although no one even knew where her husband had taken her. With the three of them in London again at least she wouldn't feel so abandoned. Not that she wanted to listen to those blasted sonnets one more time.

She touched the metal of the pendant hanging at her neck. She would leave a note for her parents so they wouldn't worry. They wouldn't understand, but they wouldn't be able to find her.

Barrett was moving on and she would go forward as well.

She made a fist and turned away from her mother and punched at the air. She'd survive whatever might happen, although she doubted she could ever truly defend herself.

During a dinner in which the physician regaled them with stories of his days at his studies and her parents listened, Barrett contributed to the conversation just enough so that they could tell he was in the same room and she said even less.

He ate, his attention more focused on the food, she thought. Except, every so often when the physician said something, he would look across at him, giving a grimace, which might have covered a smile, and sometimes a smile that covered a grimace.

Barrett had heard the stories before. She could tell when he gave a sideways twist of his head and the physician changed the course of his words.

The physician's perfectly combed hair and aquiline features would have fit well in any drawing room. Barrett's hair was on the longish side, his cravat was tied in the minimum twist and his coat had nothing to commend it. The buttons were plain dark ones, not the fashionable embroidered or brass or ones with inlaid stones. Yet Barrett captured her notice while the physician blended in with the woodwork.

But they were alike. Perhaps the chin. The jawline. Different eyes. Not quite the same build and nothing she would have noticed if they'd not been sitting so close.

She listened carefully when the physician spoke. His voice flowed easier than Barrett's, but if she concentrated, she could hear a hint of a dialect more like the man her sister had run away with. The sound of a man who'd not lived all his life among the *ton*.

Then Barrett spoke. At first thought, his words were the most lacking. He spoke directly. No *If it pleases you.* No *Quite the best I have tasted.* And yet, if she concentrated on his words, she couldn't hear anything but the polished tones of the *ton*.

They moved to the sitting room, then her father asked the physician if he could speak with him privately about a blemish on a knee. A blemish on the knee of his favourite horse. Both men left.

'Please pardon me,' her mother said. 'I must fetch my stitchery.' She put her hand on the chair arm to steady herself as she stood.

Annie looked at the servant pull and her mother waved the thought away. Her mother had ignored the pull, which was so unlike her as she usually had her chair placed within arm's length of the pull, or sometimes waited until a servant checked on her before she asked for something.

'Oh,' Mrs Carson explained. 'I am working on several projects and I want to examine just which threads I need.'

Barrett stood. 'I've some papers to look over before I send them off in the morning.'

With the grace of a dancer, her mother moved between Barrett and the door. 'No need for you to feel so abandoned, Mr Barrett. Please sit with Annie.' Her hand fluttered near the grey curls. 'She hardly ever has any visitors and it's nice for her to be able to chat with someone her own age.'

Mr Barrett stopped dead in his tracks. 'I don't think I'm her age.'

'Why, you most certainly are.' Her mother's voice dripped treacle.

He stared at her mother, but didn't speak or move, and she left.

Annie had never purposely been left alone with any male before. She looked around, unfamiliar with her mother's actions.

Mr Barrett watched Annie. He touched his cravat, not straightening it, but pulling it a bit loose, shaking his head. 'If it makes her happy, then let her do her best.'

'She's…' Annie stopped, then whispered, 'Matchmaking.'

He almost smiled.

'I don't think matchmaking works with you,' Annie said. 'You'd rather practise fighting.'

'I doubt anyone's ever tried matchmaking with me before.' He moved to the fireplace and touched the poker, nudging it, the clink of metal against stone filling the silence.

'Have you scared them away? The matchmaking mamas?' She had trouble finding words when he was so close.

'I suppose. A well-placed growl here and there and they scamper like mice.'

'Perhaps it is their inner voice shouting out to warn them.'

Humour sparked behind his eyes. 'You could be right.' He shook his head, then paused, his face losing the emotion. 'Work before pleasure. Always. Without work there is no pleasure. And should someone wish to marry me to get to my ledger books, it is too late. I have them secured next to my heart.'

'I don't think everyone feels that way.'

'I'm pleased they don't.' He studied the fireplace and she truly thought he examined the width and height of it. He tilted his head and put a finger at the point of juncture to the wall. Then he stepped back, studying, deepening the lines around his eyes.

She gauged him far closer to her parents' age than her own twenty-two years.

'Are you planning to have a new fireplace made?' she asked.

He blinked, then turned, almost as if he'd forgotten about her presence. 'Yes. One of my properties is in disrepair in Manchester and I have hired a man to correct some of the problems.'

'Surely the man you hired will know what to do.'

He didn't look at her when he spoke. 'I know what I wish for better than he does.'

No wonder the matchmaking mamas kept their distance from him. And it would not matter to him if the years passed without his marriage. He had no one pushing him not to be a spinster.

She tried to remember if he'd been widowed, but had really heard so little of him. Nothing, really. The talk was often more concerning his father, whom her father was relieved not to be meeting.

'How does your father fare?' she asked.

No raptor's eyes ever moved more rapidly.

'I heard he is ill.' Her words rushed together.

'He is getting older.' Barrett turned his attention fully on to her. 'Finally.' Another heartbeat. 'But he has many years left in him. I wouldn't be surprised if he outlives us all.'

She laced her fingers together. 'Why are you here?'

'Making the plans for your father's shops. Our business venture.'

'He won't sell.' She'd hardly got the words out before he responded.

'He already has.'

She gave a brief shake of her head, but his eyes told her she was wrong.

'Does Mother know?' Something cold brushed against her heart. Perhaps it was the look in his eyes.

'I don't even know if your father fully realises.'

She took in the words, not wanting to believe them. Her father's grandfather had started the shops, at first selling a mixture of various household items and then moving to candles and lamps.

Barrett turned his eyes from her and stared at the fireplace again, but this time she knew he wasn't studying it.

'As your father has no sons, I suggest you convince your parents that it is in your best interest to seriously consider their matchmaking efforts for you.'

'Perhaps they have… They appear to be.'

'I think I am—' whimsy danced behind his eyes '—considered a special case.'

She breathed in deeply, taking strength from the air. 'There is more to a marriage than—children.'

He dusted a bit of soot from his fingers and, though his head was down, she saw the quirk of his lips. When he looked up, they were in a straight line. 'Do not believe everything you hear.'

Heat burned in her cheeks, but she didn't drop her eyes.

'Trust me,' he said.

'Can I?'

'That is a good question. And when you think to ask it, you really shouldn't. Because your mind is telling you no. What you're asking for is reassurance of trustworthiness. A lie upon a lie.'

She waited.

'People can't be trusted. It is why we are humans and not angels.'

'But you tried to teach me to defend myself.'

'Precisely.'

He walked to her, his boots making no sound on the rug, and took her wrist, ever so lightly. The touch heated and locked her in place. Or perhaps it was the depth in his eyes.

'You need to realise, to think, to know, that forests are not full of flowers. The flowers only bloom for a short time and fade away. There are predators and prey. Hawks and little mice. You must make your own path in the world, through the brambles and around hedges. And put your own canopy over your head. Do you have any feeling for how dangerous it is for a woman to be alone in the world?' he asked. 'It is like being a hare in the forest. If you stumble down the wrong path, a fox can be waiting for its dinner and, when the dinner is right in front of him, he can hardly turn aside.'

'There are plenty of good people in the world.'

'Yes, and if you pass by fifty good people and only one person who wishes you evil, that is all it takes.'

'Why does it matter to you so much?' Annie asked.

'It is your innocence.'

She could not move. Even though he stood in front of her, he surrounded her—perhaps with the scent of leather or the lingering waft of soap that his shirt put into the air after brushing his skin.

'Market your beauty. Price it high—marriage to someone you halfway like—forget about the love rubbish. And get your father to consult my solicitor for help in the marriage contract. Consider it a gift from me.'

He looked at her wrist, held in his clasp. Then pulled it to his lips, kissed it, then his lips trailed to kiss her palm, sending pleasant shivers throughout her body. He pulled back and stared for a moment at the skin he'd kissed, then with his free hand, he clasped her fingers closed.

'Sell high and sell your beauty, not your heart, or your mind. Always be in control of your thoughts, or someone will control them for you.'

Her fingers were still in a clasp. He took her wrist and held it up. 'Open your hand.'

She uncurled her fingers.

'What do you see?' His eyes locked on hers, but she looked into her palm where his lips had touched.

'Nothing,' she answered.

'Precisely.'

He dropped her wrist and stepped away.

'Once you and your father have decided on a prospective suitor, send a note to my man of affairs. Within a few days he will be back to you with the man's particulars.'

He paused at the doorway, his boots—reflecting the lamplight—the most comprehensible part she could see. 'I need to take my leave. I've got documents I must have ready by morning. Please give your mother my regrets.'

He turned on his heel to leave and the shadows swirled as if he wore a cape. His footsteps faded.

She looked at her palm. Empty. She put her hand over her wrist. His touch remained, but when she looked into the doorway, she didn't think any part of her remained in his thoughts. He'd handed her over to his man of affairs and she supposed if she happened to see Barrett again at some social function, he would remember her enough to call her by name and give her the most polite of greetings before returning to his commerce.

Shortly after Barrett's departure, Annie's mother walked into the room, her smile fading when she recognised that Annie was alone.

'Our guest?' Her mother's brow rose.

'He has taken his leave and returned to his house.' Annie explained. She kept her eyes on her mother. Her cheeks puffed in and she looked at Annie, shaking her head, her brows up a bit.

The physician and her father followed close behind and both stepped in and looked around the room.

She'd expected her father's look of disappointment, but not Gavin's.

The physician blew a burst of air from his lips, surprising her. Apparently he'd wanted Barrett to stay longer, too. But she wasn't sure if Gavin had merely forgotten to tell Barrett something.

'I suppose I must be going along, too,' the physician said, his eyes accusing her before he gave a weak smile and took his leave. 'Blast,' he grumbled after he stepped from the room.

So, he'd a bit of the matchmaker in him as well. And she had been examined by the potential suitor and hadn't been chosen.

Her mother stepped to her. 'Did—did you anger him?'

'We got on quite well.' In a manner of speaking.

Her mother smiled. 'I hoped.' She nodded, pleased. 'And do you think he is going to come back?'

She still clasped her palm, but then opened her fingers, letting go. He had kissed her goodbye.

'I could not say for certain.'

Her mother's eyes darted to the floor, but not before Annie could see the disappointment.

'Well.' Her mother beamed, gathering herself. 'I am certain he will return.'

Annie didn't answer. It would do no good.

'I only want the best for you. Barrett is interested in you. And his house is close enough that you could visit us often. What do you think of him?' Her father examined her face.

Her mother leaned forward, eyes bright. 'He's a bit rough, Annie. But he dresses well and has a fortune and a title. And it is so nice to have pretty things.'

'He is the only man I have been near other than servants or the physician since my sisters left and I've hardly talked to any male in my whole life,' Annie said.

Her father tapped his waistcoat pocket where he kept his pocket watch. 'I'll be inviting Barrett back and I hope you think very carefully about the opportunity,' her father said. 'The man was standing very close to you when I walked in on the two of you—talking.'

'He said if there are marriage contracts with someone else—*with someone else*—Father can use his solicitor.' Annie stared at her father, trying to will the words into his mind, but she could almost see them skittering past his ears.

'He is thinking of marriage contracts?' Her father's gaze had the same look as if an apricot tart were placed in front of him.

'I think not. At least...not with me.'

'You don't understand how a man's mind works. If he mentioned marriage contracts already, he is thinking of proposing. You'll convince him to propose.' Her father clasped his fingers and popped his knuckles. 'Would be nice to have a son-in-law who has a lot of properties.' His gaze softened. 'I'm fine with no grandchildren, saves the time of worrying what they might wish to call me, and Mr Carson sounds too formal.'

'Our Annie. Married to a future viscount. Soothes the blow of Honour leaving and Laura's pitiful marriage.'

'It makes no difference, really,' her father said. 'You have two suitors now and both have good standing. You mother and I will be happy with whomever you choose.' His chest puffed.

'Just pick one and flutter around him a bit. You will be married before the year is out, and to a man with a title, or someone related to a peer.' Her mother patted the hint of grey hair at her temple and walked away, the sound of her humming drowning her footsteps.

Annie kept herself still. She would not be forced into a marriage. Barrett wasn't interested anyway. Lord Richard had told her she was the prettiest merchant's daughter he'd ever seen and she had told him she hadn't thought her father that pretty. She'd then used the ploy of having something in her eye, and left.

Not that it mattered either way. Annie had a scarf to cover her hair, a shawl and a rough-sewn dress ready and waiting in her room. The old woman would take her to see Honour and she would be with her sister in shortly over a week. Lord Richard could find another pretty merchant's daughter and marry her.

Her parents would be crushed. But they'd get over it.

At the few soirées she'd been to with her family, her mother and father had refused to give any man introductions to her or her sisters unless he had the proper lineage. Her sisters had rebelled with fervour. Annie had felt like a different kind of servant, cleaning up behind the shouts, arguments and anger that seeped to all corners of the house.

She didn't want another round of anger erupting in front of her and she knew her parents would simply refuse to consider any arguments Annie presented.

Annie raised her eyes to the ceiling and shook her head. The dance lessons had been a frivolous waste of time.

She did want to dance, though.

With someone like Barrett, only...different. Agreeable. Someone who could make rosewater smell like leather and make her wonder how it would be to touch the skin beneath it.

Chapter Eight

Barrett knew better than to tell his father to be quiet. The Viscount moved around, slamming one book after another on to the shelf. He never read the volumes— he only used them for weapons. His father enjoyed the tomes more then than if he'd actually read them.

Barrett took the one book his father did peruse— the ledger—running a thumb along the cold bindings.

He missed the Carson household with its perfect blandness. The mother worried about her head and her feet and the father hardly knew which end of a pen to use, and Annie was planning who knew what. He could understand her irritation at being trapped in a world of such sameness, but better that one than so many others.

He'd kissed her wrist. He shouldn't have.

Her wrist. So delicate. Small. He paused, all thoughts focused on Annie, recalling as much of her as he could. Her thin shoulders. The hollow at the base of her neck, a perfect place to put his lips. Her face, full of guiltless-ness he'd never seen before, and so palpable he could almost taste it.

Mentally, he traced her body, from the softness of her cheek, down the slender neck, to her breasts, her waist…

Damn. He needed that affliction his brother had tossed on him. Especially where Annie was concerned. If only his brother hadn't insisted on that silly wager.

A book thumped against the wall, bringing his mind back into the room.

Barrett had once wondered why his father didn't tear the books from their bindings in his rage. It wasn't as if he ever planned to read them. His father considered the books a sign of intelligence and a sign of wealth. He sometimes threw them, but he never burned them in the fire or tore them. The rages were controlled actions. The appearance of reaching beyond sanity, but crafted to never injure anything priceless. Only replaceable items would be damaged.

After his mother died, Barrett had realised he could be replaced. He'd overheard his father and grandmother discussing suitable prospects for marriage to provide another heir. But then his grandmother had died and his father had let the idea fall by the wayside, preferring not to be bothered with what he called the heavy-skirts.

Gavin walked into the room. 'Summers told me I'd find you here.' He dodged the book that flew by his head. 'I suppose you win. Or lose, depending on what your life might be with someone like Annie in your life. But as the wager is clearly done, I will probably be looking in on our father more. Just not starting today.'

Gavin watched the Viscount, looking ready to throw a book back.

'Don't bother yourself getting upset with his rages. It only makes them more fun for him,' Barrett said, closing his ledger and standing. 'He prefers to stir the pot and, if he can't find one, he stirs the air.'

Barrett moved closer, tossing the book into his father's chair.

His father reached to grasp it, momentarily transfixed by the ledger, then chuckled. 'Just what I was looking for.'

Gavin looked at his father. 'As we've been getting to know each other, sadly, I no longer envy you your childhood.'

The Viscount looked up, absently turning pages. 'There's two of you, isn't there?'

'As far as we know.'

'There might be another sister. A little spindly girl who cried all the time.' He shook his head.

'Do I have any more brothers?' Barrett asked.

'I've said no. I meant no. If I was younger—' He turned the page of the ledger, scouring it, his finger running the columns. 'Then you would get what you had coming for asking questions twice. And then you'd get what you had coming for speaking to me.' He turned another page. 'Not that I mind, really.'

He looked straight into the physician's eyes. 'What's your name?'

'Gavin.'

'Oh, yes. Now I remember. Your mother was such a tart. Saucy. Quite a handful.'

Their father looked at Barrett. 'And how did you find him?'

'The mail you sent me to post. I had a copy of your seal made, or near enough to pass. I often opened your letters and rewrote and sealed them again if needed. Years ago, you'd written his mother a letter telling her that you wouldn't be sending any funds her way for Gavin's schooling and to leave you alone or you'd make things worse for her. She was dying. I doubt it could have been much worse.'

The Viscount scratched his whiskery chin. 'I did send some coal her way the year before that, I just didn't want to think about her.'

'Gavin and his sister were baking bread and selling it. He'd learned to put ribbons in Doria's hair, make sure she was scrubbed and let her sit at the cart and look hungry.'

His father grunted and his chin moved back and forth. 'He's a physician. He says I am in good health. I like him. You, I tolerate.'

'High praise,' Barrett replied.

'He said you paid for university.'

'Yes. You weren't watching the accounts as closely as you thought.'

His father coughed. 'Education is such a waste when you can be making money instead. Or taking money.'

Their father pointed one bony finger at Gavin and then one at Barrett. 'Neither of you is worth the powder and lead it would take to kill you.' Then he laughed, reaching to twist the seal ring on his little finger. 'My boys. There is hope yet. A forger and a physician.' He stared at Gavin. 'I would never have sent you to school, but...' He shrugged. 'Fortunate now.'

Barrett gave a quick nod to the door and he and his brother stepped outside. 'Remember what I said. Don't turn your back on him.'

'I can see why. I thought Annie would take your mind from him. As your physician, I would say you need a heart.'

'You are not my physician.'

'Thankfully, as you would make a terrible patient. You have no patience and cannot follow directions.' He yawned. 'I thought the Carson woman's smile might sway you and she's the most agreeable of the sisters.' Gavin chuckled. 'Only a woman who has been trained to follow along with everyone else's opinions would work for a bear like you.'

Barrett stopped moving. 'Why didn't you choose her for yourself? I'm sure you could have convinced the family to let you court her.'

Gavin nodded his head. 'Her older sister. She didn't seem to like me, though. I stopped in a few months ago and Mr Carson asked me to see if I could figure out what was wrong with Honour. I diagnosed her as being with child. Turns out I was right.'

'You'll get over it.'

'Don't know if I want to.'

Barrett laughed and felt the edges of the sound. 'Father is wrong. We aren't alike. You have a heart. I am happy with my lack of one.'

'I would say you have a ghost of one somewhere in your body.' He held up two fingers pressed together. 'About this big.'

'I tried to fall in love once. A chore.'

'Madeline wasn't the right woman for you.'

'She was perfect for me. She had her own kind of ledger book and she kept an eye on what everything cost her. And if a woman like that can't keep me interested, then no one can. I was relieved when I didn't have to squire her around.'

He'd not lied. Madeline had been the perfect woman. Calculating. Aware. Always an asset on his arm. But she'd not affected his heart. She'd turned his head and then turned his stomach.

Arms crossed, Barrett leaned against the doorway. He pushed away the image of Annie's wrist that flittered through his mind. Weakness would do no one any good. Not him. Not her.

'Go back to keep an eye on the Carsons,' Barrett told Gavin. 'I've almost finished the plans I have for him and I need to check the background on the other shops around him. I plan to own all the properties on that side of the street from the booksellers to the cutlery business.'

'Mr Barrett,' the carriage driver called out, cap in hand, running to the base of the stairway.

Barrett turned to the new arrival, waiting as the man stomped his way up the stairs.

'Yes?'

'I've found out about the woman as you asked me. The old woman outside the Carson house. She's the crone the ladies of the *ton* hire to tell their fortunes.'

He'd heard of her, but he'd never seen her before. Odd that such a crone was at the Carson household. And he was certain Annie was the cause of it.

'Do you know where the fortune teller lives?'

The man nodded. 'She moves around a bit, but you can likely find her on the North Road just before the Earl of Standridge's estate. She is said to know so many secrets people are afraid to make her go on her way.'

'Just like me,' Gavin said, bowing.

'*Please* go away,' Barrett said, then turned to the carriage driver as Gavin left. 'I won't need you to find out anything else. Thank you.'

Barrett walked into the room, shutting himself alone with his father.

'So you are taking over Carson's shops.'

'Yes.'

'Didn't he have three daughters?' his father asked.

'I wouldn't know.'

His father burst out laughing. 'Of course you would. It's your business to know such things. How a man's daughters marry affects his fortunes.'

Barrett watched his father, ignoring the words. His thoughts remained on Annie. Annie—a jewel, ready to be taken by the first thief who happened upon her.

He doubted any man who'd stood as close to her as he had would not have been aroused. She just did that to a man. Without even being aware. The twists and turns of her body as she'd moved to deliver blows had been almost more than he could bear. Heat rose in his body even when he thought of it. She'd struck at him and it had been so easy to deflect her. Her parents should listen to him and get her married off to a milksop who would cherish her.

He had to get her out of his thoughts. She was little more than another society daughter who worried over the colour of her dress and spent too much time staring at her fingernails. He'd update the ledgers and get a night's sleep, or try to. Tomorrow he would wake and Annie would be erased from his mind. Gone.

Barrett watched his father study the columns of ink.

'I thought about buying Carson's business. But he

didn't want to sell to me and his wares didn't seem profitable.' The old man stared at the pages.

'He had no choice. I choked off his suppliers, raised their prices and he must now pay so much that he cannot make a profit. Not that he was making much of one anyway.'

His father nodded. 'I made a good choice when I kept your grandmother from killing you.'

'She told me I had you to thank for my life and I didn't think she meant it in a paternal way.'

He nodded. 'I had no wish for another marriage, nor the task of starting over with a new heir. Just didn't make sense to put all the effort into you and then take a chance on so many variables.'

Barrett had lived with his father's reasoning so long that he didn't question it at all. He reached over and took the ledger back. 'Let's review the accounts together then. I would hate not being able to give you a return on your investment.'

The man nodded, chewing nothing and never looking up.

Barrett sat at the desk in his father's room, gradually surrounding himself with papers. Sometimes his father stood at his side, reading, too, and gave an insightful comment. His business knowledge always amazed Barrett. His father had more ledger book inside him than any person he'd ever seen.

Finally the old man tottered over to his bed and fell asleep.

Barrett dozed, but in the early hours, a knock awoke him and he called out to enter.

Summers held a note to Barrett, letting cool wisps

of air into the room. 'The physician dropped this off a few moments ago, but he could not stay. He has been summoned to the Carsons' again. Mrs Carson is having the vapours one moment and the wrath of heavens the next.'

Barrett took the note, the paper cold to his touch. He read. Annie had disappeared, leaving a letter behind that said she was going after her sister. The old woman's cart had been seen outside the house in the night.

His father woke, staring at the paper in Barrett's hand.

'So you don't know whether Carson has three daughters, but you certainly know enough to get a missive when the mother is distraught.' He chuckled. 'Careful, Son. You're more like me than you know. Sounds like you might have a child on the way.'

He left without answering his father.

Chapter Nine

Annie had had to stay awake in order to be sure she wouldn't miss meeting the old woman and she'd not been able to rest in the back of the rickety cart. The blanket she'd sat on had been used more by animals than by people, and she'd be glad to get away from the scent.

The darkness had lingered and Annie rested with her reticule held close while she leaned on her satchel. The wheels on the cart must have nearly worn off the axles because it wobbled with a regularity that Annie had become accustomed to after an hour. They took a detour from the main road and the cart stopped at the ragged camp, but it was a true home. The grass had been worn away. Wood gathered. Chickens were scratching about. Stumps had been cut for seats around the fire. Canvases had been stretched at another firepit, making a three-sided enclosure to trap the heat and keep whomever might sit under it warm. Firewood was stacked just inside and around the edges, adding to the walled feeling of it.

When the cart stopped, she put her reticule on the

satchel and pushed them to the edge of the cart, then jumped out. The old woman walked to Annie's side and Annie snatched the reticule close.

The woman's eyes glittered and she took the satchel. 'You act as if I might steal.'

'I think you no different than I am,' Annie said.

The woman cackled. 'Then I will keep my eyes on my silver,' she said.

She put the satchel down by a stump.

'Pardon me,' Annie said, walking to the woods. 'I shall need a chamber pot.'

'Behind the canvas,' the woman said. 'It's hidden by the ivy. I wouldn't get too close as there are stinging nettles there and you'll be itching all the way to Scotland.'

Annie took the reticule with her and hurried as much as she could. Then when she returned, the woman seemed to have forgotten her presence.

In an hour or so, the soup was done and she handed Annie a bowl.

'Ed will travel with you on the mail coach,' the old woman said as they sat around the camp eating their breakfast.

'A mail coach?' Annie took a bite of the rough stew, trying to force her teeth tight enough to gnaw the last bite of meat softer. It didn't work. She swallowed the chunk.

'Yes. Tomorrow you'll both take it and when you arrive in Scotland, you'll be able to find your sister.'

The old woman's eyes darted to the road. A rider on a horse was on the road, moving in their direction.

The men in the camp moved closer to the central part, all eyes focused on the road.

The man slid from his horse, still too far away for his face to be clear. Annie lowered the bowl.

The man walked closer, his hat and the riding boots making him appear taller than any of the men around her. It wasn't only the width of his shoulders that made everyone in the camp take notice. She knew it. He walked with the assurance of having an army behind him, or maybe within him.

She'd recognised Barrett in the dark, she realised. As she'd known she would.

She could feel her body becoming smaller as he strode towards them.

She took in air, forcing herself still and to sit straight, waiting.

'Appears you have a parcel that I've been looking for.' His words were to the crone, but his eyes were on Annie.

He kept moving nearer and placed himself with nothing between the two of them. She realised he'd led the horse a few steps closer to the men. A barrier on four legs.

'My daughter. She'd be for sale, but you likely don't have any coin on you.'

Barrett didn't move. 'How much did she pay you to take her?'

'My daughter pays me nothing and she won't stop eating. She costs more than she's worth, but I feel like a matchmaking mama and wouldn't mind seeing her with a man such as yourself.'

'You should keep to your own business,' Annie spoke to Barrett, keeping her words strong.

'Right now that is you. Let's go,' he said to Annie. 'I'm tired. Your parents are worried. Your mother has had to send for the physician.'

'Tell her I'm fine,' Annie stood, walked behind the fire and put the bowl on a stump. 'The physician will take care of her. I'm not leaving.'

'You will.'

The men around her stood.

'I'll take you all on one at a time, or together. That's best. It's over quicker.'

'Don't get his blood on the rug,' the old crone said, looking at her men and kicking up dust. 'I just cleaned it.' She cackled.

Annie crossed her arms and stared at him. She forced all her strength into her legs and her glare. 'I'm going to be with my sister. She needs me more than my parents do. And if she wants to return home, I'll find a way to get her there.'

'Your sister, Honour, is going to have a baby in a few months. She fell in love with the man—Reginald—who brought wares to your father's shop. They ran away to Scotland to marry.'

Annie took a step back. That was true. Honour had told her Reginald was taking her to live with relatives while he found a house. His uncle in Scotland had work for him.

'How do you know?'

'I stayed several days in your home. Your father told me every bit of family lore and tale he knew. A letter to a man in Manchester who knew Reginald verified your father's suspicions.'

The thought of Honour having a child while being

so far from family hit Annie in the pit of her stomach. 'I must get to her now. I have no choice.'

'You do not even have her correct location. I do.'

'I can't believe you.'

'You can. I paid quite well for that information,' Barrett said, reaching out to her. 'You can't help her. You're only risking yourself. I'm taking you back to your home.'

She swung, arm extended.

He darted his head back, but she grazed his hat, causing it to fall. It plopped down on to a patch of mud, settling into the mire. He stared at the mud a moment, then back at Annie. 'I should have just let you hit me.'

'I *can* help my sister,' she said.

'If she needs help getting a hat off her head.' He shook his head, momentarily distracted.

'I told you to not swing the arm. And don't aim at the skull.' He pointed to his nose, his temple, his jaw and his chin. 'Four points to hit.' He held up the fingers on one hand besides his thumb. 'Four.'

'True love,' the old woman said and laughed. 'A man teaching his beloved how to hit him.' She looked at Annie and moved her arm wide. 'A child hits like that.' Then she moved her fist straight. 'This is how a woman says good morning.' She laughed again.

'Eyes speak louder than words and yours said plenty. You learned nothing I taught you. You did not practise at all,' Barrett said.

'I practised.'

'Not enough.' He gazed at her. 'Go back with me and I'll see that your sister has more help.'

'Why didn't you do this before?'

He shrugged. 'It didn't occur to me and I didn't

need to. You can't change the path of every leaf that falls from a tree. Your sister is where she needs to be for now.'

Annie turned and the old woman lifted Annie's satchel, holding the bag out to her.

'What's in it?' he asked the woman.

'Nothing of value,' the hag answered. 'At least, not any more.'

'That's not true. It has my jewelled pin.'

The woman poked out her bottom lip. 'I am certain it does not have a pin inside. You must have left it behind.'

Annie stalked forward, opened the case and looked inside, rummaging. Then she glared at the old woman. 'It's gone.'

'Ah. Must have fallen out.'

Annie looked from the woman to Barrett.

'I don't have it.' He lowered his chin, eyes still staring at her, and held out a hand to indicate she leave.

'My pin.' She looked at the woman, pointing. 'I have had it since birth. It was my grandmother's.'

The woman raised both hands. 'I do not have jewels for my hair. The other women would be jealous.'

'You thief.'

'Yes.' The woman nodded. 'I have a skill. And you, miss?'

Barrett reached in his waistcoat pocket and held out a coin. 'I want to buy a jewelled pin.'

'Fancy that,' the woman said. 'I have one for sale.' She pulled it out of the folds of her dress, blew on it, then wiped it on her skirt before exchanging it for the coin.

Barrett took the bauble and tucked it in his waist-coat pocket.

His eyes challenged Annie to ask for it back. Instead, she turned to the old woman.

'You were paid to take me to my sister.'

'Of course.' The woman batted her lashes. 'And if you are still here in the morning, we will do just that.' She glanced at Barrett. 'Sound fair to you?'

He didn't answer the question, but turned to Annie, grabbing the satchel. 'Let's go. You can verify everything I said about your sister by writing to her when I get you back to your home. I'll help your sister if you leave with me,' he said. 'Consider your odds, your sister's welfare and your own. You only have one good option. But it's not my choice to make.'

Annie looked at him and then at the old woman. Then she tossed her reticule to the woman. The woman caught it, almost dropping it, shock in her eyes.

'There's the rest I owe you. Thank you very much.'

'You are such an innocent,' Barrett said. She should never have given the woman more funds.

'Yes, I am,' Annie said, stalking beside him. She turned back, shouting to the men. 'Make sure she shares everything with you. I had two jewelled pins in my satchel.'

Barrett opened his mouth, but she had a look of too much innocence. If there was another pin, he wasn't staying to find it.

He looked at the bedraggled miss and his body reacted. Instantly, he swore at himself. This was not how he was supposed to feel. Something had gone wrong in his head the moment he'd seen her wrist and it still grew inside him like a wound that wouldn't heal. And he'd never had a wound that wouldn't heal.

He tugged the ribbons on his horse and stepped towards the road. Her footsteps sounded at his side.

The inn they'd passed earlier would make a good place to get the mud and filth off him and keep her safe while putting distance between them.

For the moment, he had to get her safely away from the camp.

They traipsed along without speaking until they reached the main road.

'Why could you not stay in your warm house with your servants?' he spoke, the words echoing in his mind.

'I did not ask you to follow me. Why didn't you stay in your warm house with your servants?'

A thousand answers entered his mind. None acceptable to him, but all hinging on the same fact that Annie had been traipsing off after her sister without any chaperon and the woman could not disable a gnat.

'My horse needed the exercise,' he said. 'It would have been unacceptable to get my stable master out of bed that early to do what I had hired him to do in my stead, like exercise my horse.' He softened his voice. 'Don't you agree it would have been very bad manners on my part to make the poor man traipse out in the countryside this early?'

'Positively. I would never do such a thing. I would get up myself and tackle the problem.'

'You are so thoughtful and considerate.' His face was away from her and he knew she couldn't see him look to the heavens and frown. 'You did not make me ride all the way to Scotland. I appreciate that.'

She grumbled, a choking cough sound. Apparently his sarcasm hadn't been well disguised. A faux pas. Perhaps her ire was not of the intensity that he felt inside himself, but he'd ruined a hat and his boots weren't doing much better on the muddy path.

The road was little more than a rut and would remain the same until they reached the inn and nothing would change that.

But they'd make faster time if she rode.

He tightened his hold on the ribbons in one hand, then walked back and reached for Annie's arm, but stopped midway and let his hand drop. He didn't need to be touching her. Inwardly he cursed himself.

'Come on.' He stepped over another mound of dirt and turned to see that she followed.

Annie gathered the sides of her skirts, taking a broad step over the uneven ground, and he saw the slippers she wore. Those had never been out of London before the journey.

He pulled the horse even with her and tied the satchel to the saddle. 'You can ride?'

'Not very well,' she said.

'I'll get you situated.' Although it would be impossible without touching her. Well, it couldn't be helped.

She put her hand on his arm and he grabbed her waist and turned, sweeping her off her feet and holding her in the air, putting the horse right in front of her.

He tried not to feel anything through his fingertips. But he could feel so much naked skin through the layers of dress and corset, and—no—his mind was going in the wrong direction. Chemise. Chemise, those shapeless bags of a garment that only had any form when they touched the skin underneath and called out for a man's eyes to take note.

He sat her so she could grasp the pommel.

He took a second, keeping his eyes locked on hers while he mentally pried his fingers from her waist, releasing, he knew, his nearness to a well-formed, feminine garment that could have taken a good hour of his time just to explore. Forget about how much time he could devote to everything near it. 'I'm not happy with you. I do not like being your chaperon.'

Because if he hadn't been her chaperon he was blasted sure he could get her away from any other chaperon on the face of the earth.

Turning his head, he only kept the barest glimpse on her so she could slip her opposite foot into the stirrup. She perched sideways on the saddle and he stepped back.

'Can you hang on?' he asked, reaching again for the ribbons.

'I think…not.' The horse took a step and he caught her as she slid into his arms, her foot dangling in the stirrup. His nose told him she smelled more like a saddle blanket than a woman, but everything in his hands screamed female to his inner and outer extremities. And his brain wafted the scent of bedcovers in front of him.

He put her down quickly, but the damage was done. He shoved away the thoughts of breasts, of hips, of soft curves tangling around him.

He gritted his teeth and stepped closer to the horse, taking in a big whiff of sweaty beast, leather and manure. Hoping to cleanse his mind of the scents that were dancing along inside him.

'My parents never let me ride,' she said. 'They didn't want us trampled.'

'That's thoughtful of them.' Very thoughtful, but not for him and not in this situation.

Oh, hell, it was out of his hands. At least she was, for the moment. A good thing. Certainly. But he could still feel her waist. And the chemise. He was certain it had been washed so many times that it had softened and now caressed her, hugging close.

His feelings pounded into his body and his head was trying to talk some sense into him, and it was getting him nowhere. He imagined his brain shrugging its way into the size of a peanut and telling him he was on his own.

His intentions vibrated from one side of his thoughts to the other, but his mind focused on her legs. It was as if he still touched her. He tried to push his imaginings a different direction with his words. 'Your parents need to hire a companion for you. One with eyes in the back of her head and who does not mind chasing after you in the night.'

She squared her shoulders and raised her face to look at him. 'You did not have to come after me. I was fine until you did. I'm not enjoying listening to your complaints or looking at your sour face.' She lifted the edge of her skirt to move forward. 'And I could have helped my sister. It might have taken me longer, but I could have.'

'If one of the ruffians you ran away with decided to do you harm, you would have been at their mercy.' He followed at her side, pleased for an argument. Anything was better than the thoughts of her chemise.

And then he thought of Annie being damaged at the hands of her companions.

'Do you see?' His body shook. His voice thundered. 'Do you see what you just did? You left your safe house to travel with people who would steal a pin.' Or a man who would notice softness and curves.

'It's not my fault. I am an innocent, apparently, and can make friends with all sorts of low types.' She swaggered her shoulders and he took the jab as she began to walk straight through the muddiest part of the road.

He steered her to the edge where the grass kept the mud at bay.

'Your mother is terrified she will never see you again. I am not used to being summoned by a distraught mother. Nor do I wish to take care of someone who does not know to be happy with all the baubles of life.'

The road was dryer and he kept walking. Even with the horse, he had to walk. Riding two abreast with an arm around her and her legs dangling down from her skirt would likely do what a hundred jabs at Gentleman Jackson's hadn't been able to do. It would take him to the ground. He switched hands with the ribbons and walked fast enough so that he could move the horse between them.

'Life is not about baubles.' She walked in the road and Barrett again steered her to the more stable grass. He had no idea of what it was like to live in a cage with only two others to be friends with, then to lose them.

She loved her family. She loved her parents. She didn't like having her mother at her elbow at every dance, smiling at eligible men. She was certain her mother had scared away all the ones she didn't deem eligible for her daughters by giving them that sweet *drop dead, you big hairy beast* smile. A few of the eligible ones had certainly noticed how well the Carson sisters were guarded and kept their distance.

Oh, goodness, her mother would have abhorred it if a man spoke more than four words to Annie if he'd not been someone her mother deemed worthy of matrimony.

'You have been eating too many confections.' Barrett held a limb back so it would not hit her as she walked by. 'It makes you believe in nothing but sweetness. The world is not so simple. I learned that at my father's knee.'

'He should have taught you about more than that.'

'Oh, he did.'

'I dare say you would make a horrible tutor, unless it is for boxing.' She lifted the edge of her dirt-caked skirt.

Her shoes were not made for anything more uneven than a few cobblestones and he'd begun walking faster. She pulled her dress up and scrambled to keep up with him. Now, he didn't seem to care if he left her behind. He was in a foul mood.

She'd never heard a man curse so much. In fact, she'd hardly ever heard a man curse. He strung the words together in such a way it almost sounded as if he spoke a foreign language. It didn't seem the time to remind him she was a lady and one didn't talk so in front of a lady. She wasn't even sure if one spoke so in front of another man.

And legs. She didn't know why he cursed legs.

'Would you stop with the foul language?' she asked, scurrying to keep abreast, lifting her skirt higher so it wouldn't drag on the uneven ruts. 'I do not even know what half those words mean.'

He stopped. He looked at her. He cocked his head. 'You just need to be quiet. I am not used to having a woman around. My apologies for the language, I'm just damned...' He paused, took in a breath. 'It's just not something I'm used to. Other people take care of my—female problems.'

'Well, I'm not used to being around a man and you don't hear me swearing.'

'Oh, by all means, go right ahead. It will make the trip go faster.'

'I don't think it really would.'

'This is why you are kept locked away in your parents' house. You don't understand a man's thoughts.'

'You can't tell me you planned this.'

'Miss Carson. It seems you are the one who planned this, if you remember.'

'Well, I did.'

'You take off with a woman who is a stranger—'

'She's got the highest recommendations. The servants have spoken of her for years. She saved the rag-and-bone collector's life with one of her herbal mixtures. And she sells the best shawls, which surprises me given that she dresses in rags.'

'Spare me.'

She hurried along behind him. 'I didn't ask you to come after me. In fact, I waited until you were gone before I left.'

He paused, then looked at her. He took in a breath, then he smiled. 'Thank you for that consideration. I take full responsibility. And I take full responsibility for getting you safely home which may be more than a mere mortal can handle.'

'If you can manage Gentleman Jackson's, I should be no problem.'

'You are.'

He turned and strode away, and she kept up with him even though it meant that she had to take the straighter course which was through the mud. Her slipper mired in the road. When she raised her foot, the shoe stayed behind. She turned, putting her toes down, holding her dress out of the muck.

She twisted the tail of her skirt, draped it over her arm and bent to pry the shoe out of the mud, hearing the gasp as it released its captive. Her stockings would never be white again.

He continued walking along and she stood holding her skirt tail over one arm and a muddied shoe in the other.

'Mr Barrett.' Her voice rose. 'Mr Barrett. Wait up. You are leading me through a mess.'

He turned, his mouth widened and he stared. She dropped her shoe, ignoring the squish of putting a foot inside it, and fisted her hands on her skirt and took off after him, the shoes flopping in the mud.

She caught up with him. 'I wore my sturdiest shoes, but I did not expect to walk in a swamp.' She raised her chin and wiped her muddied hand on her dress. 'Your arm, please.'

'This is not a soirée,' he said, looking at the mud remaining on her hand before holding out his elbow. 'Trotting out in the night like a babe walking right into the fire. Stumbling headfirst into it. Unable to pull yourself back until it is too late.'

She'd trusted a stranger. Him. She'd left the woman she'd hired to take her closer to her sister and trusted him.

'I have money for you to give to my sister,' she said.

She paused then, reached to open her coat and searched her spencer for the pocket she'd sewn inside. She pulled out folded notes. 'There's more.'

He took the paper, turned it over and examined it. 'How did you get this?'

'I've been selling the dresses my sisters left behind. No one has noticed.'

'I am impressed. You do have a skill.'

'I was taking the money to my sister.'

He mumbled a growl under his breath, but didn't speak at first. He held the notes up, then paused. 'Is that all you have?' He held the notes steady, then thrust them back at her. 'Keep them.'

'I shall.' She snapped them from his hand.

He just stood there, shaking his head as she tucked the money inside her spencer.

'I do not know how anyone could be so protected as you,' he said. 'I can't figure out who is the aberration. You or me.'

'In my life, it would be you,' she said.

'Same here.'

'I made a mistake.' She moved forward, her words quietened. 'Yes. I made a mistake. I see that now. I should have hired you at the beginning, but then, one doesn't hire a viscount's son.'

'No. One does not.' He raised his hand, and extended a finger and pointed to the trees canopying the road. 'You left a house of people who care for you and ran off. You risked your entire future. Your life. For what? To chase off after a sister who has no more sense than a sheep without a shepherd?'

'She is having a baby.'

'Your sisters were senseless. Your parents want better for you.'

'I'm sure they do,' she said. 'So do I.'

'You left with an old man and old woman who could have sold you to anyone.'

'No.' She shook her head. 'No. I know of her. She would do no such thing. Many other women in London have hired her for help.'

'How much do you really know of that old bag of tricks?'

She shook her head, not answering. The woman had helped Honour. Honour had made a mistake and decided that she could only redeem herself by marriage and the woman had helped her travel without anyone finding out.

'Your risk was too great,' he said.

She walked faster, catching up to him. 'Try to stop me. I have practised defending myself,' she said, moving forward.

He reached out, dropping the ribbons, one arm clamping on her like a vice.

She stopped and let herself stumble sideways into him, then she slammed her foot near his boot. He moved his foot aside and she bent her knees, causing him to step forward with the pull of her weight. Then she pushed back her head, not hitting him, but stopping then to turn and look at his face.

'Elbow,' he growled at her ear.

She regained her footing and slammed her elbow straight back, and it brushed his coat as he moved aside. 'Try bending one knee next time.' He remained behind her. 'Drop *one* knee. Lower, twist and slam.'

She tried it, turning into the elbow punch. He caught her as she stumbled and kept her upright. He felt sturdier than her house and she felt more secure in his arms than she had in her own room.

'Better,' he said, his voice husky. Her skirt tangled around his legs and he held her close with both hands.

'If I'd not been expecting it, you would have connected well.' He shook his head. 'But the sad truth is that you don't have much strength in that little elbow.'

He stepped away, but he touched the small of her back with one hand. With his other, he clasped hers, helping her make a fist. 'Next time, hold it with your other hand and shove back with all your might.'

His breath brushed her cheek and his eyes changed. Everything stilled as he continued to hold her. 'Did you notice that you keep throwing yourself into my arms?'

'Not on purpose.' She thought of the sparring. 'Entirely.' She felt a sudden burst of warmth in the air around her. 'And did you notice you keep catching me?'

A smile slipped on to his face. 'What else am I to do?'

'You have little choice there.' She shrugged. 'My pardon.'

But she didn't know if he would have done it for any woman, or just for her. 'I suspected you might come after me,' she said.

'Your parents were worried. I would do *that* for anyone,' he said. 'Well, or I would have sent someone else after them.'

All the relief at seeing him—all the pleasant thoughts of him coming to her aid—vanished.

'You would?' she asked. 'Anyone?'

'I could see how much your father and mother care for you.'

'Of course they do.'

His head bent closer to hers. 'There is no *of course* about it.'

He turned and strode away, leaving her to catch up.

She couldn't speak at first, thinking, and just putting one foot in front of the other as she trekked. Of course. Of course parents cared for their children. They might not always show it. It was nature that parents care for their children. Like mother birds care for their baby birds.

'Some parents care more for their pets than they do their children and some people do not even care for their pets,' he said.

He'd somehow become jaded, perhaps because he didn't have children of his own and never would and it had made him angry. 'How could you grow up so?' she asked.

'I had no choice. It was root hog, or die.'

'Root hog, or die?' she asked.

'It is from the Americas. Some people let their pigs loose in the woods to fend for themselves so they will not have to feed them and only see them when it is time to butcher them. If the pigs do not root out their meals, they die.'

'But you were fed.'

'Of course I was fed, our servants being well trained.' He met her gaze. 'Do you have any idea what it was like the first time my father used me to break the glass around him? He found a certain joy in picking me up and using me to clear the top of a table, delighting in the disarray. I think there was game in it for him. A certain skill in sliding me across the table to completely clear it. Finally, no breakables were left on the tables except for mealtimes and the servants placed the lamps on shelves on the wall.'

'No.' She clasped his arm.

She felt off balance and, even though her body didn't touch his, she could feel him along the length of her. He put his hand over the touch she had on his arm.

He smiled, dark and light mixed. Laughter and anger. 'It became almost a game to me as well. I learned to land on my feet or roll, mostly. Father's rages were the Sunday afternoon entertainment. Better than any theatre. It became so routine and so much blustering and rage it was a little like theatre. A farce. I didn't hate it or dread it. I accepted that it was the way things were.'

'Someone should have stopped that.'

'Who?' he asked. 'My beloved grandmother? She instigated it, often as not. My father calmed some after she died. He said he wished he'd not buried her in a crypt so he could have danced on her grave. He would have, too, and hired a fiddler.'

'Still, someone should have stopped it.'

He paused. His eyes became bland. He seemed to have no thoughts behind his words. Barrett looked at her. 'Someone should have stopped it, you say. No one was there to stop it, Annie. Sometimes there isn't anyone there to stop things. That is what I am trying to tell you.'

'I'm sorry,' she said.

He looked into the distance, then back at her. 'Don't be. It made me stronger.'

'Are you sure?'

'Yes. I don't feel pain the way other people seem to feel it. I don't care the same way other people care. I just don't. I didn't realise it until I saw the others at Gentleman Jackson's. A man's face paled from pain. Another cast up his accounts. I could not understand it. I thought them just weak. Then someone noticed how I reacted and told me I was the aberration.'

'I think that isn't a good thing.'

'I am content with it.' He shrugged. 'It is easier to play the game when you cannot be touched. When they cannot make you suffer and you can make them suffer, and they know it.'

He kicked at a stick that had fallen on to the road, moving it from their path with his boot.

'You have some kindness in you. You care about my safety.'

He looked at her. 'Until this moment, I thought I had no weakness left in me. But I see how I have let soft feelings grow in me. A mistake. They'll do me no good. They'll make me no richer.'

'Does everything have to be about wealth?'

He looked away, arms still at his sides. 'How could it be otherwise?'

Annie touched his sleeve. 'Perhaps it could be about people. Deep in his heart I'm sure your father cares for you.'

'No, Annie. For him it's all about money, more money, and the power it buys.'

She held the cloth of his coat in her hand. She had to let him know that he was mistaken. That even though his father didn't appear to care for him—all fathers cared for their children. They might not show it, but the love was there nonetheless.

She caught his eyes and it seemed as though she could see straight past the man into the child beneath all the whiskers and rough edges. And she wasn't certain the boy would have been less jaded. In fact, she feared he might have been more.

He stopped moving, reaching up to clasp the leather from the horse's bridle. Annie held his arm. He'd never seen such an innocent before. Not even in a cradle.

How could he tell her that she endangered herself with her soft-coloured view of the world? He couldn't. No one could. Her parents did right to keep her within their reach.

Annie stumbled. He steadied her and pulled her closer as she walked. 'I can't imagine living like you must have,' she said.

'Just as well. It's the past. It died away after my father realised I was bigger than he was.' He laughed softly. 'A handy thing to have. Size. And then I went to Gentleman Jackson's and studied the sport of it. Another fortunate thing is the way I learned to take a punch and land easily. It seems I have known it all my life. Like walking and talking.'

She wrapped her arms around his, her face at the cloth where his coat covered his shoulder. He needed to distance himself, but it would hardly be possible without hurting her feelings. Besides, he liked the odd feeling of walking along as a couple.

It had a feeling of…he wasn't sure what. Of companionship. Of togetherness. Of sharing a journey together rather than being alone. Perhaps even of weakness. He sighed internally.

'I can hardly walk another step,' she said. 'I didn't remember how far away the inn was.'

His footsteps slowed, making it easier for her, as he realised he'd probably been walking too fast for her.

His voice barely sounded through the air. 'This morning, did you leave your house for the adventure or for your sister?'

She shook her head. 'A little of both. I wanted to see my sister, and then I got angry at her for leaving us. Why did she not trust us enough to stay? Why didn't she trust us to take her secrets as our own?'

'Secrets,' he said. 'The eternal tie that binds families.'

'You understand that?'

'Yes. That, I understand.'

'How could I risk her not having family around when the child is born? And how can I live the rest of my life with my parents watching me as though I am the last bit of porcelain in a treasured set? They have made certain I am the wallflower at any event. My mother stands at my side and does not dance because someone without connections might swoop in upon me and whisk me away. And the ones she picks for me are insipid.'

'Life is a business and your parents want you to be well off. They care for you.'

'They wish me to walk exactly on the path they have chosen for me.'

'We all have to walk the path we were born into.'

'I cannot help being the way I am.' He heard the apology in her voice.

'I want you to stay the same, Annie. Though I understand that it's not possible.' His words flowed with the softness of knife covered with a soft cloth. 'You have a right to go out among the other people in the world. Even if the world may disappoint you.' The briefest of smiles. 'And the world *will* disappoint you.'

Chapter Ten

The inn was up ahead, but it was hardly more than a large house with a battered sign that showed a bird and a boar, if one had an imagination. A horse stood tethered to a tree.

He stopped. 'I think it will be easier for you to pass as my wife than it will be for me to pass as your chaperon.'

She stopped. 'I…disagree. I think I can…'

'Yes?'

She held out her rumpled dress and looked at him. 'You might be embarrassed to have me thought of as your wife. I'm a mess.'

He examined her face. Petal-soft everywhere. She made the smudges of mud look endearing.

'And you cannot stay in the room with me,' she said. 'That would be unheard of.'

His jaw moved before he spoke. 'Completely.' But not un-thought-of.

He had to keep his distance. 'We'll pretend to be married. You'll tell the innkeeper we're having a quarrel not long after we arrive and ask for separate rooms. It will certainly convince them we are married.'

'But I'm not a good liar. You should do it.'

'You will do it. You will succeed.' No one would ever believe his wanting a room separate from her. Not with a brain in their head. 'It has to be you.'

She looked at his face, opened her mouth to speak, then closed it. 'I don't think I can.'

He looked at her. 'We'll have a fight in front of them, then.'

She looked at him. 'That's preposterous.'

He shook his head. 'People disagree more than they agree. Whatever I say, just find fault with it.'

'Well.' She raised her chin. 'I will do the best I can.'

They walked into the inn, where two men sat talking with a woman on a bench near the wall, and the scent of bread filled the room. One of the men wore a battered wig that could have been left over from a grandfather and he had a pipe in his hand. The other had on a pair of breeches with garters holding up his stockings.

'Welcome.' The man with the powdered wig looked his way.

'Do you have a room for us to rest the night? My wife is tired,' he said. 'And so is our horse.'

'What happened to you?' The woman stood, even though it didn't make her much taller. She stared at Annie. 'You look as if you've been rolled in a barrel of mud.'

'I need liquid,' he said, interrupting to keep questions at bay. 'The stronger the better. If it doesn't singe my insides, it's too weak.'

'You been married long?' the man asked.

'Seems like a lifetime,' he answered and his eyes flickered to her. She didn't speak.

'Don't it, though,' the one with the garters spoke. 'I'm married ten years.'

'You've not been married that long,' the wigged one spoke. 'You was married this last year.' He stood and filled a mug, and put it down in front of Barrett.

'Well, it seems like ten years.' The young one laughed.

'Seems like thirty for me.' Barrett glanced at her. Her eyes flickered and her mouth opened. A stab of guilt hit him. He raised his brows, trying to give her a cue to fight back.

'My wife finds fault with everything I do,' he said. 'My wife finds fault with everything I do,' he repeated.

Her hand went to her lips and trembled.

'Here, now,' the one with the powdered wig spoke again. 'Don't be abusing your wife so.' He looked at Annie. 'She appears to be a gentle sort.'

'Too gentle,' Barrett said.

'That's the best kind.' The man took a puff of his pipe.

'Yes,' the other one said. 'My wife shrieks at me from the moment I step into the house. Be grateful you have such a quiet woman.'

'She *could* speak a little more.' Barrett lowered his chin. 'Annie...'

'I suppose I could.' The words seemed to end on a whimper and she had a startled look in her eyes.

'Annie? Would you speak?'

The man with the pipe put it down, rose and had a fist clenched. The other one followed, eyes tight. 'You leave the woman alone.'

Barrett watched the two. The wind from his fist

would have knocked them over. They were no bigger than the spindles on a staircase—put together.

He looked at Annie. He didn't want to tussle with them, or her. They'd knocked all the spirit of a fight out of him. 'My pardon.'

'Thank you,' she whispered.

'Ah, for the love of—' He turned to the wigged man, tilted his head to the side, firmed his lips and said. 'I have treated her abominably. I feel guilt to the core of my soul. I would not want to discomfort her for a moment more. Do you have a spare room for me so that I might spent the night in contemplation of my errors?'

'Oh, now...' The woman walked back into the room. She waved a hand. 'We women are much stronger than that. We forgive. Over and over and over.' She smiled at her husband. 'It is our lot in life.'

'That it is,' the man said. 'They're the salt of the earth. Wives.'

'Do you have an empty room? For me? Near her?' he asked. 'I feel that I have deeply wronged her and I would not wish her to forgive too quickly.'

'You are wantin' another room?' the woman asked.

'Yes.' Annie nodded. 'He has a sickness. An affliction. Epidemeosis. It's caused by being around me. My humours irritate him.'

The one with the garters spoke up. 'Haven't seen a husband yet not irritated by his wife's humours being out of order.' He looked at Barrett. 'Just get a pair of braces. They'll hold up your trousers and the humours won't bother you so bad.'

'I do not have an *affliction*.'

Annie blinked. 'It's nothing to be ashamed of.'

His jaw firmed. 'I'm not ashamed.'

'Oh,' the woman said, backing away from him. The man with the wig stepped behind the man with the garters. 'We can't be letting you stay if it might be contagious.' She looked at Barrett. 'You'll have to leave. Both of you.'

Barrett saw the warm blankets flittering away and a long, cold walk ahead of them. 'Annie,' Barrett said. 'It's a fair way to London in the dark.'

She nodded. 'He's fine. I just don't forgive easily as I've not been married thirty years yet.' She raised her chin. 'Why, it seems like just this very second I was married.'

'That's more like what my wife would say.' The one with the garters chuckled and sat.

'We will get you a room,' the innkeeper's wife said. 'Just the one.'

'One?' Barrett asked. He heard a damn squeak trying to sneak into his voice and corrected it. 'One. No. Two.'

'Yes. Just the one.' The innkeeper's wife took the thin towel from the counter and gave it a flop to shake out crumbs, then smiled at Barrett. 'A little quiet talking in the dark will be good for both of you.'

Annie gasped. 'We've never talked quietly before. In the dark.'

The men snickered and the innkeeper's wife took in a breath. 'Well, it is time you learned.' Her cheeks reddened. 'For the sake of the children.'

'Thank you.' Barrett turned, paused, lowered his voice, frowned and said, 'Children.'

The woman led them both out of the room, pointed to the doorway to the left. She raised a brow. 'No fussing. No fighting. I want a promise from both of you.'

'I won't,' Annie said, clasping her hands in front of her.

For the first time in his life, Barrett couldn't find words. He just nodded.

'There, now.' The older woman reached out and patted his sleeve. 'I can tell in my heart that you're a good 'un. I know we women have our moments, but so do men.' She cleared her throat and looked away. 'A little *quiet* conversation, with *tender* forgiveness, makes everything better.'

She rushed away.

He doubted Annie's cheeks would ever return to their normal colour.

Opening the door, he stood aside to let Annie precede him.

She took in a breath and raised her foot to step over the threshold, but then her movements froze.

He waited. She didn't move and had one foot still in the air.

He leaned down, his lips near her ear. 'Pardon me, but you're blocking the path.' He reached out, giving a tug on her arms while pulling her against him. He watched for her to flail him when he touched her, but she was more concerned with staring into the room. He picked her up and carried her over the threshold.

She sputtered, gasped and clutched at his arms. He moved forward, depositing her gently on her feet. She jumped back. 'That was uncalled for.'

'It's a tradition.'

'For brides.'

'And people who will not step out of your way.'

He looked at the bed, shook his head, and then at her. 'I can be tender.'

Her eyes opened wide.

'If you were wondering.'

He shut the door behind him.

'No.' She stepped sideways, remaining close to the wall. 'I wasn't.'

'Didn't think so.'

He took off his frock coat and tossed it to a chair. He sat on the bed and tugged off one boot and then the other. He kept his waistcoat on, and the cravat.

He lay down on the bedcovers and stared overhead. The very act of taking off his stockings would terrify her. He lay immobile—in all parts of his body that he could control.

Glancing at her, he realised she'd taken some of his advice and was standing a safe distance, and could leave the room with minimal movements.

He shut his eyes, wishing for sleep and not wishing to sleep. How could one sleep when Annie was so close?

Without opening his eyes, he asked, 'Do you usually sleep standing up?'

'No. I'm learning a new skill.'

He slung out an arm, reached across the bed, grasped the covers and flung them over himself. He opened his eyes to slits. 'You can be on bottom. I'll be on top.'

Not a single blush. No notion of what he'd said. Innocence. 'Of the blankets,' he added unnecessarily.

She took in a breath 'I suppose I would not want either of us to sleep on the floor.'

'You may,' he said. 'It's up to you.'

He shut his eyes again. Light footsteps. A slow sag in the bed. A bare scoot. A rustle. Innocent. Innocent.

Innocent. And earning him a special spot in Hades if he touched her. His own Hades. He ground his teeth together. Perhaps he could say his prayers. He'd heard of people who did that before they slept and this might be the night for him to begin. He would need some help. No. Even that wouldn't work. He'd be praying for the wrong things.

He flopped the covers over her without opening his eyes.

He felt her shuffling about, sorting the covers, fluttering a lavender scent from the fabric into the air. She managed to get a wisp of a bedcover over his stomach and legs. Then she snuggled back into the little nest she'd made.

He closed his eyes, wondering how he would ever fall asleep with her next to him.

'Pardon.' He heard her whisper, sounding quieter than he'd ever heard. 'Pardon.' Annie. Louder.

'You're snoring,' she said.

'I wasn't asleep.'

'Oh, yes, you were. You were snoring. Loud.'

'I wasn't asleep.'

'You were asleep. Unless you snore when you're awake.'

He realised the covers were tossed aside. He'd not known he'd fallen asleep. But then, he had been up most of two days.

'And you have taken up more than half the bed.' She tugged at the covers and he saw that he lay on some of them.

'It's a small bed.'

'It wasn't until you started spreading out and took the middle as your half.'

He sat up and looked across at her. She was rather hugging the edge of the bed.

Turning to the side, he sat up and slipped his cravat out of its choking knot. He undid his waistcoat and threw it on top of his coat, and the cravat followed. He touched his shirt and pulled it out of his waistband, and her sharp intake of breath caused him to pause.

He stopped moving for a second.

'Goodnight.' He lay down, kept both on his side and to his side of the bed, and stretched his feet. He felt refreshed. Alive. Aroused.

'Are you going to sleep?' she asked.

Anyone else in the entire world who asked that question at that moment would have got a different answer. 'I thought I might.'

'I've never slept away from my home before.'

'Ever?'

'No.' The covers rustled. 'When we were younger, my sisters and I left our doors open so we could call out to each other. I never thought I would miss that.'

Carefully, he rolled to his back. At least it was dark. She couldn't see him clamping his teeth. He raised his arm and put his elbow over his eyes. He wanted to listen to her. He did. His body did not.

'When my sister Laura became betrothed, I knew those days were over. Father had the banns read. Mother cried and cried. Father would hardly speak. They were so despairing of the match. Honour confided she felt suffocated.'

He sat up, feeling the mattress shift beneath him.

He turned away from her, stretching, shaking his body a bit, trying to change the subject within his head.

'I live with my—my father.'

'Even though he's been so mean to you?'

'It really makes no difference in my life now. He's ill. May have always been so. Who knows? He's being looked after now by a man I hired.'

He put his elbows on his knees and clasped his hands together, looking at the faint moonlight that came in through the windows.

'He drinks too much. I have had his poison reduced,' he said. 'Although why I don't let him drink himself into a stupor, I don't understand. At times, I thought of having it delivered to him in crates. Crates and crates of it. Because he can be so much easier to control when he cannot find his fist and he cannot find anyone else's face. He just doesn't stay at that point.'

She rolled towards him. 'He sounds miserable.'

'I suppose. Making everyone else around him suffer diverts his attention enough that he doesn't care. He's been better after Grandmother had the apoplexy.'

'What did you do when your grandmother died?' She remembered how he'd said his grandmother danced around his mother's body and she wondered if he'd done the same.

He moved a bit, softly shaking his head against the backboard of the bed. 'That was years ago.' He dismissed the words with a stretch. 'Servants took care of everything, except Father swamped himself with drink and I propped him up for the service, which lasted all of a minute. Then I put him into the carriage and he didn't wake up until the next day. It went much better than I expected.' He tapped his foot against the floor.

'It was a quiet day. I was able to get a lot of work done that evening.'

Closing his eyes, Barrett could feel Annie even though he didn't touch her. He didn't have to. She was so near.

But he kept himself immobile, staring at the window. Distancing himself just as he had when he was a child. He contented himself with listening, feeling, and the simple knowledge that she was there.

Annie could see the outline of his shoulder and the profile of his face. He looked strong. Stronger than anything she'd ever seen. And she'd really not minded listening to him snore. He'd not been as loud as she'd complained and the regular breathing had tempted her to sleep, but it had also teased her to stay awake.

'You know,' he said, settling back into the bed beside her, 'I've never realised how much I swear.'

When he moved, even the smallest amount, he drifted over the mattress. She could tell he tried to stay in his area, but he just didn't quite fit.

'You don't swear that much,' she said. 'Just those moments when you started out with me after leaving the camp.'

'Well, I would say I've tempered my speech around you. I'm probably speaking about half as much as usual.'

'I understand coarse talk.'

'Has anyone ever talked such around you, other than me?'

'Father says *damn* sometimes.'

'Bless him.' He chuckled. 'I say it sometimes, too. Not usually my first choice, though.'

'Well, Mother does correct him.'

'My life has been one of swearing and yours has been one of sweetness.' His breathing changed. 'I didn't have other children as companions, but I didn't miss them. I had my governess, an old sow of a creature, and she was to keep me in line. She was a distant relation. But she didn't stay long after my mother died. I enjoyed my moments alone. Most of them, anyway. They were rare. Even being locked in a cellar was a relief compared to being around Tizzy.'

Annie digested his words. Surely he exaggerated. Locked in a cellar?

'Father insisted I spend some time with him, probably to please my grandmother. I was her project,' he said.

She didn't understand the contradiction. 'But your grandmother…'

'Not my favourite person. She kept me as far as she could from my mother's parents. I was to be the heir, although she could barely tolerate that thought. I was the child she was to prepare to be Viscount even if it killed me. If I died, I didn't deserve the title.'

Surely he was having a jest at her expense, or he exaggerated as much as he swore. 'I had my sisters and we were close. We disagreed, but we were together. Almost all the time.'

It was a shame he'd not had more siblings.

The darkness in her house had enveloped her after her sisters left. Her mother had taken to the sofa and hardly moved except to moan. Her father paced. The only time either one of them had spoken had been to mourn for their lost family and then they'd remind each other that they still had her. It wasn't that she'd wanted to tumble headlong into a disastrous marriage or have a child, but she'd not planned on being a nurse-maid to her parents either.

Even as they had returned more to the routine of their days, she could feel them turning to her more and more. They'd almost seemed to devour her in their need for her.

At first she'd stayed in the attic at times to give herself a place to breathe, but when her father had asked her to move there, she'd felt too far away from the doors. Too far to go anywhere. A prisoner who could only escape by marrying the man they put in front of her. The sentence outweighed the crime.

'My father—the Viscount—always, in public, encouraged me to have an interest in books.'

His voice remained low and swept over her, capturing her attention.

'Father had some volumes,' he continued. 'Illustrated beautifully. The artists were quite good and he would boast to me how precious the books were. But then he decided he must get rid of them and he had me take them to a bookseller. When I arrived at the bookseller's and was let in the back door, I realised the books had been stolen and Father was selling them.'

She turned her head sideways. He didn't move.

'You think the books were stolen? That you, a child at the time, helped sell them? How can you say such a thing?'

'There's no proof.'

She looked at his face. Too dark to read well. Her sisters had claimed her gullible when it came to the tall tales they'd sometimes tell her. But he didn't seem to be watching for a reaction from her. In fact, he hardly seemed aware of what he was saying. She'd heard a bit of exasperation in his tone.

'It was just another day, Annie.'

'Why?'

'You need to know I'm not a saint. Never was and never will be close enough to see one's face. If something had been left unattended in a church, it could have ended up in my home. That is the way of it.'

She turned away. He'd tried to warn her that the world was an evil place. That he warned her surely was a reflection of his goodness. Beside him, she felt safer than she had before.

'I have a jewelled hairpin in my waistcoat pocket,' he said, his voice softening. He stretched his legs again and yawned so large that his jaw popped.

She opened her mouth to speak to him, and he dragged out a long inhale and followed it with an exhale. Almost an exclamation point to end the conversation.

She burrowed a bigger spot for herself and it brought her closer to him and she didn't care that he kept the jewelled pin for safekeeping. 'Thank you,' she said.

He huffed from his chest and groaned. 'Goodnight.'

The heat from his body radiated across the bed, but she didn't feel warmer. She felt she'd been pushed out of bed, or at least, far, far to the other side.

Annie woke to the sound of three quick raps at the door. Barrett was gone from the bed.

Another knock. 'Miss. Your husband sent me to see if you need any assistance.' The innkeeper's wife. Annie looked around, saw she was alone and rushed to open the door and let the woman in. She carried a tray of bread fresh from the oven, the aroma preceding her. A platter of butter and jam. A pitcher finished out the arrangement. She put the tray on the table.

'He's a mite impatient,' the woman spoke. 'And he's managed to talk my husband out of a horse with a side-saddle brought from the Andrews' house. I can understand why the two of you might bicker. He's snappish.'

'Not always.'

The older woman shook her head. 'The man is more surly than an ill-tempered dog.'

'He's just used to having his way.' Annie grabbed a roll, quickly buttered it and said, 'He's a viscount's son.'

'That thinks he's a prince,' the woman grumbled. 'And we ain't the type what princes prefer.'

She pulled out a cloth tucked into the waistband of her apron and wiped her hands on it. 'You'll be leaving him again, miss, unless you have much more patience that I do. Only next time, take my advice. Plan better.' She stepped out the door.

Annie rushed through breakfast, then hurried downstairs to a man standing with crossed arms, who'd not shaved in several days, had slept in his clothing and looked as if he might chew up the devil himself and spit him out.

He took Annie's arm and led her outside, handing her a strangled rag of a bonnet.

She took it, surprised that he would be thinking of her complexion at a time like this, but strangely pleased. The couple was wrong about Barrett.

'The sun is hardly shining,' she said.

He gave a growl from the base of his throat. 'But there's enough of it to see your face. I don't want you recognised when we arrive.'

She stood in front of the horse—a beast that looked no different than a hundred other horses she might see along the way to London. She touched its brown pelt and looked at its uninterested eyes.

She patted the horse again. She really didn't want to get on it and go back to her old life. She'd rather liked having Barrett with her.

From behind, two hands grasped her sides and lifted her straight into the heavens and out of her breath.

Before she knew it, he'd told her to hang on and stood ready to catch her for the first few steps of the horse.

'Secure?' he asked.

She nodded, aware of the determination in his face and in his hands. He couldn't make it any more plain that he wanted her out of his life.

After the way they'd talked last night, she would have expected him to be friendlier. But instead he seemed even more distant. Perhaps he regretted telling her the things he had.

She could hang on to the horse, but it was Barrett she kept wanting to reach out to. He'd been a part of her adventure and he was returning her to the sameness, and she'd miss him. She wanted to soothe him. She'd always been able to talk her sisters into a better mood.

'Thank you for securing the horse for me.'

He gave a half-nod and didn't look her way. She was on the other side of his feelings. He'd closed away that friendliness they'd shared in the night.

He moved around her, preparing to leave, but she could tell he'd already left her in his mind.

'You didn't have to come after me. But I am glad you wished to help my parents.'

He looked at her. 'I felt sorry for them.'

The edges of his words knifed into her. She turned her head away from him. He felt sorry for her parents. Such compassion. 'I understand.'

Chapter Eleven

The closer they came to London, the more she sensed his distance from her. The lines at his eyes deepened and his lips firmed.

Her father was the same way when he was angry, using silence to punish. But he wasn't her father and she didn't feel like tiptoeing around his feelings. And she'd not hurt her parents on purpose. She fell back into her old habits, hating when someone seemed angry. Not wanting to displease them, or feeling uncomfortable in their silence.

'I left a note for my parents.' She examined the road, holding on more snugly to the reins as the horse neared a rut.

He looked at her, eyes tight, but his face loosening just a bit. 'They thought you might have been at my house, or that I might know where you were.'

'I told you that I purposefully waited until you were away. They only thought of you because you seemed friendly to me when you taught me to defend yourself.'

'Your parents have no real notion of life. Or people.'

'They imagined a life of grandchildren with fancy

names and a family growing larger and larger with smiles growing larger and larger, and all of us under one roof and sunbeams in every corner and it's not turning out like that.'

'No life is perfect. But yours is better than most.'

'I am sorry for the struggles you've had.'

'Don't be. I'm not.'

She wanted to jab back at him. To ask if that included his mother's death. But she wasn't soulless. And even if he wasn't sorry for the struggles in his life, she knew he was sorry for his mother's death. He couldn't help but be. And perhaps that was why she felt the distance from him. Perhaps he was angry she'd worried her parents.

'I have been the sunbeam for the family my whole life. My sisters knew I would soothe my parents when they left. It's the way it's always been.'

'Your sisters didn't give a thought about you or your parents.'

'How can you say such a thing? My sisters followed their hearts.'

'By now the broken bits of those hearts are likely scattered along like ashes behind them. Desire fells innocents faster than any other disease.' He stared through her. 'And it can fell old rogues, too.'

'Do you fit into that category?'

The horse kept plodding along and Barrett finally answered, 'I fit into a group all my own.'

She examined him. 'And your age?'

He waited, knowing that when he looked at others his age moving about in the *ton*, he saw the gulf that existed between them. He had more the feelings inside him of the lower class, with his stocky frame and the battered look of his hands. But when he looked in the mirror, an heir's face stared back at him.

'I'm twenty-seven.'

Her lips parted and she stared, trying to determine if he lied. 'Twenty-seven?' She touched the side of her eyes. 'Twenty-seven?'

His lips turned up and the lines at his eyes increased, but he didn't truly smile. 'I started living my life at a much younger age than you did.'

He was not as old as she'd thought. Much closer to her own age and yet he reminded her of the music boxes she'd seen at an exhibition. Some were rather rough and had intricate parts that made no sense to her, and yet when the music started, she wanted to listen forever and examine the working parts and figure out how the music had been made. They seemed impossible and so did Barrett.

'I don't think I've started living yet and I don't wish to live my whole life watching my parents. The same house. The same roof...'

'You're safe there. The refuse on the streets can stick to your clothing for a very long time.'

'Your whole life you have had freedom.' She rode, pulled along by wanting to see deeper into his gaze. Except for the darkness under his eyes he appeared no different than the first time she saw him.

'With it comes a cost.'

She raised her brows.

'There can be a certain loss of innocence.' He tilted his head back so that his lids dropped as he looked at her. 'Can I tell you what the flavour of chocolate is like? The burn of brandy? Can I tell you how the loss of innocence feels? I've heard that you must lose it enough so that you don't retain any to make you bitter for what could have been.'

'Have you innocence left?'

'I never had any to begin with.'

'So why do you care about mine if it has served you well not to have it?'

'Rose blooms are rather senseless to me. I feel nothing for them. But why should I want to see them crushed under someone's soles?'

She didn't answer. He talked as if she were going to run off the edge of a cliff just to see the feeling of plunging to the earth. Everything had risk. Even doing nothing had risk and sometimes that was the biggest risk of all.

And he was taking her back to her home where she would have two choices—the best one being to remain in the attic. The three rooms would almost be like having a little cottage of her own. 'I suppose life is not all soirées.'

But she would have to attend soirées now if she wanted to leave her house. She doubted her parents would trust her alone. Her best hope might be the attic, rather than with her mother sleeping between her and the door.

A stab of irritation flashed inside her. Her sisters could have stayed closer. They really could have.

Even as she thought that, she knew why they hadn't. It never felt good to be on display with an imagined sign over your head listing your wifely qualities and a parent waiting for the highest bidder.

The horses reached the outskirts of London and her bottom ached at the thought of riding through the streets. She'd wanted to be out, but not on an old nag and wearing a drooping bonnet that would have looked better on the horse.

'I cannot be riding into town without a chaperon. Particularly in the middle of the day.'

'Yes, you can,' he said. 'Neither of us looks reputable enough to be noticed, nor quite disreputable enough to be observed, and the bonnet hides your face. When we get to your house, I'll slip you inside.'

'The rear door shouldn't be attended well. I can enter there.'

He rode with her to her house and slid down from his horse. He moved around, reaching up to help her from her mount. His hands touched her sides, warming her. He lifted her up into the air and then down from the horse.

Her feet went out from under her—she'd been so lost in his hands—and he caught her. She looked up and her world changed. She reached out, grabbing him to stay aloft and then stumbling when she gazed into his eyes.

He stared at her, this giant of a man, and then he gently removed his hands, leaving her the feeling of being abandoned.

She dusted herself off, unable to stop her hands from brushing away the places he'd touched.

The wall that he lived behind was well in place and the fortress wasn't welcoming.

'Are you able to walk?' he asked.

'I think so.' She took a step and he steadied her elbow. 'I've not ridden much before.' It was easier to stand near him for a few moments, his hand on her elbow.

'I suspect you've not done much of anything before.' He took the reins and tied them on a gatepost at the side of the gardens, then led her until they stood at the rear door.

He put out a hand to still her and guided her so she looked into his gaze.

'I considered marriage once.' His voice rolled like a breeze over a meadow.

Everything faded from her view, except the look on his face. 'I cannot imagine you in love.'

He chuckled. 'I wouldn't have called it love. I would have called it Madeline Trotter. I was quite in her thrall. Perfection. A courtesan's body and a courtesan's heart, with quite the lilt to her voice. I was busy at the time and was up to my eyeballs, trying to purchase Fortnum & Mason, which sadly did not happen. Plus, I was investing heavily, trying to increase the output at the ironworks.'

'You smile even now as you think of her.' She turned. The door was at her back and he was at her side.

'I laugh at myself. It felt as if I was having to open another sort of ledger book deep inside me and that was acceptable. Theatre visit—check. *You look lovely today, Madeline*—check. I moved through the motions. So I put off the proposal. I was busy. She would wait. She did. The man of affairs wanted to earn a bit of my favour and alerted me to an obscure change in funds from my father's accounts. Very craftily done. Madeline Trotter had been put in my path by my father. I must say he did quite well.'

'You had a matchmaking papa. I'm not surprised. Most peers want heirs.'

'Most certainly, but when I understood my father was involved, I no longer saw her as a suitable wife. My father's foresight and finesse impressed me on that occasion. As a rule, I had only seen force from him. Now I saw how he'd managed among society. He'd decided he needed an ally in my camp and saw her as an opportunity. I believe he felt certain he could severely discredit her in society should she not go along with any of his schemes.'

He tilted back his head. 'I learned a bit more of the game with little effort. I decided not to ask her to marry me. Her loyalty had already been purchased and I couldn't know if I ever truly had it, nor that it was something I count on.'

'You couldn't marry someone you couldn't trust.' She rested her hand on the door frame.

'I don't think you understand how the game is truly played, Annie. I didn't tell her. I didn't change anything except my plans for marriage. It took her quite some months to suspect we were not going to wed. In the meantime, I had an adoring woman at my side who seemed to float on my every word. I had but to lift a finger and she'd jump to my bidding—but she caught on.'

'If she was so devious as you say, I'm surprised she didn't try to take revenge.'

'She couldn't. I brought up the subject of my father and she couldn't be sure what I knew about her. She played the game as a professional would. She folded her cards, wished me the best and moved on.'

He took her chin and held it so that she could not avoid his eyes. 'I tell you this so you'll have no illusions about me. And you should take very close care that you don't have them about other people. You will be far better off to be like the Madeline Trotters of the world.'

'But if she'd been true, and not guided by funds, perhaps you would have married her.'

He shook his head. 'Perhaps. But would that have been a good thing for either of us? And how do you think she would have felt when I visited your father's house and became entranced by his daughter?' He took Annie's hand and kissed her wrist, before reaching around her to open the door for her, completely surrounding her by his form. She had no choice but to go inside.

He could answer the question he'd asked Annie and he knew her conclusions were wrong. Madeline wouldn't have particularly cared if his attention had moved elsewhere as long as her status hadn't been affected.

He was the one who had the problem with his fascination with Annie. He'd wanted to warn her away and knew the warning had been ignored.

The passion that could even mislead him had reared its head and stood at the edge of his sight, laughing at him.

Barrett smiled, feeling no humour. They were all prisoners, of a sort. He could not leave his father for long, uncertain of what the man might try and knowing that he could control and contain his father better than any other. A duty ingrained in Barrett.

He paused. Perhaps, in some wasted memory of his father's mind, he knew exactly what he did and finally controlled the son who'd always railed at being dominated. Perhaps his father had finally found a way to keep Barrett under his thumb.

No matter. It worked.

He had to keep his business and his father at the forefront of his mind. He couldn't be distracted by Annie.

Barrett could feel the risk for himself, though. The

pull of her goodness. The very things he'd warned her about were not as extinguished inside him as he'd believed. He could not be misled by the desire he warned her about. Love. A word created to make sense of foolishness and passion, and cause people to destroy everything of value in their life, just as the drink could. Even themselves.

Their footfalls sounded throughout the quiet halls. Annie looked in her mother's sitting room. 'They're not here.'

'I suppose they are searching about for you.' He examined her. 'When they come home, if they see you so bedraggled, it will take years from their lives.'

She held out the hem of her skirt. 'I've never worn such a muddied garment.'

'I'll wait for you in your father's sitting room.'

'You're not going to leave?' Relief showed on her face.

He couldn't. Battle lines might be drawn. True emotions could surface. He could protect Annie again.

Annie studied him. He could see in her face she'd not really listened to a word he'd said, nor even understood that he was telling her that she was better off not being embroiled in his life. He wasn't sure he should be enmeshed in his own life, and yet he could never step out. It wasn't just that his father held him confined. He'd lost his innocence too early and when he saw Annie, he could not reach through the invisible barrier that kept them in different worlds. Nothing inside him could traverse the distance.

Chapter Twelve

Barrett kept an ever-so-proper distance between himself and Annie as they waited for her parents. She should not be alone for this.

A maid had stopped in the doorway, eyes taking in the scene. The servant had explained that Annie's parents had left suddenly, but hadn't given a reason.

A clatter on the stairway alerted him that her mother had arrived. He tensed. Mrs Carson rushed into the room, a whirlwind of jewellery and fabrics. Her face wreathed in lines. 'My baby is back.'

She grasped Annie's shoulders in her gloved hands. 'Why did you do this to us, Annie? Why?'

Then her mother saw Barrett. 'You brought her back, didn't you?'

He nodded.

She turned again to Annie. 'If not for Mr Barrett… we might never have seen you again. We went to your cousins' houses, hoping to discover who'd helped you leave, but no one had heard from you. Where were you?' She pulled Annie closer, clasping her daughter in a tight hug.

Annie patted her mother's back. 'I just wanted to see Honour. I don't want her alone when the baby is born.'

Her mother's voice wavered. 'You could not. Childbirth is no place for a gentlewoman. Why, I would not have attended any of my children's births if I hadn't had to. It was ghastly.'

'Oh, Annie. What are we to do with you?' her father asked, stepping into the room.

Her father turned his head away. Carson had had tears in his eyes.

'You must promise us, Annie. You must promise you will not do something so foolish again.' Her mother stepped back, removed her gloves and used one to dot her brow, seemingly unaware she didn't have a handkerchief in her hands.

Barrett examined the tableau, seeing it, but not understanding the lack of emotion. Where was the shouting, the ruckus, the threats?

'You will not leave the house again without your mother or me with you. You must understand.' The gruff voice of her father, breaking a bit.

'Father. I do understand how much you care for me.' Annie's calming tone. 'I took great care to leave with a kindly woman who could chaperon me.'

'When we thought…' Her mother's voice, with a gasp at the end.

Silence.

'We cannot bear to lose you.' Her mother again. 'I cannot believe you tried to run away.'

Barrett turned, just as the mother fell into a chair, knuckles at her mouth. She still held her gloves in the other hand.

He'd thought the Carson family cared for Annie and yet they were treating her almost as if she'd done nothing more than been late for dinner. No wonder she had such innocence. The family itself showed no deep emotions. Perhaps they didn't feel them.

Without speaking, he moved to the door. Outside, he shook his head, standing for a moment, waiting for the crash of glass.

Instead he heard sniffling from either her father or her mother. He wasn't sure which. Perhaps both. He stopped. Her parents were more innocent than Annie.

'Annie,' her mother spoke. 'You have no idea how much we love you. I thought I would truly die when I discovered you gone.'

'Without any of my daughters here…' her father's voice again '…there wouldn't be a reason to keep on living. Not for either your mother or me.'

Barrett left, their voices echoing in his head, while he still kept an ear out for the sound of breaking glass. Finally, he heard it—the second he stepped into his own house and up to his father's doorway.

Annie watched her father and mother eating silently and slowly. Honour and Laura's empty chairs sat across from her.

At least her parents had stopped sniffling. And just as she expected, her mother was planning for Annie to sleep on the sofa in her sitting room.

She waited until her mother had finished eating. Annie put her fork on the side of her plate, arranging it exactly as she wanted, then she spoke. 'Mother, perhaps I made a mistake.'

Her mother turned to the footman at the sidebar and signalled him to leave. The door closed behind him.

'Perhaps more than one,' her mother said.

Annie braced herself and said the words she'd never expected to hear from her own lips. 'Mother, I spent the night in an inn pretending to be a married woman. A pretence—only—of marriage so no questions would be asked.'

'You'll be staying at your mother's elbow the rest of your life.' Her father's voice cracked with emotion. He pointed a finger to the ceiling. 'We've tried to be lenient and you see where it has got us. You will not run away again. You will be with either your mother or me, or you will marry Lord Richard or someone of his ilk.'

'A pretence? No actions?' Her mother waved her hand in front of her face. 'Although any mother would be daft to believe such nonsense in a situation like that—except the physician did say...'

Annie drew herself tall. 'Mr Barrett has kissed my hand.'

Her father rotated towards her, his body remaining in a straight line, but his face contorting.

'He has kissed my hand several times, and my wrist,' she added.

Her mother looked at her father and rapped her fork on the plate, catching his attention before he spoke. 'It is not wise to believe a child when she says nothing happened, but then again, this is Mr Barrett and you know what the physician...well, he said what he said when he suggested to send Barrett for Annie.' She cleared her voice.

'But—' Carson sputtered.

'Dearest Husband,' her mother interrupted, looking down the table, 'you know what the physician said to you privately about the unlikely event of Mr Barrett having an heir. That snails just couldn't fly and, barring a miracle cure—which he had searched for these past five years—Mr Barrett would never fly. Never. He wanted you to know in case you worried about Annie should Mr Barrett find her and the two of them be alone. And he wanted to be sure you knew that there could never be a little viscount.'

'It was rather lovely when he kissed my hand,' Annie added.

'Your hand?' her father said.

'A special moment,' and she hated sharing it, but she wanted her parents to know that he had treated her admirably and she was no longer the innocent they believed, but neither was she not an innocent. 'He seemed to be telling me that it would never lead to anything else.'

'The plain and simple truth of it. Mr Barrett is the safest man in London for Annie to be with.' Her mother wadded her napkin and threw it on to the plate. 'And no five or six-month healthy babes to be born.'

'I cannot believe you pretended to be married.' Her father shook his head at Annie. 'That is abominable.'

'Again,' her mother reminded. 'Uneventful... Affliction... No surprise grandchildren.' She picked up the discarded napkin, straightened and folded it. 'A man who will inherit a sizeable estate kissed your daughter's hand. Perhaps his deepest expression of affection.'

'Father, no one knows. I learned my lesson and

Mr Barrett said he has started plans to get Honour to return.'

'It is not that simple, bringing your sister home,' her mother said, arranging the napkin again with tactical precision. 'We will have to pretend it never happened. We cannot stand for the disgrace. Your father has worked so hard to keep the family name upheld. If it were only her…well, then we could work something out. But there is a child. My grandchild. A niece or nephew for you. We don't want it branded with a bad name for the whole of its life. I can adopt it later. I have told everyone that Honour is visiting my sister.'

'Your sister passed away.'

'I left that part out.' She paused.

'Barrett said he can bring Honour home now and I am sure that we will somehow fix it so there is no disgrace for the child.'

Her mother sighed. 'I have already written to Honour and explained that we will work to get her and the babe home with no one the wiser as to who its mother is. And when I recall that my sister has passed on, I'll also mention her grandchild who needs a home. So far, Honour has refused to consider all the options your father and I presented. She just wanted to chase off after that man. It doesn't matter to me. She can have a husband on two feet—or we can have a nice stone erected with the proper dates and a suitable name. That way there's a record. I know of a good stonemason who will not ask any questions.'

'Three daughters,' her father held up the correct number of fingers and touched each one. 'Three. And all of them—'

His wife looked at him. 'They did not get that from my side of the family.'

She stared across the table at her husband. 'Annie will be marrying Mr Barrett.'

'I think he has to agree to that,' Annie said.

'The planning is in the details,' her mother said.

'He is an heir,' Annie reminded them. 'His family has been in society longer than ours and has a higher place. We are only cousins of cousins of an earl. Barrett is not someone who can be forced into anything. And I don't think I will get a lot of empathy if he decides to bring up the little detail of my running off in the night and his bringing me home.'

'You didn't run away.' Her mother glared at her. 'You were here the whole time, dearest. We were stitching. The whole of the *ton* knows your father and I never let you out of our sight. You were here. All night. That is how to remember it.'

'The physician knows I was gone,' Annie said, 'and perhaps a servant or two.'

'Nonsense. The servants know to keep quiet. The physician knows Mr Barrett is a snail and snails can't fly. Therefore, he also knows that you were safely asleep in bed.' One brow cocked up and one brow remained in place. 'Correct? Safely in bed?' Then she looked away and muttered, 'We just cannot mention whose bed.'

Annie looked at one parent and then the other. She nodded. 'Mr Barrett took care not to touch me and he snored.'

Her father put his head down. 'The poor, poor man.'

'Perhaps I am ready not to be a wallflower any

more,' Annie said. 'Perhaps I need to open my eyes to the world around me.'

'Lord Richard?' her father asked, hope in his eyes.

'I'm not ruling out dancing with him.' She looked at her mother's napkin. 'I would not rule out a harmless flirtation either.'

Barrett's concentration hadn't returned and neither had his ability to sleep through the night. The only night he'd slept well since seeing Annie's wrist had been the night he'd slept beside her. He had to get her out of his mind once and for all.

With her back at home, she'd be in her own little cocoon, safe from all the predators who might prey on fragile innocents.

Carson had sent a note, thanking Barrett profusely for all the assistance he'd given on matters of late. Hoping again for Barrett's invaluable advice. Noting how much his presence brightened the spirits of the entire family. Requesting a visit from Barrett, and mentioning that, if it were inconvenient for Barrett to travel, Carson would stop by when he and his family were out on calls.

Another matchmaking papa. Barrett put his elbows on his desk, fingers steepled together, and rested his forehead on his hands.

Every time he shut his eyes, he saw Annie. And every time he listened, he heard his father's voice, either real—from the Viscount's room shouting out some nonsense to Summers—or imagined, slinging some profanity into the air.

Barrett didn't want Carson in his father's lair.

After hours of his father's ire seeping through the

walls and Summers walking into Barrett's room to show him the remains of a meal dripping from his clothing, Barrett stood. He'd get the Carson family out of his mind once and for all. He'd put a rift so deep between them that Annie would hate him.

Hate, that was a real emotion, and even that could weaken a man. Emotions were weapons and humans were victims.

He had to get Annie out of his thoughts instead of letting her linger inside him, like a scent from a spring-time garden that rested in the air, filling the senses with delicate purity and an amazement that, after the desolation of winter, the earth could replenish itself.

Annie reminded him of the earliest wildflowers, so delicate a single touch on their petals could mar them. He only knew how to deal with dandelions. A wisp of air and they went in all directions, spreading the seeds and returning with vigour.

He sprinted downstairs and sent for his horse, waiting, trying not to listen to the commotion in the rooms above him.

Telling Annie goodbye would be his own solution as well, he thought, as he checked to make sure the cinch was tight on his horse's saddle. Destroying their friendship would save him from the temptation of returning to her over and over, until she decided she was little more than another Madeline Trotter in his life. Another beauty on his arm. Another woman to fulfil his checklist as he went through the motions required to appease her, while his life continued on alone. Another stolen book with hand-painted illustrations to put on the shelf and to pull down to show others how well-ordered a viscount's life was.

With a foot in the stirrup, he jumped into the saddle.

It was tempting—to lead her along a false rose path, propose and marry. But should he do that, a Madeline would work so much better. She couldn't be crushed by the world that sat inside the walls of Barrett's home. Annie had an innocent's view of love. The flower-petal arrangement, not the mire of walking through the stables. The superficial view of her parents—who shed a few tears and expected roses to form from the moisture and everyone to dance arm in arm down the lane with birds tweeting about and no foxes with empty stomachs patiently watching and waiting.

He would tell her. Show her. That his life wasn't right for her. She needed one of the bespectacled men who had plush carriage seats, umbrellas close by, and an assortment of collapsible fans to match their attire.

His horse splashed through the puddles in the road and Barrett wiped the sweat off his brow with the back of his hand.

If he could show her one second inside his father's mind, she would run to the attic and lock herself in her room.

He would end all thoughts she might have in his direction and he would end his thoughts of her, too. They both needed to be on different paths and he'd make sure they were.

Chapter Thirteen

In Carson's study, the older man's gaze softened. 'I have not impressed upon you how much we appreciated you bringing Annie home to us safe and unharmed. I cannot repay you enough. You're the only man I trust near her.' Carson lit his cheroot after Barrett refused one. 'Not all men are like you.' He stumbled over his words. 'Not all men have an—'

Barrett raised a brow.

Carson coughed. 'Upstanding. Good decent men.'

Obviously Annie's father was every bit as oblivious to the world as his daughter was. The man had closed himself away as well not to have heard of the women who had flitted through Barrett's life. Not to have suspected that Barrett knew more about Carson's business than a casual observer would.

But the man could see the virtue in Annie. He could see how easily a few soft words and a smile could lead her into danger.

'Of course, you're welcome here any time.' He took a puff of the tobacco. 'If you can convince Annie how much we love her and how important it is for her to be protected, I would be very grateful.' Carson's eyes registered the thought of Barrett's interest in Annie. A not well-hidden hope appeared in his eyes.

'I'll think about what you're saying,' Barrett said. 'In fact, I would like to take Annie on a stroll to Lincoln's Inn Field today. It's a perfect day for a walk.' It was, if you didn't count the clouds overhead and the extra coolness in the air.

Carson jumped to his feet and had the bell pull in his hand before Barrett finished with the sentence. 'You can take our maid, Myrtle, as a chaperon,' he said. 'She can follow along behind. Just don't lose her.' He paused, his hand on the bell. 'Really, don't lose her. She gets distracted easily.'

Barrett waited and Annie walked into the room, causing his insides to jolt. Comparing her to anyone else had been a mistake. Much like comparing an artist's rough sketch to something created by divine inspiration. Annie was the creation made to dissolve resolves and drop mortals to their knees.

But it didn't matter. The art would stay safely locked away from Barrett's world. He would remember her and, in time, he would sleep again.

Lincoln's Inn Field bustled even with the feel of moisture in the air. A group of three ladies walked along, two carrying umbrellas high, the third one hand in hand with a small child.

The iron rails of the fence surrounding the square absorbed the sunlight, making them appear warm instead of forbidding.

A man driving a curricle along kept his distance, not disturbing the moments of quaintness.

'The world seems so alive,' she said. 'It's been years since I've been here.'

'I've been through a few times, but never paused long.' He walked with his hands behind his back, left hand clasped over his other wrist—because if he did not, he feared he would ask that she take his arm.

To be that close to her would cause him to pull her closer and closer and walk with his head bent to hers and that would be near to announcing a betrothal in such a public place.

Myrtle trotted along behind, humming, speaking to the others nearby and, without meaning to, drawing attention away from Barrett and Annie.

A man with about two sprouts of hair sticking up on each side, ragged, wearing an eyepatch, sat on the corner next to a dog that had an eyepatch as well. When he saw Barrett glance at the dog, the man pulled out a finger and pretended to shoot at the dog. The dog rolled over on its back. 'Go for the sympathy now, Rouser.' The little dog whined on an outward breath and then whined again.

'You're a good one,' the beggar said. 'Now get well and sing us a song about how happy you are.' The little dog hopped up and barked.

Barrett reached in his pocket and took out a few coins and tossed them into the cup.

'Well, would you look at that, Rouser?' The man rattled the cup. 'Look. Coins.'

Rouser jumped over to the man and the man lifted the dog's eyepatch. Then the beggar held up the patch and light shown through it. The beggar smiled at Barrett. 'The hard part was getting her used to the patch, but now she expects an audience when she wears it.'

'And is yours real?' Barrett asked.

'All too real, but I don't mind. The day is grand. The people who walk along are always in a pleasant mood. I've a good life and try to see as much with my one eye as other people see with two.'

Annie walked forward, reaching out her gloved hand as she knelt to pat the dog. 'She seems a good companion.'

'She's my joy,' the old man said, smiling. 'I think she'd miss the people if I tried to keep her away.'

Annie straightened, told the man goodbye and walked along with Barrett. 'I can hardly believe the freedom. Everything seems so bright and alive.'

He looked overhead and saw absolutely nothing of interest, but the air did feel fresh on the dreary day. 'Lots of clouds.'

She studied his face until he touched her elbow and moved her onwards.

'I have a feeling my father would be pleased if you were to have dinner with us tonight,' she said.

'I can't.'

The smile on her face faltered.

He didn't want to let that smile fade. He thought back to how many smiles he'd seen in his life. Not a lot.

Another turn and she would be at home. 'Just one more thing,' he said, stopping her again. He realised he'd done that so many times on their walk. A stop for a few seconds here. A stop for a moment to examine a bit of iron, or a second to look at this or that, or the man's dog. Another check to see that the maid was following. Anything to keep her with him longer.

She paused, waiting.

'Never mind,' he said, watching her eyes gaze at

him. 'Never mind.' He touched a finger to her cheek, feeling the softness deep in his chest. A mistake. A mistake he'd never forget, but one more added to the ledger would not matter.

He'd been about to tell her that he couldn't court her. That he could give her a bit of freedom that day, but he could never bring her into his father's house. The risk would be too great. And for him to leave his father alone, that was a risk, too. If his father ever found out that Barrett cared for her, her life would be in danger. But he would not let her into his world of shadows, darkness and greed.

He needed to leave, but he couldn't force himself. Just as he was giving her a taste of freedom, he was giving himself a taste of a world that wasn't his.

He walked back to her parents' house with her, a puppy on the string, following the smile in Annie's eyes and unable to leave. He pulled her closer, taking both her hands in his, almost losing her fingers in his grasp, but feeling them with his being.

'You have won over both my parents.' She paused.

'They are immaterial to me.'

'And I beg your pardon for not seeming grateful for your efforts on my behalf.' She shrugged. 'My parents trust me with you, because you brought me home. I assure you they do not normally leave me unattended.' She turned her face away. 'And your medical condition seems to reassure them, particularly since my sisters have…'

'I don't have a medical condition.'

'Mother explained it to me very carefully. It is nothing to be ashamed of. It happens.'

'I don't have a medical condition.' A tiny lift of his shoulders.

'Very well…' she turned '…you don't have a medical condition. Call it whatever you wish.'

'The physician was having a jest at my expense.'

She could read nothing in his expression. 'Well, it doesn't matter to me, either way.'

'It matters a tremendous amount to me.' His chin tilted down but his eyes remained on her.

'Are you here because my father asked you?'

He laughed, a low rumble that reached inside her. 'No. I don't care what your father thinks.'

'Yet, you're here.'

'I saw your hand, and heard your voice, and walked away. And yet I keep coming back. And I curse myself for it. But it will not continue.'

'So flattering to me.'

'I don't know why I tell you the truth. Perhaps that's why I keep coming back. I can speak what I think with you and it's not the same.'

He saw the moment she took it as a compliment and yet he knew it wasn't in the way she took it. Without a doubt he could have finessed his way so deep into her father's good graces and then spoken pretty words to her and she would have been in his arms easily. And he could have walked away. But he didn't like crumpling things just because he could break them. He saw no reason to expend the energy. No satisfaction in it.

'The stronger prey on the weaker. If you look at the animals in the forest, it's just the way of it. You can't change it. And your innocence to me is more fascinating than the softness of your skin, or the look of your face. I've never seen it before. Never, in such a way as you have it.'

'You hardly know me.'

'I know your purity. It's rare. At least to me.'

She didn't think anyone had ever examined her face so carefully, yet he didn't really seem to be looking at her.

'Why do you consider me so innocent?'

'Because if you knew what risks you took, you wouldn't have left with the woman. To go out alone into the night with someone you hardly know.'

'I don't say she's golden. But she is someone who has been around most of my life. My sisters told me stories of her before they left. She helped Honour leave.'

'It isn't worth the risk to be wrong. You could lose everything. Your life. Or your spirit. You trust too easily.'

She watched his face. 'So can I trust you?'

'With your life.'

His heart pounded. He told the truth. He would go to the ends of the earth to find Annie if someone threatened her life.

'Sweet, don't look so amazed. You can trust me with your life, but there are so many other things that you have I'm not so sure you should trust me with. Things which may be as important as life.'

She didn't move.

Her face looked up at him. The sun-mixed shadows giving her a radiance that made him believe, for half a second, in angels.

And how could you not kiss an angel? But to kiss an angel was surely a sin.

She pulled him along with her innocence and he followed willingly. Her artlessness surrounded them and he could feel it. That trusting belief in him.

She stepped forward, her skirts kicking up and touching his trousers, connecting them.

'I mustn't let you think that I can court you,' he said. 'It's not possible.'

'I don't care about your affliction.' The gentleness in her gaze almost taking him out at the knees. 'I really don't.'

He took in a breath. 'I can't court you. I can take you out of your prison today, but you must find a different gaoler and a different path. I have my work. My father. The things that have kept my attention my whole life. You have been a bit of a respite, but we live in two different worlds.'

'Only because I haven't been allowed out in society. I've always been a wallflower, even in my own home. But, I'm willing to learn to be a part of your world. I would like to. I have already told my parents that I want to go to soirées.'

Soirées. This was not about a simple dance or two. No, she would never wish to be a part of his world. It would destroy her and the only thing that could destroy him would be to see such a thing happen to her.

But she would never understand the evil that he'd seen and felt. The evil that had deadened his heart and tried always to get the upper hand.

'If you were in my world, then perhaps you would change so much that neither of us would recognise each other.' He tried to put softness into his words. He couldn't tell her what his mother's face had looked like within minutes of her death. How he'd remembered that, but not the way she smiled, or how she looked on any other day. And how she'd called out to him in her last moments and he'd not answered.

'An innocent tossed into a maelstrom might not withstand the winds as someone who'd done nothing else but live in a storm their whole life,' he said.

She turned, dipping her head. 'What if I could withstand them?'

'But if you couldn't…'

He reached out, twirling her, and then stopping her at an arm's length away.

She clutched at his waistcoat. He took the fingers and pulled them to his face, shutting his eyes and holding her hand to trail her touch along his face. 'I find you more appealing than anything or anyone I've ever seen. You are the only poison I've ever wanted.'

She shook her head. 'I can't be poison and an innocent at the same time.'

'Said the innocent one.'

Chapter Fourteen

He studied her face, committing it to memory and knowing he was foolish to do so. He didn't need to torment himself with something he couldn't have. But he wanted one pleasant face in his memory.

'Why do you notice me? Why did you come after me?' she asked.

'You're the innocence I never had. I never believed in. And I see it in your every movement.'

She swayed closer to him.

'No.' The softness in his voice stopped her, and the finality in the word.

'After Mother died, I decided I was old enough not to have a governess. I took my grandmother's favourite necklace, the one she wore every day, and hid it in Tizzy's winter coat.'

His grandmother was never one to let things slide away peacefully and brought in the stable hands to search the house.

He'd been quietly playing with his toy soldiers when his grandmother had stormed into the room after Tizzy. The eruption had been quite flaming. He'd thought he was sending Tizzy to the gallows.

He'd seen the moment Tizzy figured out who'd framed her. 'Get out,' he'd shouted, shaking a fist. 'Get out, you thief.'

His grandmother had been startled and, after a second's thought, Tizzy had made her escape.

That was the moment he'd learned to play. His grandmother's face had puckered and she'd studied his face. She had suspected him as well and then she'd grinned.

He stepped back, keeping his focus locked on Annie.

'I am my father's son.'

'Did you ever think you might have your mother's blood in your veins as well?'

'Perhaps. But I fear it has been diluted.'

He tilted his head down because he didn't want her to see his eyes, then he stepped through the door to the house, waiting for the sounds of Annie following him.

The only thing that touched him was the smile in Annie's eyes and he could feel the sunlight from her even when he turned away.

He breathed in and out, his thoughts lost to the world and to himself.

He waited in the hallway until the maid caught up and he gave the servant a glare that sent her scurrying and almost colliding with the butler. Another look of distaste was all it took for Barrett to have Annie alone.

A beat. 'Can I show you what felled your sisters? What fells even the strongest men and has caused more heartache than all the battlefields in history?'

She watched him as he moved closer, taking up all the space in her world.

He cradled the tip of her chin. The feather-light

touch trapped her, sending an awareness of her own skin and her beating heart deep into her.

He leaned forward, leaving the softest kiss on her mouth.

And then he deepened it, lingering, tasting, exploring the contours of her lips, filling her with so many sensations she could not sort them. Her thoughts faded as she tasted the slight saltiness of him, the hint of lemon and a tartness she couldn't place.

He leaned forward, moving closer, his hands at her waist now, keeping her upright. The kiss enveloped her and he pulled her body against his, his hardness pressing against her, and one hand clasped her neck, securing her without pressure, just the heat of his touch.

When the kiss stopped, the sensations didn't and she remained motionless, but his mouth trailed down to follow the path across her skin set by his fingers, moving the shoulder of her clothing aside, lingering where the barest skin covered the ridges just below her neck.

He stopped and clasped her shoulders, and his lips traced just above the bodice of her dress, leisurely taking his time with the juncture where skin met cloth.

He moved back, but one finger traced the trail of his lips, burning fresh into her skin. 'Desire feels like love, looks like love from the inside and even tastes like love. Applied often enough, it can temporarily erase the senses to make a case it is love, but it isn't. Ever. Love is the fancy word it hides behind. Rather like a sturdy tree, in which a large, dark cat is hiding, waiting to pounce and devour the prey beneath, sometimes only leaving dry bones behind. The tree is there, but it only provided a perch for the predator while the prey moved closer. Love is the biggest lie of life.'

His eyes, darker than she'd ever seen them, stared.

He stepped back, bowing. 'Thank you for these moments. And remember you can get them easily from any male you find halfway palatable.'

'No, I can't,' she said.

He stilled. He had to change the look in her eyes. He had to turn it to hate.

'I made the men who sold their goods to your father sell to me instead. He could only buy at higher prices. It caused your father to lose so much that he could not maintain his profits. I then moved in and bought his shops for less than what they were worth.' He paused. 'That is who I am, Annie. That is what I do.'

Then he gave her a dismissing glance and touched the door to leave. 'I took your father's business, gutted it and then bought it for almost nothing and am rebuilding it in the way I wish. It was another day's business to me. And I've lost not a moment's sleep and I feel absolutely no remorse at all. None.'

The shock in her eyes gouged him in such a way he could feel it on all sides. He blinked away the look of hurt on her face, cursing himself for putting the vision in his memory.

Then, as he had learned when he was a child, he closed his mind to any feelings of pain.

He turned back, making sure not to look at her face. He looked at a mirror on the wall and hated what he saw. 'It was all folly on my part. You were a folly. A diversion. No different than any other woman who has been in my life, except you're an innocent. A waste of my time.'

Then he walked out the doorway and shut the door with a click that echoed in his head.

He stepped away, closing his feelings down and pushing them further into the recesses than he ever had before. He'd secured Annie behind him. She was a moment of his past. Not even a memory to think about.

He strode out of the house and barred her from his mind.

He'd ensured she would want nothing more to do with him and he'd erase her from his memories. She *had* been a folly. A frolic. A moment of madness on his part to trifle with someone so naive.

She'd been a distraction. A lapse. A trivial matter.

He was a good distance from her house when he realised he'd left his horse behind.

Annie ran to her room in the attic. She wanted her heart to stop beating. She wanted to scream. She couldn't face her parents in this agony so private that she could not share.

She ran to the window and put her forehead against the glass, shutting her eyes and trying to shut her heart away from the loss and humiliation that Barrett had given her. She had been senseless. Utterly senseless.

Barrett had no heart. He was cruel. He could just as easily not have said such hateful things.

She opened her eyes. A movement below the window caught her attention. The garden looked as peaceful as it always had and a man stood untying his horse. Not any man. Barrett.

Using both hands, she thrust up the window with all her force. She leaned out, gripping the sill. 'You're hateful. Horrible. I want nothing to do with you ever again.'

She slammed down the window, the crash jarring her body. She moved out of sight and slid to the floor.

She put both hands over her face. The horrible man. Horrible.

That horrible man who tasted so good when he kissed her.

Touching her lips, she ran her fingers over them. Desire. He knew what he spoke of.

But then she understood. She'd thought him aroused earlier, but surely she'd been mistaken. He'd even told her the physician jested about the affliction. Barrett had tried to convince her Gavin lied so she could never reveal the secret.

He'd said all those things to protect her. He'd known he could never be a true husband, or give her children, or fulfil any moments of desire other than the kind he had shown her with a kiss. He'd told her to find someone halfway palatable and marry him. He'd wanted her to find happiness and was willing to sacrifice himself to do so.

He could have easily not said the words. He could have led her along the same path her sisters' beloveds had led them, only to introduce them to the truth when it was too late to step back. Barrett had warned her for her own good. She realised that.

Her father's business had been in trouble long before Barrett arrived. Her mother's father had left a sizeable inheritance to his only living child. It kept them when there were no profits. She'd heard her parents talk of it many times.

And Barrett had seen the scene with her mother and

father and known how upset she'd made them. He'd thought her the same as her sisters.

She pushed herself to her feet and ran to the window. Barrett had left.

Her stomach plummeted.

And she'd shouted out hateful things out the window. He would never, ever forget that.

She put her hands over her face. She understood completely that he could not forgive that. He'd been so mistreated in his life and she'd behaved no different to him than his father or his grandmother.

She'd been a shrew who'd shouted out the window. A disgrace. An embarrassment. The one woman in his life who had treated him kindly—his mother— had died early.

Annie knew she'd been much more like his grandmother.

She might have been an innocent, hardly equal to the demands of society, but she'd shouted out the window like the lower classes. She would learn. She would learn how to be more like Madeline Trotter.

Moving to her nightstand, she picked up a bottle of perfume Honour had left behind. Lavender. Then she touched her other sister's perfume bottle. Lilac.

Then she picked up her own, something she'd had her mother request for her, and it had taken months to arrive. A French blend of jasmine that she'd never worn and was now not her preference. She held the liquid up, between herself and the window, watching the light refract. She wanted rosewater.

Chapter Fifteen

Annie walked into the main sitting room. Her mother had her foot propped on a silk pillow. Her father sat at her side, reading to her. He'd never been one to concentrate on his properties much, often abandoning any ideas soon after he'd talked himself into them. When they didn't seem fresh any more, he lost interest.

'I wanted to court Mr Barrett, but he has left and said he has no fascination with me.'

Her mother gasped. 'He can't not have interest in you.' She sat straighter. 'He asked you out on a walk today. What did you talk about that upset him?'

Her father's lips moved into a line and his eyes narrowed in speculation, but not in surprise. 'I was certain he wanted to court you. I mean, the man moved into the household for almost a week. We don't live far apart and I'm not that interesting. It had to be you.'

'He doesn't want to court me. That was to tell me goodbye.'

Her mother opened her mouth and put a hand to her chest as if she meant to deny the words, but didn't speak immediately. 'Has he ever courted anyone?' she asked her husband.

His eyes were half-closed in concentration. 'He once seemed to be courting that conniving witch of a woman, Madeline Trotter, who would sell—' he looked at his wife '—would sell about anything to anyone for a good price. Now *that* woman should be in trade.'

'She is,' her mother said, blinking twice. 'Which goes to show that Barrett is not that wise where women are concerned.'

'He told me he wouldn't come back,' Annie insisted.

'You can't have children with him.' Her mother reached out and adjusted the pillow. 'The physician would be a better man to court.'

'If I never marry, it's unlikely I'll have children.'

'Well, it's not all the joys you'd think.' Her mother wiggled her toes, then put her head against the chair back and rested her eyes.

She looked at her mother. 'I need to get out more.'

Her mother touched the ribbons of her dress decorating her collar, straightening. 'But are you interested in marriage? Or is this a folly as your sisters had and that caught up with them?'

Annie didn't answer.

Her mother turned to Carson. 'It's your turn. I don't know what to do.'

'Don't count on me to catch the two of you in a compromising position.' Her father snorted. 'That little device is well off the table.'

She rolled her eyes and ignored the heat in her cheeks. 'Barrett has no wish to marry me. He practically embroidered it on a pillow and propped it in front of my face. Or at least, that is what he says. That he has no wish to marry. He likes to work. It fills him with deep happiness, or whatever is inside him.' She thought of the chunks of coal in the fireplace. 'Perhaps his insides are black.' And perhaps coal could ignite.

Her father straightened his back. 'And he does have strange ideas about how one should work all the time.' Her father tilted his head down, shaking it from side to side. 'You already sound like him. A little too direct. If he has walked away from you, you should let him go. A man who thinks in profits must see you as a value high above others or you will be leading separate lives from the moment of the wedding breakfast.'

'If he doesn't wish to court me, then I would like to see if anyone else wishes to court me. It would be good to know.' Perhaps someone who could make rosewater smell so masculine it could make her insides burn.

'I might like a living son-in-law in London,' her mother said, she picked up a handkerchief from the side table.

'I would like to dance,' Annie said, 'and I would hate to think of Barrett believing that I am one of those insensible women who might be like Madeline Trotter and fall for the first viscount's son who notices me. I would like him to know that I am carefree, happy and could care less that he does not want to court me.'

Sticking her head out the window and shouting at him had been a mistake, but she could show him she really wasn't like that. He might understand, but even if he didn't, she was tired of living in the attic. And the black-hearted Barrett had best hope his heart was truly black, or she intended to make it glow red-hot. Innocence. She was leaving that at the window.

She looked at her mother and then at her father. 'I will likely end up a spinster. But not one whom no one wishes to court. Just one who doesn't wish to court. There is a difference. I would rather not be dismissed so easily.'

'I understand. After all, you are twenty-two. And don't speak to us as if we've not tried to find a husband for you. You just haven't cooperated,' said her mother.

'Except for Mr Barrett,' her father said, neck craning to the door as if he expected Barrett to be standing there. 'I still think he wanted to court you, Annie. I would have never let him move in had I not thought so. I mean, really—' he held out a hand '—what other reason would he want to stay here for if not wishing to know the family better? I didn't want another child conceived under my roof. I moved you upstairs so I could be certain his motives were more honourable than dishonourable.'

'You must consider the bachelors of the *ton*.' Her mother fanned her face with the handkerchief. 'You would make a good wife. You have all the requirements. Good teeth. Hair that stays in place. Your arms look well in the summer dresses.'

'So will you help me put these arms to good use?'

'Yes. And your head. Don't forget to use the head,' her mother said. 'They come in handy in a courtship. Just ask that Trotter woman. But don't show your hand. That is never good until it has a ring on it.'

'Mrs Carson.' Her father's face tightened and he glared. 'Don't be telling your daughter such nonsense. You never said such a thing to Honour and Laura.'

'Perhaps I should have,' she said. 'Dance carefully, Annie. You'll be the one living with the consequences.'

Barrett sat at his desk. Telling Annie goodbye in person had been like telling her spirit to enter his thoughts and not leave. He reached into his waistcoat pocket and took out the jewelled pin. He'd meant to return it to Annie, but he'd not been able to part with it.

She'd been wearing it the first time he saw her face. At the top of the stairs. Her hair tousled just enough to be glorious. A simple jewelled pin above innocent eyes.

He took a last look at the jewel and put it back in his pocket.

He put his elbows on the table and both palms over his face. He shut his eyes and rubbed them, trying to get Annie from his mind. He was just too tired. That was causing him to lose his concentration. He did not need any more thoughts of the Carson household.

Annie kept chasing him through his dreams and he'd rarely dreamed before. But those were better than the waking moments when he realised she was not to be in his life.

Instead he was to have a life of guarding his father and keeping the man from destroying everything they both had worked to build. His father likely would tear down all his holdings just for spite.

His father had tried to escape twice in the past few days and Barrett couldn't get anything but a gleeful laugh when he asked his father why. A new game. To be played until his father tired of it.

Annie's face appeared in his thoughts. To hold her would be so comforting. But wrong. He couldn't bring her to his father's house, ever. The risk of having his father find out he cared for someone was too great. He could never risk focusing attention on her so much that his father reacted. Annie could be hurt. Or killed.

His brother opened the door.

'How is Annie?' Barrett asked.

'Oh, good to see you, Gavin,' his brother mocked. 'Please do come in and have a seat.'

Barrett put down the silver pen he used, opened the drawer and pulled out one of the feathered quills he'd used in the past. He tossed it straight at his brother. The feather flew to the edge of the desk and then spiralled down to the floor. 'That's how well your humour flies with me.'

Gavin picked it up and held the quill. 'Better than yours does with me. I just looked in on the Viscount. He called me Barrett and slung a plate at me. You should have him put away.'

'Tried it. He escapes. Woke up one morning and he was opening my bedroom door. I almost didn't see the knife, but I knew something was odd by the way he kept one side away from me.'

'Why do you put up with him?'

'I've lived this way my whole life.' He laughed to himself. 'And I expect that the afterlife will be more of the same.'

'Well, better the heir than me,' Gavin replied. 'Oh, and there was something else I meant to tell you. Something I forgot.' He closed his eyes and used the nib end of the quill to scratch his cheek. 'What could be something from the Carson household that I might forget?'

'Gavin. Did I ever return the honour when you knocked me on my—?'

'You had it coming.' Gavin threw the quill up into the air, letting it flutter to the ground. 'Just like the fact that you might be invited to a wedding some day. Have you heard that Mr Carson has plans for a new son-in-law?'

Barrett jerked his head up. Then he realised that Gavin must be speaking of Annie's sister, Honour. 'I know you were fond of her.'

'Not really.' Gavin locked his knees and seesawed for just a moment, hands behind his back. A spark of amusement appeared in his eyes. 'I think it would be the one you are fond of, Annie.'

'Annie has never courted.'

'Doesn't mean she isn't planning to.'

'I wish her all the best.' He kept his face card-player-straight.

'I believe she is on her way to finding it.'

'And why do you think I view her any differently than any other woman I have spent a brief amount of time with?'

'You didn't expect anything from her. She's the only person you've ever spent more time than the minimum with who did not have to repay you. We all pay a stipend to you, one way or another. Those invitations to Lord Allen's soirées. Tell me those are not an effort on his part to keep his landlord happy and tell me that you don't go for purely business reasons.'

'What of it?'

Gavin's eyes held the same look of their father's before he lashed out. 'Even I. You paid for my education and now I weave my way around society and help you find out the weaknesses of people.'

'No one forces you to live to the height of your profession.'

'You mentioned that my skills were great, speaking in the right ears, and then I became welcome in the best households. I'm like a stench in the air, bringing the buzzard to the carcass. You are so much like the Viscount. I see it now as I am around more.'

'Perhaps you should keep your visits to him and stay away from me.'

Gavin turned to the door, putting his hand on the wood. 'How would you exact your revenge?' He faced his brother. 'I've seen you take it with your fists and with your funds.' He paused. 'A whisper that I'm not a good physician? That someone else is better?'

Barrett stood. 'You know me better than I thought. Tainted blood runs in both our veins. You can't escape it either.'

'And how could I take my revenge on you?' Gavin asked. 'By kissing Annie?'

'Take any revenge on me you please and I'll give it back. Touch Annie and I'll break you. A thousand times over.'

'Oh, you can trust me. I'm family.' Gavin backed out. 'Somehow I think I'm forgetting to tell you something.' He gave him a bow and pulled the door shut behind him as he walked out.

Barrett jumped up, moved to the doorway and opened it. 'Gavin,' he shouted.

His brother didn't turn around, but whistled a few notes before letting them fade.

Barrett had risked his life for the money to send

his brother to school, methodically stealing from his father, and nothing was free. He gripped the door, but let his brother continue down the stairs.

Their blood was tainted black. He'd noticed it in Gavin, too. The façade. The pretence of being just what the person in front of you expected, while pursuing your own goals.

'Oh,' Gavin said, stopping and turning around. 'I don't appreciate your sending me after her sister. I may not go.'

'You'll go,' Barrett said.

'Yes. I will.' He faced Barrett. 'But this repays you. No wagers, no bargaining. No more. My life is my own from that point on. I don't even wish to see the Viscount on your schedule. I know him now as well as I'll ever need to.'

'Your life has always been your own.'

'As long as I did exactly as you directed. You may be my brother, but I detest my father and you're little better. You think everyone is a bit of meat for you to drain the blood out of. Even our father. You can't tell me you don't have a certain joy in keeping him locked up.'

Barrett ignored him.

'Oh, now I remember what I was going to tell you.' Gavin's words popped into the air, like a burr sticking into the skin. 'Lord Milsap's soirée.'

Barrett stared at his brother, waiting.

'Should be quite the event,' Gavin inserted, putting a hand on the doorway. 'Lots of music. Lots of dancing. Lots of—you know, the type of stuff you thrive on—business being conducted with drinks in hand.'

'I wasn't planning to go.'

'Well, that may be for the best. It turns out that Lady Milsap saw Annie at the dressmaker's when she was having new gowns made.' He slowed his speech. 'At least that is the way her mother recounted it to me when she preened about how her daughter will be attending a society event—Lord Milsap's soirée.'

'Annie?' He raised his eyes. 'She's attending?'

'Oh, yes.' Gavin's eyes had the same shine of their father. Even he had not escaped. 'Carson has confided, not so confidentially, to me and about a hundred others, that he would like to see his gem of a daughter on the arm of a true man who appreciates her beauty and her good sense to not fall for a certain viscount's son. Apparently Carson intends to secure a husband for his youngest daughter. You know the man talks when he's nervous. He also talks when he's angry, particularly if he feels someone has overlooked his daughter.'

'My Annie is—'

'*Your* Annie now has two husband-hunting parents, a new interest in cosmetics to hide the shadows under her eyes and what I would classify as a case of revenge on her plate.' Gavin's eyes blinked, asp-like. 'She appears to be planning to take herself straight to the first eligible man with a title equal to or greater than yours, or a fortune equal to or greater than yours, or maybe just someone breathing. Who knows?'

'Not Annie. You're lying.'

'You convinced her quite well that you were throwing her over. And you even taught her how to think like a member of our family.' He raised his chin. 'Be proud, Barrett. Be proud.'

Barrett responded with venom and Gavin backed

out of the hallway, chuckling. 'Hoisted with your own petard, eh, Barrett?'

Gavin left, whistling.

Barrett looked straight ahead. He was still standing, but he was tumbling into a choking abyss.

He'd seen Annie's wrist and helped her make a fist, and found himself being pulled into her path. She'd captured something inside him and he'd had to fight to get away. But he hadn't escaped completely.

Annie. Was it asking too much to have one person that he could trust completely? One person he could speak freely with for the first time in his life?

But to pursue her would be using her, and bringing her into a world she had no idea existed.

He tried to push the thoughts of Annie as far back in his mind as he could. He did not need more weakness in himself. But if he could have one thing it would be a person whom he could trust in his life.

Yet that wasn't possible. He could not trust himself, so no one could trust him.

Barrett walked back into the room he'd left, and moved to his desk. His boot caught the leg of the desk and he crashed forward. As he righted himself, he shoved his arm out and swept the papers around him on to the floor. He returned to his chair, the desktop in front of him smooth.

He didn't care if he was just like his father. He couldn't escape it.

He reached into his waistcoat and took out the hairpin in his pocket and placed it on the table, staring at it. The damn pin. Sunlight seemed to glisten over it, even with the curtains pulled.

'Mr Barrett,' Nettie's voice squeaked from the doorway. She held a tray in her hands, eyeglasses sliding to the tip of her nose and the scent of the steamed vegetables reaching Barrett. 'I thought you might like to eat something.' She took one step forward, then stopped, ignoring the scattered papers around the desk.

'I'm not hungry.'

She took another step forward. 'You need to keep your strength up.'

He pressed his lips together. No one had ever told him before he needed to keep *his* strength up.

'Perhaps the roast,' he said, indicating with his eyes that she could sit the tray down.

She moved forward, seeming oblivious to the clutter on the floor as she stepped over it.

She propped the tray at the edge of the table and set the roast beef in front of Barrett, and then a wine glass, and arranged everything around the pin as if she could not see it.

He put one finger on the pin and slid it towards Nettie. 'See that this is returned to the Carson household.' He held the pin trapped against the table and he didn't raise his hand from it.

He spoke. 'It's for her own good.'

Nettie held the tray in both her hands, staring at the fingertip trapping the pin on the table.

'I'm sure it is.' She waited a moment.

Nettie stepped back, then she turned and bustled to the door. 'I can return it later,' she said, a chirping cheerfulness in her voice as she left. 'Leave it anywhere I can see it and it will be gone before you know it.'

He slid the pin back and put it in his pocket.

Taking the fork, he stabbed a piece of the meat and

bit into it. Tasted like it had been boiled in swamp water.

The fork clattered to the table and he stood.

He would only attend the soirée to return the pin. It wasn't as if he would need to talk with her for more than a second.

And if she was husband-hunting, then she might want the jewel to wear for her courtship. She seemed to place great stock in the pin, not wanting to leave it behind when she left her home. He touched his pocket. And he certainly didn't need any kind of memento of Annie Carson.

'Barrett… Barrett…'

The voice carried through the walls. His father summoned him.

He stood. He would die alone. He could not risk having a child who might grow up to become like his father, or treating a child as he had been treated. His grandmother had shared tales of the ancestors linked by blood and the shared evil that ran through all their veins.

He had heard the stories all his childhood. Of his great-grandmother who'd killed her husband in his sleep. Of an uncle who'd smothered a wife and poisoned her lover.

Every day he'd been told of the virtues of revenge.

He could not put a princess in a world of evil, particularly if it flowed in his veins.

He thought back, trying to remember when he had cared for someone and when he had ceased to have feelings. He supposed he'd cared for his mother, not that he truly remembered much about her except the day she died.

He took the decanter and used three fingers to grab the small glasses.

Nothing would make his father happier than to destroy someone like Annie.

He walked the gallows steps to his father's room and opened the door, and could tell by the look on Summers' face that it had been a long day. His father lay in the bed, dressed, covers sprawled about, yawning, eyes half-closed.

Barrett stopped.

The Viscount held his hand out. 'Share the drink, Son. Share the drink.'

Barrett put the decanter on the table by the chair and poured three drinks. He handed one to Summers, in part to make his father wait. Then he gave his father one.

His father smirked at Barrett. 'Not like you to be gone as much as you have. New tart in town?' He sized up Barrett. He smiled, a bit of drool out of his mouth. 'You and that other one look exactly like I did at your age. And some day you'll look just like me.' He laughed, spitting on to the floor. 'Better get to work if you want to have a caring son like you to coddle you and lock you in your room.'

'I've made you richer.'

'And I don't even have to pay you. You steal your wages.' The man shrugged. 'You always have to have a thief around. A fact of business.'

'Was it a fact of business to backhand me when I was a child if I didn't steal enough for you?'

'Yes. I gave you the childhood I never had. I took you into my work and taught you everything. Everything. I let you carry important messages.'

'You let me set up smuggling rings.'

'I knew you would succeed.'

'I was only fifteen and would have been hanged if caught.'

'Oh, but you were much too smart for that. Besides, I'm a viscount.' His brows rose. 'I could have had you freed. Someone else would have been hanged. Not my son. You were too valuable in increasing my holdings.'

'I took risks.'

'Good ones.' He sniffed and it turned into a sneer. 'The fittest survive. You had to earn your place in life. It's not that you're honest, Barrett. Just that it became easier for you to pretend to be. The wealth grew and you needed more time to manage it. You didn't have time to get your hands dirty any more. So don't lie to yourself.'

Barrett shook his head and poured himself some of the brandy. But he didn't want to drink it, so he left it on the table.

He gripped the chair back and leaned closer to his father. 'I told you Grandmother pushed Mother down the stairs and you called me a liar, even when you knew it was the truth.'

'It would have changed nothing. An accident is an accident. You cannot count on someone to break their neck when you push them down the stairs.' A cough racked his body and he clasped a fist and put it against his chest. 'My mother did not go so gently on me as we did with you.'

His father rolled out of bed and poured himself another brandy. 'I could have left you locked in the cellar until you died. Or I could have said I sent you away and I could have waited another year or so and brought the other rat back.' He shrugged. 'Behind my back you gave the other rat an education.' His father cackled. 'Two sons born within weeks of each other. A lightskirt and a heavy-skirt and both having a baby at the same time.'

He'd learned about Gavin when he was around eleven. Irritation at his father and curiosity had driven him to discover more about a brother his own age. He'd searched out Gavin's mother.

Gavin had a toddling half-sister he cared about and she'd easily accepted Barrett.

Barrett had witnessed the relationship Gavin and his sister had. They'd not considered it unusual, this caring they had for family. Not family loyalty, as he'd had preached to him, but concern for each other. Gavin had watched over her as closely as Barrett watched his father, but the duties came from different places.

Barrett had made offhand boasts to let his father think he was going to a brothel. Instead he'd travelled to the four bare walls that Gavin and his sister shared and pretended to be a part of their lives. He'd known they existed on funds they earned from Gavin's baking and their taking the cart to the street corner and selling the breads from it. And they'd considered themselves fortunate for the walls and the coal to bake with.

He'd tried to talk Gavin into trusting him and, when that hadn't worked, Barrett had pointed out how much better Gavin could provide for his sister if he had the right friends and the right patron. That had been a bargaining tool that Gavin could not refuse.

The education for Gavin had started as a bit of curiosity, but had been a good investment in so many ways. People hadn't realised who Gavin's true father was—they'd always assumed he was the son of the man who'd taught him to speak well.

His father laughed again. He lay back on the pillow and shut his eyes. 'The only time you ever took me by surprise was when you were in the wine cellar. I never could figure out which servant was giving you food while you were locked away. You were there a week once and I didn't expect to unlock the door and have you charge me with a broken wine bottle.'

'It was eleven days. After the first time, I stole the key and had it copied. I put it back and no one noticed. I was safer in the cellar than in my own bed. Finding my way around in the dark gave me something to do. I was not giving you or Grandmother the satisfaction of breaking. I would have died first.'

He stared at his father and saw his own face, lined, and his life wasted. A life without Annie was no life at all. He wanted to do the right thing by her and step away from her, but the ache inside him gnawed at him more than he believed possible.

The empty look in his father's eyes haunted Barrett.

Now Barrett looked across at the speculative eyes of his father. Barrett chuckled, picking up the glass. 'To your health,' he said. 'May you live long and die a natural death befitting your actions.'

'To yours.' His father held out the glass. 'May you have the pox and no one to share it with.'

His father gulped down the drink and Barrett sipped his. The dull ache in him lodged in his chest. He couldn't bring Annie into the house.

To have lived in another life and to have Annie in that world. A world that didn't exist—of goodness and decency.

Of Annie lying in his bed. Of her hands, soft, caressing his chest.

When she touched him, he could forget everything but her. She freed him from his past, soothed the present moment and gave him hope for the future.

With Annie in his life, he'd never end up like his father. He couldn't. Annie took his mind from himself and gave him something precious to look at. Something more important to watch over than any funds growing in an account.

Without Annie, he was nothing more than a poor replica of his father.

His father ran his finger along the scar on his own chin. 'I should have paid more attention to you. Then I might have noticed you were a forger and a thief.'

'Your son.'

'I never once said you were a bastard.' His father laughed. 'The only thing I never called you.'

Barrett tilted his chin down and looked across his nose at his father. 'Oh, how I wished.'

'No, you didn't. You liked the fight. You'll miss me when I'm gone.'

Barrett smiled. 'Not for long.'

'You've got a sweetheart. I saw the notes that other rat gave you on the Carson family. Which one is it?'

Barrett looked at his father. 'Why do I need a sweetheart when there are so many other women in the world?'

'To us.' His father held up the glass again.

Barrett took a sip.

Oh, there was no us. There was no sweetheart. But there was Annie.

Chapter Sixteen

Annie tried not to bite the inside of her lip. The wall-flowers were together, chatting away. She gave Julia and Diana a wave. Meg gave her a strained smile.

Her own upturned lips were not as natural as she would have wished, but if Wellington's soldiers had risked the town of Waterloo, then she could dance.

She turned to the unmarried men who'd gathered on the other side of the room. The music would begin soon and she'd be on the dance floor, hopefully with a partner.

'Oh, there's Earl Winsley,' her mother whispered. 'He's not met you. His four sons are married, but you never know when one might become a widower.'

Annie allowed herself to be dragged along and found herself in conversation with her mother and Winsley.

'You're so thoughtful,' her mother said, and then the edges of her eyes hardened. She stared over Annie's shoulder.

Annie turned, following her mother's gaze.

Barrett had walked into the room, looking as if he'd

taken his valet to the tailor's shop with him and just emerged, sparing no expense. His face might have thinned, but it added to his austerity and authority.

She turned away, hoping he hadn't seen her. She pulled up the edges of her gloves and met her mother's eyes. Her mother also pulled up the edges of her gloves. When the conversation ended, her mother led her away from Winsley and to the refreshment table. 'Show those teeth, Annie. Smile. And do let your arms flash about,' she whispered.

'I simply don't know what I would do without you,' her mother stated loudly as they moved closer to the punch.

Annie spotted Lord Richard. 'Let's detour in his direction,' Annie said. 'I'd like to dance with him.'

'Finally,' her mother whispered. 'I would have insisted Barrett visit us years ago if I thought it would point you in Lord Richard's direction.'

'Yes,' Annie said. 'He'll ask. I'll dance and have a grand time, no matter if his hair pomade smells like sausages. No man watching will be worried about being refused for a dance.'

'I'm sure someone more pleasant will become a widower soon and remember how lovely you look in summer wear.'

'I'm not counting on a widower,' Annie said, clasping both hands around her mother's arm and leading them straight to Lord Richard.

He asked, Annie accepted, and she kept her back straight and made sure to enjoy every last utterance and when he turned the conversation to pork and all its usages, she agreed. It even helped in dancing, she told him, because it gave the dancers something to speak about.

Admiration flashed in his eyes. 'You're delightful.'

Which was a slightly different look than she noticed in Barrett's eyes when the dance happened to turn her in such a way that she could see him. She would have expected a bit of smugness in Barrett's face. Perhaps relief. Or happiness that she had taken his advice and started a search for a husband who would be willing to show up for a wedding ceremony.

Barrett joined a group of men. They were all in conversation, drinks at hand, seemingly oblivious to the world around them. But if Barrett's jaw weren't so cleanly shaved, she would have bet his last whisker that he wasn't really attending the conversation. She would have thought business talk would have put a happier look on his face.

When the dance finished, she took Lord Richard's arm as he started to return her to her mother's side. She stopped walking and he had no choice but to stop as well. 'Dancing with you was so lovely,' she said. 'And except for the fact that it would be unseemly to dance too much with one partner, I'd love to dance again. Do you happen to know of anyone who might wish to dance with me so I can perfect my steps?'

'Have you been formally introduced to Charles?' he asked.

She nodded.

'He hates asking women to dance,' Lord Richard said. 'Fears he'll murder their toes, but…'

'I have sturdy feet.'

He led her to his friend. 'Miss Annie quite loves to dance.'

'That's good,' Charles answered.

'You are…so thoughtful.' Everyone was so thoughtful. 'That is so kind of you to ask me to dance.'

Both Lord Richard and Charles opened their mouths, but didn't speak.

She put her hand out, taking Charles' arm after she pulled it nearer.

'Uh…'

'Do go on to the dance floor, Charles,' Lord Richard said. 'The lady is waiting.'

Charles looked at Annie's hand, then her face, and led her into the dance as the music for the next reel began. 'I'm not the best of dancers,' he said.

'Then this will be practice for us both.' She spoke softly. 'All I care is that you keep your feet moving.'

He leaned closer to whisper, 'That I can do.'

'You have quite excellent posture,' she said. 'I've noticed that before.'

'And so do you, Miss Annie, if I may be so bold.'

She laughed softly. Dancing was more fun than she expected. Perhaps Barrett should try it above glancing in her direction. 'Oh, by all means.'

'Charles, you really should dance more often,' she said when they met in the dance again. She did not want to continue to live her whole life in an attic.

'You're an easy person to dance with, Miss Annie.'

'That is a beautiful compliment.'

He blushed. He had the kind of complexion that held on to redness to the very last instance, which she was grateful for, just in case they were being observed. It might be a good thing to the other men, to think she was a woman who could embarrass a man. She didn't know and she didn't care.

When she helped him recover from a missed step, he seemed so grateful. He truly was the perfect dance partner. 'You just did that to get me closer,' she said. He smiled again and his cheeks reminded her of a particularly glorious sunrise.

When the dance ended, she remained close to him. More people seemed aware of her than she'd expected and she didn't like the feeling that people were watching her. She'd wanted it to happen, but that didn't mean she enjoyed it.

'Did I injure your foot while we were dancing?' Charles asked. 'I can help you to a chair if you wish?'

She laid her hand over his arm. 'That won't be necessary. I'm fine.'

Charles led her back to her mother's side. 'Annie is the best dancer I believe I've ever stepped on to the floor with,' Charles told her mother.

Her mother beamed, her head nodding as she spoke. 'She is so thoughtful. Sits by me for hours, reading to me.'

'And what books are your favourites?' he asked Annie.

'I just read one by Eliza Parsons.'

'At my request. To me. Aloud,' her mother said and then looked over Annie's shoulder, before glancing back at Charles.

Annie hoped her mother wouldn't say she was thoughtful again.

'I never give the housekeeper any instructions either, as Annie has taken over that duty for me as well. She's beyond compare.' Her mother's gaze iced over. 'A treasure. Simply. A. Treasure.'

Barrett was behind her. Annie knew it without looking. Her mother's face gave it away.

'I understand that completely,' Charles said.

'I thought I might dance with—'

Barrett's voice from behind her.

'Oh, thank you.' Her mother stepped completely
around Annie and held out her hand. 'I've hardly
danced a step all evening.'

He raised one brow, but reached out his hand to
her mother, and pulled the back of her hand close to
his lips. Kissing the air. 'A dance with your daughter
would be wonderful.'

Barrett looked every bit of his elevated birth. Even
the simple tie of his cravat contributed to his status,
almost seeming to shout out that he didn't need to
spend any extra time on something so frivolous. His
eyes commanded the room.

Annie gave a small pivot on the heels of her slippers. He knew how to ask people to dance as well as
she did. And to refuse, just as she was about to do.

Annie schooled her face to look uninterested and
turned to Barrett. 'I must decline—' she put her hand
to her bosom '—as I have just agreed to tell Charles
about the book I've been reading.'

Her heart thumped so loud she hoped no one could
hear it or see it throbbing in her throat.

'By Eliza Parsons,' Charles said. 'Have you read
any of her novels, Barrett?'

'No. I've been busy.'

'Oh, you would not be interested at all.' Annie
turned from Barrett and peered at Charles. 'It has a
castle and no one wants to go to the upstairs at night
because that's where the ghosts live.'

Charles raised a brow. 'Sounds interesting.'

'I couldn't do it justice in the telling,' Annie said to Charles. 'I must lend you my copy.'

'I'd like that,' Charles said.

'Well, now that we've got that settled,' Barrett said, holding out his arm for Annie's hand. 'Dance?'

Charles excused himself, probably a bit intimidated by the ferocity in Barrett's eyes.

'I really can't,' Annie said. She lowered her voice. 'I have epidemeosis. A rare case. And the physician has said I must not get too tired. Why, just this very morning he said that if I danced with the wrong person, someone who could upset my humours, it could be very disastrous.' He had actually said that and then winked at her.

Her mother gasped. 'I thought you were cured,' she whispered.

'I didn't want to tell anyone.'

'Of course,' Barrett said. 'That epidemeosis is serious.'

'I now have a severe case.' She turned to her mother. 'I believe the physician reminded me to be in contact with people I've not been in close quarters with before. He said it will build up my resistance.'

'Well, Annie...' her mother reached out, patting Annie's arm as she glared at Barrett '...I will tell your father and we can take you home.'

'Not until I dance a few more times,' Annie said. 'Please introduce me to people I don't know, that's healthiest.'

'I would prefer to get you home,' her mother said. 'The air in here has soured a bit and I'm getting a headache. I will get your father.' Her mother flounced away, moving between them with her elbows extended as she went in search of her husband.

Barrett dodged, then closed the space she'd left behind. 'I wanted to return this to you.' He reached into his waistcoat pocket and held out the pin, keeping the fingers of his gloves cupped around it so no one else could see it.

She frowned, recognising it. She didn't move.

'You have to take it. It's yours,' he said.

The one her grandmother had given her.

She raised her chin. 'No, thank you.' It would not do her future dance prospects any good for anyone to see her accepting something from him.

'It was your grandmother's.'

She looked at the jewellery. 'That doesn't look familiar.' She shook her head. 'I can't imagine where you received this, Mr Barrett. I lost mine on a walk in the countryside.'

'I must have been mistaken.'

'Happens,' Annie said. 'None of us is perfect. I want to beg your pardon for shouting out the window. I was upset that your horse may have left manure behind.'

'That is truly unforgivable if my horse did such a thing, but perhaps not as much as what I said to you.'

The words swirled into her and erased all the memories of the things he'd said. That and his eyes. The man had eyes she could drown in. Lashes to tangle herself in. And she couldn't think what his lips looked like except they'd felt better than any silk in the world.

'We had a peaceful walk and were merely two people who decided that their paths should not cross.' She looked around the room. 'Particularly as there are so many other ventures in this town to consider.'

'And are you determined to consider those ventures, Annie?'

'I could not say.' She raised her brow, telling him with her eyes that she *would* not say. 'Did you not teach me to strike back?' She kept her voice innocent.

'Against physical harm.'

She put two fingers to her chin. 'I suppose I might have confused that and not realised there were limitations.'

'Do you not understand that I considered your best interests?'

'Yes. I do. And I agree with you.' She looked around the room, realised Lord Richard was watching her, and smiled at him. 'I'm considering the same.' She moved her head so no one else could see her lips. 'Lord Richard is a dear and Charles blushes so easily.'

'Richard isn't any sort of *dear* and Charles' blushes are possibly why he spends so much time in the darker haunts of London.' Barrett's face lost its softness, but it didn't lose its appeal. 'So he doesn't embarrass himself by what he does.'

Charles hadn't made her toes curl and he'd not stepped on them, but still, they felt rather flat when he was around. And Lord Richard, the fourth son of a duke, was pleasant to dance with when he spoke in a language she could understand. But she didn't want to spend her life asking him to translate—she feared the translation would lose a considerable amount in the telling.

Barrett didn't even need to speak. Even the way he snored was soothing. A quiet rasp with a bit of a rumble at the end.

Barrett watched her and it didn't feel as though he was actually looking at her, but seeing her spirit and her heart in a way no one else had ever done before. As if he could see a part of who she was that even she couldn't understand.

'Well,' she spoke, then sighed, but she looked straight into Barrett's glare when she said, 'I'll be sure and tell anyone I might find interesting that I'm so very innocent. That way I will not be taken advantage of.'

'When butterflies pull carriages full of that horse manure through the air.'

Her chin went higher. 'Could happen.' She took a step back. 'You and I have been talking far too long and I don't want to discourage any future prospects. Besides, I feel that blasted epidemeosis.'

He lifted the pin and turned it into the lamplight before putting it back into his pocket. 'I'm shocked to find out your affliction returned.'

'Me as well.' She stared at him. 'If I remember correctly, the physician decided the quiet night hours will help me regain my health.'

She took a step and then looked back. Her mistake—looking back—but she'd known she would have to take one last look and it wouldn't be enough.

And then beyond that, beyond anything she saw in his eyes, she remembered the little boy he'd mentioned. The one who'd been used to clear the table and grown so used to it that he expected it. The child who had a grandmother who might scar him with a poker.

And she remembered the kiss.

'I might unlock the side door for a breath of fresh air tonight. And I suppose, in the dim light, the pin might look more familiar if I were to see it again.' She paused, then spoke, almost to herself. 'I really must get over this affliction,' she said, turning away.

'You're not choosing the easiest way.'

'I'm not perfect, Mr Barrett.' She inclined her head.

'Neither am I, Miss Carson.'

Her stomach jumbled a thousand different ways, but she turned to leave as if the world had parted just for her.

Another man walked up to speak with Barrett. Barrett and the man discussed a new waterwheel he wanted to purchase for a country venture.

At the edge of the room, she paused and turned a bit so she could take one last glance. Again, she couldn't keep herself from looking back. Whenever he was in a room, no one else mattered.

The man handed Barrett a filled glass and spoke. Barrett nodded. He truly didn't look as if he had a care in the world, or as if he had a thought of anything but business.

But she knew that even though he was looking forward, his eyes saw her, just as he had schooled her to do when she struck out.

He brushed his hand over his waistcoat pocket.

She straightened her shoulders and walked by him, and looked at him from behind the other man's back, her chin at an angle definitely not recommended for fighting. His face changed, a flicker of a smile flashed in his eyes.

And her heart did a thousand little warm jabs and she wondered she could still stand, but she managed to leave with her head held high and the memory of a smile that had only been for her.

Chapter Seventeen

Annie touched the key in the lock and paused. She turned it, warnings exploding into her mind, but none of them strong enough to stop the turn of her wrist because they all seemed to warn her of how Barrett's arms would feel around her.

She knew she wasn't letting Barrett in as much as letting herself out.

She opened the door and Barrett leaned on the side of the house. He pushed himself from the wood. 'I thought it was four a.m. that you waited for the epidemeosis cure.'

'Isn't that what time it is now?'

'Probably a quarter to a half past.'

There was no way she would have opened the door early. She'd been standing on the other side, counting slowly to a thousand so she wouldn't appear impatient. 'I'm sorry to have disturbed your night's rest.'

He walked through the doorway and put a hand at her side, pressing the dressing gown close. 'Annie, you've been quite proficient at that.' He took the key, touching her fingers, and turned back, locking the door. He put the key on the hook beside the door.

She turned to him. 'Did you realise you glared at Lord Richard and Charles?'

'I did not,' he said. 'I hardly noticed them.'

He stepped closer and lowered his voice. 'I only remember seeing you at the dance. I meant to return the pin that you had that apparently was never yours when you had it in your satchel.'

She stopped. 'Do not pretend you didn't know what you were doing when you stood by me in the corner. Everyone there was watching us.'

'Were they?'

'And you knew it.'

'I didn't mean to stop the others from dancing with you. I just couldn't bear that you might do something foolish.'

'Unless it is with you.' She crossed her arms.

He nodded. 'If you're determined.'

They stood, duelling with their stares, and she didn't know who was winning.

'I can't stop thinking of you. Even when I look at the ledgers,' he said.

'I wouldn't consider that a bad thing.'

He looked into the distance. 'It isn't. Just odd. The ledgers and business have always brushed away everything else.'

'I understand. It's a little bit of the same with me. I wanted to escape my room, and my world, and see what is on the other side of my walls. When I think of you, it seems the walls have disappeared.'

'There are no walls around me.' His gaze caught hers again.

'Are you sure?'

'It is the truth of me you're seeing.'

'It could be,' she said. 'I think you judged me much like a property you were interested in buying. And after one close look, you backed away. One look and you were pulling a different direction. Because I was such a very different kind of investment.'

'You were. Before I'd ever seen you, Gavin kept insisting you were a perfect wife for me. Gavin swore that I should consider marriage, and that you were a woman who did exactly as your parents requested, but then he had no idea you were planning an escape.'

'A journey. A life.'

'He talked about your sister Honour, but he kept saying that I should see you. That you'd been kept secluded and were someone that I should court. I didn't want to court anyone, but I gave in. And he was right. But it doesn't change anything.'

She took a step closer, trying to read his features in the dim light. 'The physician sent you to me?'

Barrett nodded. 'He meddles.'

'And he selected me?'

'He's a physician. He gauged you healthy and knows all the families about. He claimed you to be the pick of the crop.'

'You were willing to let someone else choose a wife…or tell you which crop to harvest?' How cold. 'And you consented?' A little squeak had sneaked into her voice.

'No, I wouldn't let him choose my wife.' He touched her arm. 'But he mentioned you so many times I could not help but go see you. And he said you were a planner. You didn't have the vapours, but tried to keep the others from flittering too much.'

She closed the distance. She'd suspected something

else, particularly since he'd just said the physician had claimed her healthy. 'The epidemeosis, a total lie?'

His lips parted and his head tilted to the side. He straightened the hem of his coat sleeve. 'I requested a meeting with you alone. I'd seen you by then and wanted to see you again. I wanted to talk with you. The people I hire arrange things for me. It's their job.'

She *was* an innocent. At least, much more of one than she'd realised. How could she have been so friendly with a spy and the man who set him upon their family?

She moved closer, understanding why he'd taken the time to show her how to defend herself. They'd let two predators into the house. One, Gavin, and the other, Barrett. And she'd never suspected a thing. Nor had her father or mother, she was certain.

She had been more innocent than she'd ever expected. She couldn't believe the world worked in such a way. No wonder her father didn't do well in business. The man was honest.

'Where did you see me at first?' she asked. 'After Gavin mentioned me. I don't travel about much, have only attended a few balls, and I was mostly under lock and key for the past five years.'

He studied her face. 'It doesn't matter.'

She jutted her chin. 'It does to me. I am a merchant's daughter. Not of the peerage. Where did you see me?'

'At your house.' He shook his head. 'I didn't plan your illness, but after I heard your laughter, Gavin did. I thought it clever of him to get me a chance to talk with you.'

'The physician—'

'You may believe him if you want. And he is honest, but not with that diagnosis. It's a family tradition. The meddling. The manipulation.'

'I knew you looked like the physician. Sound like him.'

He nodded. 'My half-brother assists me in business. Learned to speak properly as a child, when one of his mother's lovers who didn't have children thought him close to a son. But then the man lost interest in the mother and Gavin as well.'

'You've had a spy in my house to spy on me? Or my father's business? Which is it?'

He stepped back and put a hand over his waistcoat pocket. 'Both. At least, after he noticed you. It was your father's business at first. I wanted to know the truth of it before I purchased it. People tend not to tell the truth when money is concerned.'

'I would agree.'

'Your father has no sense of finances. Nor of family. He kept you locked away, then allowed a stranger to move into your world.'

'I would agree that his financial decisions can be questionable, but he does try hard with the family. He cares for us.'

'But he put you away in the attic.'

Raising her chin, she said, 'Considering who was in the house, I wouldn't say it was a bad decision.' She stepped in front of him. 'But, you said to trust my instincts. My instincts don't tell me to fear you.' She reached out, her fingertips grazing the lapel of his coat before she lowered her hand. 'But they also tell me that you have a stone wall behind your eyes. I cannot think why you are even standing here.'

'I apologise for Gavin being in your house. And for

the spying. I should never have done that to you. But I didn't know you then. You weren't Annie to me. You were Carson's daughter.'

'You also spied on my father.'

'That, I don't regret.' He frowned and gave a half shrug. 'Business and all.'

He leaned against the door, pulling her closer, his voice softening. 'And I don't regret you, Annie. Without Gavin alerting me to you, I wouldn't have noticed you. I couldn't have. You were hidden away.'

'For good reason. I don't know who to trust.'

'Don't trust anyone. Ever. One bit more than you have to.' He ran his hands up her arms, the warmth of his touch blazing into her. 'But I would lay down my life for you, Annie. Just not my heart.'

'It feels like I have your heart when your arms are around me.'

She curled herself against him, resting her head against his shoulder and clasping him around the waist. After a few moments, he enclosed her in his arms. They stood together, her face buried against his chest.

But he didn't respond when she'd told him she felt like she had his heart.

She raised her chin and his lips closed over hers, sending a moist kiss into the recesses of her soul.

The kiss lingered, lengthened and blocked out everything, filling her with light and the warmth of sunshine.

Finally, she stepped away. She knew why he didn't wish to court her. She had to tell him and make him realise that it didn't matter. 'You must understand,' she said. 'I am completely fine with the fact that you will never have children.'

'It's not—that simple.' He took in a breath.

'I understand.'

'Based on the look in your eyes, I don't think you do.' He shook his head, and tipped up her chin and kissed her. 'Gavin lied about that as well. He thought your father would not be so careful about us being together if there was no risk of childbirth to you.'

'Then why do you not want to hold me? After you hug me, it is as if you put as much distance as possible between us. I see it in your face. You act as if it hurts you to touch me.' She put her hand over her mouth. 'Not that, I mean, I'm a tart. Or care about such things. When I invited you here tonight, I thought it would be impossible to—be close.'

'Annie, I would very much like to spend a long, slow night in a warm, wide bed with you.'

'I did enjoy sleeping beside you, too.'

He shook his head from side to side, choosing his next words. 'I think you're the purest thing I've ever seen.' He put his hands on her shoulders, then he gently put a finger on her chin and lifted her face to look into his eyes. 'When I warn you to take care, it's because there are men who are like me in the world.' He spoke in a whisper. 'A lot of them, and I don't want one of them to take advantage of your unsophistication for a place in your arms. I don't want one of them to touch you who doesn't care about you.' He frowned. 'I don't want anyone to touch you.'

'Then why do you not want to court me?'

'Because I don't want you hurt.'

'Then don't hurt me.'

'The only way I can be certain of that is to step out of your life.'

'Nonsense.'

He took a step to the side and stared into her eyes. 'I think the marriage your parents share is insipid. It almost turns my stomach. And I suspect you would expect some of the same in a marriage.' He shook his head. 'Your father trots in circles to please your mother.'

Annie nodded. Her mother appeared to be the fluff in the marriage and the family had always treated her as such. But she'd been an heiress and the one her sisters had avoided when they decided to leave home. Her mother seemed not to have thoughts at all, but when she did think, it was with an iron will and the directness of an arrow going straight to the centre of a target.

'I don't want to have a marriage like my parents… I mean, I do, but…only similar.' Laughter bubbled in her throat, a blend of humour, irritation and confusion. 'I cannot imagine you asking me three times if I would prefer a carriage ride to the park, or an evening at home, or if am I sure what I would wish to have brought to me.'

She hated her parents tiptoeing around each other, always seeming to lose any senses when the other person was in the room. Her mother used the sofa like a throne or a deathbed, depending on the day. And the rest of the family always followed along and Annie had soothed everyone when her mother was upset.

'I suspect anyone having you for a husband and expecting the event to be smooth,' she said, 'might have the same luck as planting thorn bushes in a garden and expecting beautiful blooms to sprout.'

'True. My business comes first, second and last.'

'And you are the business in its entirety.'

He didn't answer, but raised a brow, indicating she might be foolish to believe anything else.

She had one of those wind-up machinations in front of her. The Barrett version. All starched and pressed and with only moving parts that one could see working and nothing flesh and bone beneath.

But perhaps he didn't know that something else was inside him, too. She doubted he'd let anyone, ever, in his life any closer than she was.

And if she pushed him out the door, she doubted he'd ever let anyone get half as close to him as he'd let her become.

She put a hand on his chest, over his heart, and really, she felt nothing beating.

It seemed that he could read her mind and the look in his eyes challenged her.

'What do you have inside?' she asked. 'To fill the space?'

'Ledgers, I suppose.'

'That is better than absolutely nothing. You care for something.'

'I've never pretended not to have a fascination with increasing my wealth.'

'A fascination?'

He nodded, unspeaking.

'At least you are free to move about when you wish.'

He snorted.

'You are,' she challenged. 'My attic world,' she said, turning. 'Let me show you the room.'

He grasped her hand, stilling her. 'I can't go to your room with you.'

'Your feet don't work?' she asked. 'You can't raise

your feet? Should I get Gavin to attest to this, or would
he twist that to his purposes?'

'I can raise my feet,' he said. 'Extremely well.' He
leaned closer, eyes direct. 'I can raise my feet as high
as they need to go.'

She blinked, a dismissal, and led him up a darkened
hallway, into a smaller, bleaker corridor and then into
a small room. He ducked his head under the doorway
when he went inside.

Barrett looked into the room. For a small place
under the eaves, it was appealing. Two chairs, a table,
and some books. Two lamps turned low. No bed.

'I have a sitting room, a room for my clothes and
one for my bed. It is like a small house, but the ceil-
ings and walls of each room are so close that I'm forever reminded of being confined.'

All he could think of was the one room with a bed
that must take up the whole space. He needed to give
her the pin, tell her goodbye and leave. He would leave
as soon as he gave her the pin.

He looked at her and breathed in a light floral aroma.
Perhaps some scent from the soap she put on her hair.
So fragile. The only thing in his life that he couldn't
easily turn from. The only thing. She kept telling him
of the cramped feel of her room and he kept thinking
of her bed and knowing it had more than enough room.

He reached out, taking her wrist and holding it up.
A slender reed, so fragile he could hardly believe it.
He looked where his hand joined hers. She quietened.

He could not tell her of the wager with Gavin. He
could not tell her he'd seen her wrist and heard her
laughter and it had pulled him along like a wheeled toy

on a string. But then when he saw her and realised her beauty and her frailty, he'd known she wasn't strong enough for his world. He'd known it best for her to be secluded. The safest place of all for her, in her family's home. And he knew he could keep her there, if she would only listen to him.

The touch of her skin infused life into his body and destroyed his resistance. He'd suspected from the very first that would happen. And he did not need to ruin her any more than he had. He'd made a blasted mistake and he didn't need to make it worse.

'Where did you see me first?' she repeated.

'I only thought I saw you,' he said.

'You can't think you see something. You either do or you don't.'

'You were in the hallway at this house and only in my vision for a moment. I couldn't see you. But I could see the innocence in your movements and hear your laughter.' He dipped his head. 'Your laughter. I'd never heard a sound like that.'

With a free hand, she put a palm flat on his chest. This time he'd not prepared himself. His defences ripped from his body. All he could do was gaze at her.

She dipped her head. 'I can understand that since I'm a merchant's daughter, it might cause you to dismiss me. I'm not a business asset. Will never be.'

He touched her chin to raise her eyes back into his view. 'You are not just any merchant's daughter. You're Annie and never has there been a better view in my eyes. Never. Than at this moment.'

His grasp on her wrist loosened and slid down to cup her elbow, and then lower to rest at her waist. Barrett couldn't keep from touching her face. 'You've never even seen evil. The one thing your father did correctly was keep you safe. But he should have let you see that the world does not have your best interests at heart. It only holds their own.'

'He has kept me a prisoner.'

'For your own good.'

'And you would do the same? Lock me away?'

'Your father does not have locks on doors to keep you in. He has them there to keep evil from destroying you.'

'I'm locked away, but I would like us to be friends.'

'My body doesn't react to friends the same way it reacts to you.' He needed to step back. To keep her safe and secure, and let her keep believing that people did have good in them.

She turned away.

He reached out, the light touch of his fingers on her arm stilling her. 'Annie, at the soirée did you want to dance with me?'

'I did. But I didn't really. I wanted to speak with you when no one was around so we could talk of things that matter and not the folderol you must say when a crowd is around.'

'I wanted to dance,' he said. 'Just that moment. A waltz though, a chance to swirl you through the air and keep you close for the memory of dancing with you.'

'There isn't enough space in here for a waltz.'

He moved closer, turned her to him and took her hand in his. He pulled her palm to his face and placed a kiss in it. 'There is plenty of room.'

Then he held her hand high and put his other at her back. With his lips close to her ear, he hummed the music and led her in the confined dance. Leading her around the room, he kept holding her nearer his body.

Finally, he stopped.

'We must tell each other goodbye and mean it,' he said.

'Or we could continue to be friends,' she answered. 'Why is that not possible?'

She moved against him, holding him tight in her arms. Their clothes crushed between them. Flashes of heat erupted in him and he closed his lips, tightened the muscles of his jaw and put his hands at her waist and pushed her away as he stepped back.

'Because we are too fascinated with each other to merely be friends. Ever.'

He reached into his pocket, took out the pin and carefully placed it in her hair, weaving it into the locks. He took his time, savouring the feel of the soft wisps of hair and the nearness.

'This is how I wish to remember you. A nymph in the night. A treasure to dance with. A beautiful innocent.' He stepped away, reaching for the door.

He felt her hands clamp around his arm and she swung her body between him and the door. 'You are leaving. Just like that?'

'I have to leave. There's no marriage in me. No tender feelings. But I cannot look at the most beautiful thing I've ever seen—the most innocence I've ever seen—destroy it and go on. And I am going on. I'm going back to the world I've lived in always.' He took her face in his hands and moved close. 'You are too perfect.'

'I think you've mistaken me for someone else,' she

said. 'I'm one of the Carson sisters. We are not known for our discretion. Rather our indiscretion.'

He rested his face against her, feeling heartbeats pounding in him.

'I've missed you, Annie. I've missed you all my life.'

'I'm here now,' she said, leaning into his kiss and the caresses that went from his heart to his hands and against her and then back into his body again.

Hard and aware of every flicker of her movement, he ran his hand to the front of her dressing gown and untied the knot as if he were unwrapping a gift. Even the fastening of her clothing seemed to understand his need for her, falling open before he could imagine.

All his sense of business and rightness and everything else fled, but the desperate need to touch her skin.

When he looked at her, he forgot all about doors to leave through and darkened windows and even the warmth of sunshine, because Annie warmed him more than anything else and all the way to the edges of his heart. To look into Annie's eyes engulfed him in her touch.

He took off his coat and his waistcoat.

Raising her hands, she unpinned her hair, letting it fall around her shoulders. She took the pin he'd given her, and slipped the pin over the side of his waistband. 'I don't need this right now.'

She took the lamp and walked through her bedroom door.

She was freed of the constraints of society for the first time in her life.

Pulling him close enough was impossible. Touching him enough eluded her.

'You will not be able to go back to the innocence you had.' Barrett pulled away and the intensity in his eyes engulfed her.

She lowered her eyes to follow the trail her fingers made from the side of his face, over his cravat and down his arm. 'I can never go back. It's already too late to return. My world changed forever the moment you told me to make a fist.'

She didn't want to let her mind stay in the dark attic. All she wanted was Barrett. The scent of him entranced her and she pressed against his coat, pulling him closer. She couldn't breathe unless she touched his skin.

Their fingers tangled at his waistcoat buttons and his husky laughter reached her ears. Gently, he moved her hands aside and, in the time it took for him to run his fingers down the placket, he had the buttons undone. He shrugged his clothes from his shoulders and took her in his arms.

The warmth of his chest surrounded her, a fortress of man stronger than anything she'd ever imagined.

Barrett held her close, taking his time with the sleeves on her chemise, lingering over each movement. He slipped the garment from her shoulders, pausing, taking a breath. Bending down, he kissed the soft skin of her shoulder, his lips lingering.

Letting the dressing gown fall to the floor with the chemise, he caressed her breasts from behind, pulling her against him, the fabric of his trousers brushing her.

Then he turned her, lifted her in his arms and took her to bed. She couldn't feel the sheets or any of the covers. The only thing that she could see, feel or taste was Barrett.

Running a hand along her hip, he traced the rise and fall of her body, breathing life into her with his kisses.

He was spice and life and her body felt more alive than it ever had before, and free. She'd escaped the prison and found her freedom in his kisses.

He touched her, trying not to miss any part of her, learning the magic of her body, and letting it infuse him with a magic he'd never known before. Annie soothed all the storm clouds he'd ever felt and the magic appeared in her face, and nothing else was in the world but them. His eyes questioned her and she answered him by lessening the distance between them.

He moved above her and, with all the control he'd learned, he gently moved inside her, easing his way slowly, taking care so he could watch her eyes and then brush kisses over her face. His cheek rested against hers, and he held her close and tried to make a moment neither of them would ever forget.

Lying beside Barrett, she could feel the peaceful blanket of security around her.

Annie rested her hand against Barrett's chest and savoured the moment of closeness that seemed to erase all the emptiness in life before she'd touched him.

'This was most wondrous,' she said.

She couldn't tell him how much their moments had meant. She had no words for such an experience. Shutting her eyes, she snuggled into him. She'd finally reached into his heart.

She propped herself on one arm, keeping the covers over her. She took his hand and pulled it to her lips and kissed the fingers, then nipped one.

He pulled her down against him and hugged her

close. 'I can't stay much longer. The servants will be about.'

Those weren't the exact words she wanted to hear. She'd give him another chance. 'This meant something to you?'

'Of course it did.' The truth of his words soothed her. She treasured the knowledge.

'But we must get back to our duties.'

She listened to his words again in her mind, studying them, trying to put them in a different order or somehow make them sound like what she'd wanted to hear. She must have misunderstood.

'Think of my life. I have no duties that matter. I say soft words to my parents to make them believe all is well and I stare at the walls. I live in someone else's house and someone else's world.'

'Can you not make it your own?'

It was as if a cat yowled inside her, but she pushed the feelings away, soothing herself by running a hand along his arm, reassuring herself that all was right. He would understand. Surely he would.

'It doesn't fit, my world,' she said. 'I'll always be the baby of the family and my parents don't mean disrespect, but they dismiss my thoughts. They bat my feelings back into the crib if I so much as hint at a thought—then they tug at me when they need someone to bolster their own feelings. If I disagree, it is as if I am a mouse who just grew a giant claw and it shocks them deeply that I might swipe out with my opinion.'

'I am not a man to release you from these walls. I would only place you in others.'

Her hand clenched. 'What others?'

She held her breath, waiting to see if he would say

the walls of his home. If he married her, it wouldn't matter if he did think to shut her away. She would have a carriage at her disposal. He attended soirées and as his wife she could stand with the wallflowers and it would not matter so much. Nothing would matter, as long as Barrett was in her life. As long as he knew she was in his.

'The walls that protect people from my world. I have to take care of my father. I can't leave it to the others. He would destroy them or innocent people. No one can handle him like I can. No one.'

'I'm sure that's true. But I can help.'

And she could. She'd spent her life helping her parents and her sisters get along. Making peace. She could help with his father.

'No.' He moved out of bed, clutching his trousers from the floor. 'He would see you as another opportunity, a weakness in me. He can't use you.'

She sat, her arms crossed over the covers. 'Trees gain strength because of the winds that push against them. I have been sheltered, but I want to stand on my own feet.'

The air suffocated her. She'd just shared the most closeness she'd ever shared with anyone ever. She was hoping he'd stay until the last moment of the last second he could remain and keep their encounter secret, yet he was more concerned with leaving.

'You cannot enter into my father's household. He doesn't need another toy to bat around,' he added.

She certainly could understand how a toy that might be battered would feel. 'Do you think that is what he does to you?'

'Perhaps. Perhaps it is a game we both play.'

He put on his trousers and sat beside her, touching her hand. 'Whatever it is in my household—game or bitter fight to the death—you cannot be involved.'

'But if I wish it?' Why could he not agree, or ask if he might visit her again? And where were all the fluttery words of love that her sisters had talked of over and over and over? She tightened her fists on the covers and drew her knees closer to her body.

He shook his head. 'I would not let you walk into a fire just because you wished it.'

Annie pulled away and lay on her back, staring up at the ceiling. 'Why would you not want me to be happy? Why would you not wish to place the world at my feet?' Or at least place a soft word into the air. Or promise to return to see her again with a decision of the second they would be together. Did he not understand how this affection thing worked?

He stretched his opposite arm away from her, then placed his palm against the back of his neck, pausing for a moment and then reaching to rest his fingertips against her arm.

'Because the world wouldn't be at your feet. You would be at its mercy and it would trample you. You cannot have your reputation ruined.'

He'd forgotten she'd risked running away to be with her sister. *Conveniently?* she wondered.

Her thoughts clashed against each other. 'The only trampling is done by you and against my feelings.'

She had heard stories of ruined women and now she knew how they felt. She'd thought she'd shared

the most precious moments of life with Barrett and
he had apparently missed that.

'I don't want to hurt you. I don't want you hurt.
I want you to have all the best of this life. The best
of food, clothes and the house you have always lived
in.' He stopped talking and seemed to be choosing his
words. 'I can't take you from this life and put you into
my own. It's not a pleasant world. My mother died in it.'

'You want me to have all these things and yet you
do not want to give me yourself.'

'I've told you, I want the best for you.'

'In your case—' she directed her gaze at him '—I
will take an exception. I would settle for less than perfect. Much less than perfect.' She tightened the covers around her.

'Thank you.'

'Don't you have somewhere to be?' She blinked,
directing him to the door with her eyes. 'That house
where you live…the one with walls which are not welcoming, but which you cannot wait to dash back to.'

He leaned down and touched both her arms. 'You
have to understand. It's for the best. I could not see
you hurt. You think you feel pain now. It is only a little
discomfort compared to what my world could bring
you. I'll see you often, but I can't have you hurt. And
I cannot risk the moments that might bring a child
into the world.'

'You are not asking me to be a wife. And I don't
think you're asking me to be a mistress.' She took in a
deep breath, feeling it become a knot in her stomach.
'What options does it leave?'

'I don't know.'

'Do you love me?'

Was she mad? His thoughts jumped into his mind before he realised they were there. Love? Love? What did she want love for? It was an evil way to manipulate people. Once they loved you, you could use them as you wished.

'Do you love me?' she asked, voice shrill.

'Of course.' He firmed himself straight and forced the words from his mouth. 'I love you.' The most foolish words he'd ever said, but if she wanted to hear them, then he would say them.

She jumped up, realised she was naked, searched the floor and grabbed the first thing at hand: his coat.

Momentarily, conversation flew from his mind. A waif stood in front of him, swallowed by his clothes. Her image burned into him and, even in the dim lamplight, he could see every fold of the cloth and every curve of the skin.

'I'm so thankful you didn't choke on those words as you spat them out.' The waif disappeared and Annie returned to view.

With the accuracy of a hawk pinpointing a perch on which to land, the words flew from his mouth. 'I won't be used,' he said. 'Not by you. Not by anyone.'

'We're not talking about that. We're talking about love.'

'We are talking about that.' He raised his shoulders high. 'Why would you care if I love you if not to use me? If it is all about unselfishness, then why does it matter?'

He touched his chest. 'I am here. I am kind to you. What else matters? The fluffy bows I draw around the words? The ones to manipulate?'

'I do not want to manipulate you.' She pulled the coat closed tight, but didn't release the cloth.

'Not unless it is to get me to tell you I love you.'

She had one foot in front of the other and leaned her weight back, balancing, adding distance between them.

He turned. He could not bear the hurt, anger and accusation in her face. He saw framed lace on the wall, a ladies' fan and a butterfly, covered in glass. Art his father would take delight in crashing to the ground to watch the shards appear. Beauty he would destroy. If his father discovered someone cared about it, he would take joy in the destruction.

'You need to have someone who can give you a life of peaceful dreams and happiness.' A life without his father and a life without the spying and trickery.

'And you cannot?'

'I must work until I am exhausted. The memories that live within me can't be awoken. Moments of stillness like this… It opens the door to the unrest inside me. I have to hold the past at bay. My duties come first. They must.'

'I would have thought that perhaps I could take your memories from the things that disturb you.'

They stared at each other across the bed.

'You have. But I must continue to live and take care of the duties I have.'

He looked at the coat, decided he could manage one night walking home half-dressed. If memory served right, it had happened before.

But never with anyone standing there—a waif— in his coat.

He drew himself tall. If that was what she wanted, so be it. He would put the blasted bow on the words. 'I—'

He waited for his words, forming them. 'I am here.'

'With one pound note meaning you tolerate some-one and five pound notes meaning you love them, how many pound notes would I receive?'

'Eleven.' There. That should satisfy her.

'That little inner voice is telling me that you mean one point one.'

'Well, it's considerably more affection than I've ever given anyone else.'

She walked over, extinguished the lamp, darken-ing the room, and then her footsteps pattered nearer and she thrust out the coat to him and walked away, moving back under the covers. 'I can get affection from a pet.'

He thought about trying to tell her again those words of love she wanted. But it would be wasting her time and his. He couldn't say it the way she wanted to hear it and he doubted he felt anything the way she expected him to feel it.

The door was closer than she was.

Barrett left, moving to the exterior door, striding outside and following the dark path to his house.

Putting his head back, he closed his eyes as he walked. None of his feelings could leave his body from where they were trapped inside. Something had taken hold of him, giving him a wax-like coating, hardening over him, and his thoughts churned inside, controlled by the barrier that wouldn't let them escape.

He wanted to be with Annie. Craved the feel of her inside his arms. Wanted to feel her against his skin. Wanted to shut out everything and hold her close.

* * *

When he arrived at the façade of his house, he kept walking.

He'd forced the foolish words of love from his lips after holding Annie in his arms. Words he'd hated to say. Words of weakness and surrender. But he'd said them for Annie. And she'd tossed them away like scraps on to the ground.

He turned to the right and then after a while to the right again, the wind brushing his face, and then again, and then again. When he passed his house again, he kept walking. Then he stopped—feeling the circular route of his path and the circular route of his life.

Something broke loose inside him and he changed direction, completing the same path but in reverse. If his life was to change, he would have to think differently than he had been. He considered how he had done things in the past and how he could do things in the future if he were to take the opposite path.

Morning dawned and he noticed the servants leaving the houses on their errands. A few coaches on the street. A magistrate laughing companionably with a woman who had once approached Barrett with a proposition. Another man leaving the door of his house and jumping into a town coach.

He watched the people, seeing them as people and not as chess pieces. Not as particles to be moved one way or another to suit his purposes,

But then he understood that a part of him would never change. His past would always be inside him. He could choose the direction he would point his future to, but even though he could choose the direction, the world would conspire to do as it wished.

When he finally stopped in front of his father's house, seeing the walls brightened by the rising sun and morning's fresh glow covering the walls, he saw his gaol. He'd been locked inside his whole life.

He made a decision before returning to the prison.

Chapter Eighteen

His father watched him. The man had been prowling around Barrett, sniffing like a wolf looking into a flock of lambs. Watching for a weakness. A blink. 'Which daughter is it?' his father asked. 'Which is it you're sniffing after?'

Ice touched Barrett's chest, but he looked his father in the eye. 'All of them, of course.'

The old man scratched his chin. He looked out the window, eyes lost in thought. Then he turned to Barrett. 'You thinking of marriage?'

'What? Marriage? What is that? A noose around your neck that never kills you but just stops you from being alive.' He quoted his father's words back to him.

'Eh,' his father said. 'I know when you're planning something. It's a woman.'

'No. It's not.' Barrett met his father's eyes.

'You've never been as good a liar as I am. I'll tell her what you're really like.'

Barrett didn't speak.

'You can't marry,' his father said. 'You're not my legitimate son. If you marry, I'll tell the world.'

'It doesn't matter now. No proof, either way. They'll say you're insane.'

'No. I'm mad.' He laughed. 'It sounds better.'

'So it does,' Barrett said and put the food on the table at his side. He rested in the chair, letting his eyes close while he listened to his father muttering.

A pillow flew by his head and he picked it up and tossed it back on to the bed.

He stared at his father. 'This may be your house, but that doesn't matter as I've taken it from you. This is your house in name only. I've lived in it my whole life and it is as much mine as yours. Summers and Nettie are loyal to me and I can make sure the new servants they've hired are as well.'

'I kept the wrong child,' his father sneered. 'And I should have tossed you under the wheels of a carriage.'

'Too late now.' Barrett smiled. 'I'm not walking in front of any carriages with you around.'

Barrett dozed throughout the night and opened his eyes once when the sun rose, then he drifted back to sleep.

A sound woke Barrett, but he didn't move. He heard his father leaving the bed, slipping out the door and shutting it with a quiet snap. Five times he'd baited the trap and five times his father had slept through the night and long into the morning.

He opened his eyes and looked at the empty bed, waiting, hoping he'd hired just the right man.

He rested one elbow on the chair arm and his forefinger over his lip, then he leaned back and shut his eyes, waiting for footsteps.

When he heard running on the stairs, he kept his eyes closed until the door opened.

He stood, internally braced.

His father walked in with a smirk on his face. 'I brought the magistrate, Barrett.' He turned to the weathered man with him. The man took in three breaths without releasing any air when he looked at Barrett.

The Viscount pointed to Barrett. 'I want him out of the house. Now.'

The magistrate looked like he'd rather be in a fiery pit at that moment. 'Begging your pardon, Mr Barrett, but I believe the Viscount has a right to his own house. If I'm not mistaken, it is his house.'

Barrett looked at the magistrate. 'You've known of his rages.'

'Not a crime in a man's own house.' The magistrate paused.

'Entailed,' the Viscount snapped. 'And a good thing, too. He would have robbed me of it if he could. He's always hated me and I've done the best for him. He's wanted for nothing.'

'I've increased your fortune tenfold,' Barrett snapped at his father. 'I've robbed nothing from you. Only added to it.'

'Only for yourself.' The Viscount raised a fist. 'Only for yourself. You took my money little by little. I didn't see it happening until a few years ago. As soon as I realised what was going on, you locked me in a room and brought people in to keep me there. You gave my staff a choice, be loyal to you or they would be out of a job. Well, things are changing.'

'Mr Barrett. If you won't go, I'll have to get some

help.' The magistrate spoke. 'A man has a right to live in his own home.'

'And take those little rats with you. Summers and Nettie,' his father called out. 'I can't stand the sight of them.' The Viscount trembled in his excitement.

'You can't keep me from here,' Barrett said. 'I'll be back.' He stood, unmoving except for his lips, and he stared at his father. 'Your blood is in my veins and my grandmother's blood as well. Take that for what it's worth.'

The magistrate reached for Barrett's arm. 'This is a sad day when a son acts so to his father. You can't threaten a viscount in his house. Or lock him in.' He jerked Barrett's arm. 'You'll leave now and I'll see that you won't be back.'

Their steps thudded down the stairs and to the front entrance. The new butler gave a nod as Barrett walked by and the new housekeeper stood just beyond his shoulder, the scar above her eye telling of her youth on the docks.

After they stepped through the door, and before they moved in sight of his father's windows, Barrett turned to the little man. 'Are you certain you can watch over him?'

The man grinned at Barrett, but he didn't loosen the hold on his arm. 'Yes. I've spent my life fighting bigger men than me. I did as you said and hired two others. With that and the new servants you have inside the house, he shouldn't move a whisker without us knowing. I'll be sure to convince him just as you said. He'll believe we're protecting him from you.'

'If he starts getting difficult, get a message to me

and I'll visit, and you can toss me out again. I'll raise a bigger conflagration than any he's ever done.'

The magistrate moved closer to Barrett. 'Don't worry, he'll hear no good of you from my lips.'

Barrett nodded and stepped in the direction of the street, out from the eaves of the house, and could feel his father's eyes staring into his back. Jerking his arm from the magistrate's hand, Barrett stalked away from the man. 'Leave me be,' Barrett called out. 'You're making a mistake.'

'Nothing worse than an ungrateful son,' the magistrate shouted after Barrett. 'The Viscount deserves better than you.'

Barrett didn't look back. Freedom burst into his veins. He turned his head down and kept his feet steady as he walked away, each step leaving his past behind. He'd been released from his gaol. His lips turned up and he lowered his gaze more, not wanting anyone to see anything different.

Annie. He could hardly wait to see her.

Chapter Nineteen

'Mr Barrett is here,' the maid said, walking to stand by Mr Carson's chair. 'The sitting room.'

Annie looked up from her breakfast. Both her father and mother looked at the maid and then back at Annie.

Annie's eyes widened. She'd been thinking of him all morning. She'd received a gift from him two days earlier with a brief note wishing her well. She was certain the man of affairs had picked out the small statuette of an angel. The note had been all the style of Barrett, hoping it found her in good spirits and with warmest regards.

Warmest regards.

She was fairly certain he meant it.

In fact, she imagined him pausing as he wrote it and trying to decide if it was too much sentiment.

'Well, I know he's not here to see me,' her mother said, dotting her mouth with her napkin. 'He did not want to dance with me last week. The cad.'

'I suppose that would leave Annie.' Her father peered at her. 'Let's see what he wants.'

She stood, gripping her napkin, holding the fabric tight.

'I don't think he holds you in warmest enough regards,' her mother said.

Annie tensed. She knew her mother would not expend herself to look through Annie's things and Annie had only told Myrtle.

'I'm not really pleased with his inability to see what a treasure you are, Annie. If you don't get a proposal from him and he doesn't fall to your feet and kiss your slippers after not seeing you for so many days, I'd doubt that regard just a bit.' She stared at her daughter, clenching her teeth between each word. 'And if you kiss his boots, you'll be kissing them the rest of your life and, I assure you, you will get tired of the taste of leather.'

Her mother stood, took her father's arm and the three of them moved to the sitting room.

Barrett stood, completely lost to her behind the distant look in his eyes.

'I'm no longer living at my father's house,' he spoke to Annie, then turned to her father. 'I've told my man of affairs, and then I realised there was only one other person I wanted to tell.'

Her father looked at her. 'I suppose that would be you because I don't particularly care where he lives.' He took his wife's arm. Her mother glared at Barrett and marched out of the room.

Annie closed the distance between them. 'Why did you decide to leave?'

'As it stands, he threw me out.'

She tightened her hand around the napkin. 'Your father? Threw you out?'

'He had the magistrate do it.' Barrett held out a hand little higher than his shoulder. 'A man twice my age and half my size. I know when I'm outmatched. I left.'

He threw his head back and looked above. 'But he was in on my plan. I hired a new butler and a house-keeper, then instructed them to give me a mild criticism in my father's hearing while I was away from him. Nothing too severe to raise his suspicions.'

'Where are you going to live?' She knew. She knew when she looked in his eyes he would propose to her that very day.

'There's a small town house, hardly bigger than your attic. Overpriced. I bought it. The roof leaked and the rugs were stained, but furniture will be delivered to the lower storey by tonight. I've arranged that it will be finished within a month, though preparations are in place to fix the worst problems today.'

She waited, expecting the question, straightening the cloth in her hands.

'It's as if a weight is off my shoulders,' he said.

'Have you put your difficulties with your father behind you?' She folded the cloth, then tightened her hand around it, uncaring that it needed to be cleaned.

'I'm leaving my father to his own devices. If he doesn't survive, I've accepted that. Without me, he would have drunk too much, murdered someone or been murdered. When I left him on his own, even for a short time, he always caused more trouble than I wished to deal with.'

His father would be a part of Barrett's life as long as he lived. Her father still talked of his parents and they had been gone a long time. 'You can't get away from him completely and stay in London.'

'I know.' He walked to the window and then back to the place he'd stood an instant before. 'I could have done this years ago. But it was as if I couldn't see it until after I left your room. It's not that I ever cared about him. It's duty. Instilled in my being. A son to his father. And I am his son. I can't step away from it, but I don't have to let it take my life from me. He is my father.' He shook his head. 'I suppose it is part of being a man's heir. The bloodlines connect you even when nothing else does.'

'Or perhaps it really is a love deeper than you can feel.'

He smiled, whimsy in his face, then his eyes narrowed and he shook his head. 'No. I know what I feel deeply for him and it isn't love.'

Perhaps he didn't intend to ask her to marry him. In that moment, a proposal stopped mattering to her.

He looked at her, but she knew he didn't only see her. He saw too much of his own past.

'I'm not living under his roof any more. I overstayed my welcome from the moment of my birth, or I was just someone he could use.'

She considered what it would be like to live a life with a man who carried such scars he couldn't see past them.

'I have treated him fine,' he said. 'That doesn't mean I want to see him every day of my life, or even once a year.'

She looked down at the cloth, aware of a place where the hem was coming unstitched.

'I had to get out of his house to even consider your

being a part of my world. You haven't learned from birth to avoid the bites. A child raised in the countryside learns what stings, what bites and to watch where it puts its foot down. In London, we learn who to avoid. How to avoid cutpurses. It is second nature. Survival. You learn early or you die.'

'So you learned early what stung and bit.' He'd mentioned considering her as a part of his world. She didn't think that counted as a kiss to her slippers.

'I learned early to sting and bite.'

She waited, the silence ticking in her head along with the grandfather clock in the room.

'I'm thinking of marriage.' He spoke, each word precise.

She put her hand to her throat. 'So am I, by coincidence. Although we may not be thinking of the same marriage.'

His eyes tightened and his stance widened.

'Do you plan to pick me for the vase on the shelf? The marriage on the ledger books?' she asked.

'No.'

'You've told me you learned the movements society expected from you. Perhaps you learned this even from the womb. And I believe you watch others. You mimic the kindness and it works to get what you want. You are every moment the predator, watching the prey. Do you care for me at all? I mean, much like a favourite coat? As much as your man of affairs and his ledger books?'

Annie's words thundered inside him. He'd expected her to be pleased. To be happy. He had her blasted pin in his waistcoat pocket.

How could she ask such a thing? Of course he cared for her. He had since he saw her wrist and heard her voice. He reached for her hands and took them in his own.

'I want to watch over you every day. To protect you. I cannot walk away from you. Not even now. I have to see you safe. It is as if you're in my veins.'

She stepped back, her hands leaving his, and a cool draught wafting where her touch had been. 'Um... those veins that carry your father's blood?' she asked.

Her words jabbed into him like a knife.

He reached a hand out again, hardly believing Annie could say such a thing.

She took another step away. 'You see me as a weakling. Just as you did your mother. A helpless person. A person whose life ended badly because she went into a world of evil she didn't expect. I'm not so weak as you think I am.'

'You must be strong to be in my world.'

'I'm not so sure a woman has to be sturdy to be your wife. Perhaps she needs to be innocent and weak. That way, you can always protect her and keep her in your grasp.'

'I see nothing wrong with wanting to protect you.' He could not marry anyone he wouldn't want to protect. 'I've protected Nettie from my father's rages. I would have protected anyone who needed it.'

'Life is not a battle. Not always.'

'Not for you. Your father and his funds have been between you and the world. Locks on doors have kept you safe. You haven't been tempered by the fire that strengthens armour.'

'You didn't marry Madeline. I've seen her before.

She is perhaps a female version of you. More concerned with what the people around her can do for her than anything else.'

He looked at Annie. He agreed with her assessment of Madeline. She didn't need him as Annie did. Annie was so frail she had no idea of how weak she was. Believing herself strong, yet little more than a puff of wind could topple her.

'You think you are doing the honourable thing, by offering marriage and protection,' she said. 'I am another person for you to watch over. You took care of your brother, his sister and your father, and now you are planning to take care of me.'

He walked around Annie and moved to the curtains, only slightly open. He pushed back the cloth. Light washed into the room. He saw nothing beyond the panes.

He took a quick look over his shoulder and Annie still examined him. He turned his back to her, something he never did when another person was in the room.

'Duty. Honour. I have my father's honour as well.'

She waited.

'Yes. Oddest honour. If he blackmails someone and they do as he wishes, he doesn't expose them. I once asked him why. He said that if he had a reputation as someone who released information after being paid to keep quiet, then his threats would lose their effectiveness.'

'And you? Your honour? What honour do you have? Truly? Inside you?'

'I didn't want to be a better person than my father. I only wanted to best him.'

'Even in his dishonesty.'

He untangled the cord at the side of the curtains. 'I wanted to best him. In all ways. And I must keep out of a gaol to do so.' He stepped away from the light, letting the shadows surround him. 'My brother, Gavin, did convince me that, with his help, I would not need to do anything that might warrant investigation into my life. Before his mother died, she had managed to provide for them, but she'd become too ill and could no longer sell her body as she had. The life had worn her down.

'Gavin wanted the respectability. He told me I teetered too close to the edge. A simple stumble and too much would collapse. He told me that my father waited for a misstep. Wanted me to destroy myself. I listened, because he was right. I couldn't risk stumbling, because then my father would win.'

'Family is not a competition.'

'It is the first competition, perhaps. The competition for a person's attention who sees you as a parasite who must be weaned away.'

She didn't move.

'My family was not like that.'

'I know. Normal. Boring. Your sisters were like little goslings tumbling out of the nest, to be led around with a mother at the front and father at the rear, or something similar. And then they fled the nest.'

'You do not even know what a good man is. You see compassion and all things decent as weaknesses.'

'Life is too short to be good. Success is not for the weak.'

'It isn't that you're a prisoner in your father's world.'

She put her hand on his forearm. 'You are a prisoner in your own world. There's only one person in it.'

Cold chills started at his heart and reverberated inside him. He stepped forward and touched her shoulder, and warmth replaced all the coldness in his body.

For all that he told her about his uncaring heart and his lack of compunction to do anything but make a profit, this woman did something to him in a way that Madeline never had. Madeline would have been the perfect wife should he ever need a smiling face to help him administer poison in any form—powder, penned or behind the back.

Annie didn't even know poison existed. She'd never truly discovered how to manoeuvre and manipulate, which fascinated him and made her an easy target in his world.

'You have now decided to be married,' she said.

She dropped the cloth in her hands. Just dropped it to the floor. That was not indicative of a yes to his proposal.

He had to explain to her just how much he needed her.

'I've been alone all that I can remember. Even when my mother was alive, I only saw her in short moments. She wed my father for his money and paid with her life. I would not have a marriage like that, Annie. You would always be safe.'

'I will consider that.'

He relaxed, but then the inner voice inside him warned him not to.

'I can give you everything, Annie. I can. Easy enough. Marry me. I'm going to have a home. I've purchased it already and you can furnish it as you wish.'

* * *

'This is easier to refuse than the dance.' She looked at the spot on the third finger of her left hand and held out her closed hand. 'I won't be having time for a marriage.' She looked inside her hand as she opened it. Still empty. 'I was thinking about getting a new sofa for the attic room and that will be keeping me busy.'

'I never thought to be refused,' he said. His eyes flickered. 'I have never been refused an indecent proposal and the only decent one I've made, I am turned down, if I understand you correctly.'

'Well…' she turned and moved to the door '…you do come a close second to a new sofa, but you lose out terribly when compared with the attic.'

She walked out, shoulders up, chin high, opened the attic door and went up the stairs. She moved over to the warped pillow on the tattered easy chair, and fluffed it.

She could move back to her own rooms any time. She was sure of that. But the windows gave her a better view of the world as it passed her by.

She had refused a marriage proposal, if one could call it that. She had doomed herself to spinsterhood. She'd chosen a sofa over Barrett.

Remembering the wallflowers, she sighed, wondering if she'd regret the refusal.

Sitting in the tattered chair, she closed her eyes. Love turned her brain to mush, just as she'd feared it would. Just as it had worked on her parents and her sisters. She wasn't any different than they were.

But she refused to be a jot on the marriage ledger.

She pressed her lips together. No man or woman could ever say she'd wed to get out of an attic or out of her parents' house.

Without the love she wanted, on her own terms, she would choose to live alone.

The pain growing in her heart and spreading throughout her body would fade, eventually. Barrett would become a memory and she would refuse to let it grow larger or take up any more room than a speck of dust. He'd been an adventure. A moment of freedom. A chance to dance.

And if her sisters returned, she would hold her chin high and lead them along a stronger path. They would never know the pain had writhed inside her as well. She'd be their example and push away their suffering while concealing her own. They'd never know.

Picking up her notebook, she began making a list of all the reasons she could be happy in her attic room the rest of her life…

None.

She could not jot down one. Her own ledger book was empty.

When Barrett's anger faded, he looked at the open book on his new desk. The numbers made no sense, and with good reason. They were not the right ones, or were they? He wasn't sure. He closed the book.

What didn't smell of mildew in the room smelled of paint. The rotted boards would be replaced soon and he'd thought to have that done by the time of his marriage.

That had not worked out as expected. Perhaps he would have had better luck had he been the third son of a duke and could speak a phrase in six languages.

His man of affairs chattered away about the new house while sitting on an overturned box.

He could still imagine Annie's wrist the first time he'd seen her and the weepy look in her eyes when she looked at him the last time, before her anger flared. *Sofa?*

He'd been honest and she hadn't believed him. If he'd lied, she would have believed it.

He'd not lied to himself and thought all he did was for someone else. Everything he did was for the last number on the last column at the end of a ledger.

Money was the root of all power and the only way of keeping Annie secure. Without properties, he could do nothing for her. Without properties, he was nothing.

Even sending Gavin to university had, in some deep part of Barrett, been the beginnings of gaining a true foothold in the world.

Thinking back now, he was pleased Annie refused him. His life would be simpler. He would find someone less innocent and be honest with her, and he doubted he'd be refused a second time. He didn't need such innocence. Another Madeline would suit him well, assuming he could marry her without becoming ill.

But just the thought of getting a marriage licence with anyone but Annie's name on it bit into him like lye scalding him from the inside.

He put his elbow on the table and put his forehead in his palm.

If he'd never found out about Madeline and he'd married her, then none of this would have happened with Annie.

But he could never wish it away.

He would carry this inside him forever and, no matter how alone he felt, the memory of Annie would be with him always.

He slid his hand down and cupped his head while raising his eyes.

The man across the room still talked.

Barrett interrupted. 'And a sofa.'

The man's mouth paused and he stared at Barrett.

'Did we decide on that?' Barrett asked.

'You said you preferred to go without one for a bit.'

'Two. Muted colours on one for the main sitting room. Do whatever it takes to get flowery print on the other.'

Then he paused. 'Just one for me,' he said. 'Deliver the other one to Mr Carson's house. He needs one for the upper storey. The one with the flowery print.'

The man of affairs wrinkled his brow.

'Yes. The sofa with a flowery print.' He'd give Annie a gift to remember him by. Flowers. And her sofa. 'Delicate flowers in some comfortable colour, if such a thing exists. Be sure to send the furniture to the Carson household and be absolutely certain a note is included that it is for the attic room.' He looked at the pen. 'Wait. I'll pen the note now.'

'If this is for a woman,' the man of affairs inserted, 'please consider putting a bit more, um, inflection than in the last one.'

'What was wrong with it?' Barrett raised his eyes. 'I wrote it and signed it.'

'Yes, Mr Barrett. I watched when you wrote it. But in my courtship, my wife preferred something a bit more admiring in the note.'

He touched the pen to the ink, eyes narrowing in question. 'With warmest admiration?'

'Well, I suppose we would not want to risk being too sentimental.'

'You saw how Napoleon's letters were bandied about. Such nonsense.'

'You can trust me that you will never have to worry about that.'

'Fine,' Barrett said, tossing the pen aside, listening to the clatter. 'Just find and deliver the sofa.'

Annie lay on the sofa. She ran a hand over the fabric, unable to see the hideous flowers on it in the darkness. Other than the design on the upholstery, she liked the furniture.

All her life she'd watched other people. Her parents. Her sisters. Cousins. They'd all seemed impulsive. Always acting smitten when they thought they were in love. She just felt betrayed, abandoned and lost. She'd not let her heart rule her head. She'd not expected to feel so miserable.

She'd thought she was chasing freedom when she left her parents' house with the old woman, but she'd found it in Barrett's arms and, just as he'd said, it had turned to dust in the light.

That mindless world of feelings that she'd always looked down her nose at other people for experiencing had opened inside her. And now she felt it and wanted nothing more than to be with Barrett.

But not as a jot on a ledger sheet.

Not as an adventure.

The mindlessness had invaded her. Lying on the sofa made her feel close to him. She existed just to think of him. Love had hit her, and she didn't know what to do with it. That mindless insensibility of warmest regards.

Only something so senseless as love would make

her do such a thing as to refuse his proposal. If they'd met properly and he'd danced a few reels with her and then proposed, she likely would have accepted and moved happily into his house and his ledger book.

Barrett had sent her a sofa when it would have been so much easier for him just to say he loved her. An easy lie.

He'd told her that his father had locked him in the cellar. She doubted he'd ever get out.

Chapter Twenty

Barrett stood at the side of the dance floor, a glass in his hand. Gavin hadn't stopped his visits to the Carson household. Afterwards, he would trot right over to Barrett's and give a detailed accounting of what was happening behind those closed doors—just as he had before Barrett and Annie had met.

Barrett had nearly ground his teeth to the bone trying to decide whether or not to forbid Gavin to speak of the Carsons again. But he couldn't.

And now Barrett stood in a duke's house, watching three of the four sons being ever so ducal and thoughtful to all the guests, one of whom was particularly unaware of his presence.

Annie stood with a group of women and didn't look his way. The women's conversation appeared whispered with their faces close together. He noticed an irritated head swagger occasionally from one of the women. He imagined someone getting verbally skewered, although he didn't think it was him. But from the dark glittering eyes and the deep conversation, he doubted the words were kind.

Mr Carson walked up to Barrett, filling the air with the scent of shaving soap. He cleared his throat.

'The sofa arrived a few days ago.' He raised a brow. 'I tried to send it away, but the men claimed they'd not made a mistake. Annie took it.' He shook his head. 'I couldn't imagine…the colour of it.' He touched the side of his neck with one finger, loosening his cravat. 'I would happily have it corrected, but Annie refuses. There is a defect in the upholstery. I'm sure of it.'

'It was a gift to her. She said she needed a sofa for the attic.'

Carson looked at his daughter, whispering with the others. 'Probably wasn't as wise as you'd thought to teach her to fight back.'

'Go to the devil,' Barrett said.

Carson smiled. 'You should have crawled on your knees to get her to marry you.'

Barrett turned to Carson. 'Yes. Across broken glass. But I doubt she would have noticed.'

Carson's eyes wavered at the words, uncertain. He sniffed, then moved to his wife and took her to the dance floor as a new song began.

Too late to start the dance, Annie wandered over to the man with the red face. Barrett caught his eye and gave the man a glare. From what Barrett could surmise, the man seemed reluctant to speak with Annie. He kept looking Barrett's way.

Her eyes narrowed and she glanced at Barrett. He felt himself being impaled from across the room. He nodded to her. Her gaze sharpened even more.

She strode over to Lord Richard and had less wallflower and more warrior in her stance.

Lord Richard held out an arm to her and her smile

beamed. It might not have reached her eyes, though. Those eyes, he thought, had a bit of spite in them.

He hated to think how she would be looking at him had he not asked her to marry him.

She danced with Lord Richard, speaking rapidly to him, and when the dance finished she left him. She found the wallflowers and took a glass of punch to each of them. The women's eyes widened as they took the first sip. One coughed. The hostess was not known for having watered-down punch. And then Annie began herding them, or that's how it looked. She moved them closer to Lord Richard and his cronies.

The next dance, all the wallflowers had partners and Annie had another glass of the punch.

'I wouldn't drink so much of that if I were you,' Barrett said, after walking to her.

'I'm having a good time. I refuse not to enjoy myself.' She took another sip, answering him but ignoring him as well. 'It tastes like something you'd put in a lamp, so it must be good.'

'Did you get the flowers I sent?'

'Yes. I sat on them.' She glanced across the floor, seemingly enthralled by every dance step.

'Would you like to waltz with me?'

'No. I have other plans. Punch, and a lot of it.'

'One waltz.'

'I've done that. The joy I felt then could never be exceeded. Anything else will be dull by comparison. Businesslike, you could say.' She took another sip. 'Now, please pardon me, I have duties to attend to.'

'Husband-hunting?'

She pressed her lips close together. She put the glass in his hand and patted the back of his fingers around it. 'I could marry if I choose to. If I can persuade the men to dance with the wallflowers and have everyone smiling, then I would imagine I can garner a proposal. But the attic has more to offer.'

He looked at the empty glass and then at her eyes.

'No one is going to rob me of a moment of my happiness. Your father robbed you of your childhood. Don't let him rob you of your life. Don't give him the power to keep taking. You're not a child any more and neither am I.' She stuck her chin as near his as she could get. 'Your father preys on the weaker, does he not?'

Barrett nodded.

'Well, that lets me out.' She cocked her head to one side. 'I'm not weak. And as the days have passed, I've only got stronger. The one who has the power to walk away can make the better deal.'

'I'd like to know your terms.'

'I'll draw up something.'

She took a step, wavered and put a hand on his arm. 'I don't know if I have the power to walk away right at this moment. The punch was toxic.'

He put his hand over hers. 'Then stand with me and I'll enjoy your company for a while. I do want to know your terms, Annie.'

'I shall give them to you.' She wavered. 'But not now. The room is spinning and there's two of you, and they both annoy me.'

'I will call on you tomorrow.'

'Not at four a.m. Front door. Reasonable time.'

Barrett walked into Annie's house. The butler accepted him as a member of the household, taking his hat and moving to put it away, and led him to the sitting room.

Within minutes he was in the sitting room with Mr Carson.

'I'm here to see Annie.'

Carson interlaced his fingers over his waistcoat and his eyes, from his sitting position, peered down on Barrett. 'She's out shopping. With her mother. You must have really angered her. She never shops with her mother. They even took the physician, claiming she has some disease that might flare up. I think she was punishing him for something.'

'I'll wait.'

'Ah, go right ahead,' Carson said, raising both palms. 'She's much more like her mother than it appears. My muddle-headed wife with delicate feet isn't really so muddle-headed.' He lowered his chin, but raised his glance to the ceiling and settled back into the chair, hands clasped over his stomach. 'So should we talk about my business?'

'I'd rather not.'

'The weather?'

Barrett levelled a stare at him. 'If you wish.'

Carson began speaking, but within minutes the one-sided conversation had turned to Annie, and Carson recounted his memories of his daughter's childhood.

Barrett leaned forward, listening, the words resounding inside him. He'd never imagined such a world of sunshine and roses and posies. Carson grabbed a handkerchief and dotted his eyes once.

Annie's world. Suddenly, he knew how to win her. He knew how to win her heart. He swallowed.

He spoke just enough to keep Carson talking of Annie.

But then Carson wound down and he leaned back in the chair, shutting his eyes, yawning and clasping his fingers together.

When Annie finally walked into the sitting room, Barrett stood. Her father sat in the chair across from Barrett, arms crossed, head drooping. He opened his eyes, then pushed himself up with his hands on his knees.

'I'm sure there is more conversation to be had here, but not by me,' her father said, eyes showing his age, plus a few years. 'Come along, Mrs Carson.' He held out his arm for her. 'I'm going to go for a walk.' He complained as he walked down the hall, 'I have been conversing with Barrett to kill time until Annie arrived and, to my utter dismay, he didn't leave.'

Mrs Carson clasped his arm and stepped along with him. 'The shopping trip was not as much fun as your discussion, I'd wager.'

The physician remained in the room. He put his hand on the back of the chair. 'Oh joy. The love-smitten couple.'

Annie shot him a glance and so did Barrett.

'I suppose I should leave before I am impaled by your eyes. Um…too late.' He bowed, moving backwards. 'I have feet to rub.' Before leaving, he gave a long look at Barrett. 'Thank you for that, by the way.'

Annie realised her life had changed forever. Barrett, who had always been an apparent wall of impassibility, had changed also. Some of the lines at his eyes had softened and now she might believe him under thirty.

'I don't think he's as nice as I thought him,' Annie said of Gavin as he stepped out of the room.

'No, Miss Carson,' Gavin called over his shoulder. 'I am not.'

Barrett shut the door. 'No one is as nice as you think them.'

She examined his face. 'Did you select the sofa?'

'I've not seen it.'

'Oh, you must.' She opened the door and looked out to make sure Gavin was gone. When she didn't see him, she clasped Barrett's hand and took him up the stairs.

Opening the door, she led him into the room.

'That is the ugliest piece of furniture I have ever seen.' He walked forward, examining the flowers, which looked more like bright weeds, and the vines, which appeared to be choking the blooms into submission. He raised his eyes to her. 'I saw the bill. I paid good money for this.'

'You were robbed.'

'Quite badly.' He ran a hand along the fibres. 'But on the good side, this is the only such furniture in London. I have been assured of that. Plus, it doesn't bite.'

He walked to the window and did not look at her. 'I do beg your pardon for the sofa. Though I think I must ask for a gift from you.' He didn't look out the window and he didn't seem to be looking anywhere. 'I never told anyone my mother's last words,' he said to Annie. 'I don't know if I imagined them, but I don't believe I did.'

Then he turned to her. 'She mouthed the words *Help me.* I couldn't move at first. It seemed the world stopped—but I ran to her and I didn't know that she was injured so badly. I thought she would tell me what to do next. She never said another word.'

He held out his hand, palm open. 'Help me. I don't know how to love. I don't know how to have the family you accept so easily that you would try to escape it. Give me direction and I will take it.'

She moved forward, touching his fingertips. 'You make me sound selfish, taking for granted what you never had.'

'Perhaps we can both help each other. I can help you see the wonder of a family and you can help me have a family. A real one. Not a purchased one.'

She clasped her fingers around his hand, resting her forehead on his shoulder. 'Your business can never come before me in your heart and I don't know if you know how to put anyone else first.'

'I understand.' He did. The last few days he had not been able to think of anyone or anything but Annie. She'd filled every moment of his thoughts while he waited—trying to figure out how to reach her and how to win the woman of his heart. 'I have not cared at all for a single moment of work because I could only think of you.'

He pulled her into his arms. 'If I don't have you in my life, Annie, then nothing else matters.'

'I love you,' she answered, and her thoughts didn't fall away. She didn't turn into a shadow of herself. She'd never felt so aware and so alive.

He stepped back, eyes locked on hers. 'I will love you with every beat of my heart for the rest of my life. I have never loved anyone before and did not know what pain was until I felt you did not want to be with me.'

He held her so tightly that she could feel both their hearts beating together, and she shut her eyes.

Moving back, he took her jewelled hairpin from his waistcoat pocket and held it to her hair.

The tip of it brushed her temple, sending shivers into her body as he wove it into place, moving it slowly among the locks. 'I always imagine it in your hair.'

With the gentleness of strength, he took her face in his hands and kissed an even softer brush against her lips.

When he stepped back, he reached again into his pocket. He held a ring, with rubies and sapphires, the same as she had in her hairpin.

'Will you marry me?'

He took her hand and slid the ring on her finger. 'I plight thee my troth. I give you my loyalty borne of love and my faith in your heart, and I put my own heart at your feet, because nowhere else will it rest.'

He closed her hand over the ring. 'Even if you say no, you have a symbol of my love to hold inside your clasp forever.'

Chapter Twenty-One

Annie knew Barrett should be at his appointment to receive the special licence and she moved back to her room, shutting the door firmly behind her, anxious for the moment that she would marry Barrett. From her sitting room, she walked to the bedchamber. Myrtle was to be along any minute to help Annie with the corset.

She pulled the dress she was to wear from the wardrobe.

Her outer door clicked and she didn't turn around. A chill settled over her, warning her.

She heard footsteps but didn't turn, pretending that fear wasn't invading her body. 'The pearls with it?' she asked, trying to think of what weapon she might have at her disposal.

'I don't think you'll need them, you little society twit.' A bony hand clamped on her upper arm. An old man's voice rasped in her ear, chilling her as the scent of his breath choked her. 'You're not taking my son from me.' He jerked her backwards, causing her to stumble and her dressing gown to tangle in her legs. 'He's all I have.'

Barrett's father breathed in lunging gasps.

Her throat tightened and she scrambled, her legs working to put her feet on the floor. Her thoughts raced ahead into nothingness, but she forced them back, urging herself to think. His arms held her vice-like and he used all his strength, hauling her back.

She remembered what Barrett had taught her and, the moment she regained her balance, she struggled to collect her wits and her strength. She made a fist with her right hand, clamped her left over it, twisted by bending a knee to drop her weight and shoved her elbow straight back with all her might. 'No,' she shouted. 'No.'

A crack sounded.

An *ooft*.

And a dead weight hit her shoulders and she stumbled forward, out from under the falling form of the old man. He crumpled and she ran to the door. When she opened it, she realised he wasn't behind her and he thrashed on the floor. He grasped where her elbow had connected.

'You broke my ribs.' He lay on his back, clasping his side. 'Help. Help.' He croaked out the words while he writhed. His cries for help lessened to a whimper.

'Don't you ever touch me again.' She stood at the doorway, ready to run.

'You heathen witch,' he spat out. 'You vile...' His eyes narrowed. 'You're just like my mother was.' He stopped, falling back to the floor, writhing. 'Someone. Get the physician. I'm dying,' he called out again and then gasped at the pain.

He shut his eyes, whispering through the pain. 'You will be a perfect wife for my son. Your children will be little monsters.' He smiled, eyes watering. 'They'll carry the family line. My legacy will continue.'

Barrett crashed into the doorway, jerking Annie aside, moving her further from his father. He turned her to face him. 'What happened?'

Annie couldn't speak.

'The woman. She hit me.'

Anger formed in Barrett's eyes. He moved towards his father.

Annie jumped between them. 'No, Barrett.'

'You keep her away from me,' his father shouted. 'She attacked me for no reason. She broke my ribs.'

Barrett took her arm. 'What happened?'

'He came up behind me and I hit him. I did hear a crack. I may have hurt him.'

'You did,' the Viscount said, grasping his side. 'It hurts when I breathe.'

Barrett pulled her close, holding her against him.

'Who let you in?' His question thundered in the air to his father.

'No one. The window was open below stairs. I was just going to wish her happiness with you.'

'No, he wasn't.'

Barrett put an arm around her. 'I know how he twists things, Annie. It's always the way of someone like him. The bigger the lie of blame they can place on the innocent person, the more they like it. It's not just with his fists he attacks, but with his lies and anything his mind can grasp.'

Gavin dashed into the room. 'I heard a thump. It jarred the house.'

'Help me up.' The Viscount reached out a hand. 'This is turning into a family gathering.'

Gavin leaned in to reach around his father to lift him into a sitting position. The Viscount screamed in pain when Gavin lifted.

'My hip,' the old man cried out, face pale. 'Something's wrong with my hip.'

Together Barrett and Gavin lifted his father and took the man upwards and on to the bed. Gavin examined his father while Barrett turned to Annie.

'I just hit him in the stomach,' Annie said, stepping away from Barrett to rub her elbow. 'It may have—I may have hit him harder than I meant, but he startled me. My arm aches.'

'His hip is likely broken,' Gavin said over the old man's whimpers. Gavin shook his head and respect glimmered when he looked at Annie, then the old man's cries caught his attention and he turned back to his father.

'He must have done it when he fell,' Barrett said. He glanced at Annie. 'How hard did you hit him?'

'I just barely—I don't know.' She touched her elbow. 'It does feel a bit tender.' She reached up to her shoulder. 'And it's aching. I've practised with the maid. Trying to show her what I've learned. I couldn't think. I just reacted. I didn't mean to hurt him.'

Barrett snaked an arm around her waist and held her close. 'You fought back.'

'And I'm safe. Alive,' she said, hugging Barrett.

'Sometimes that's all that matters. Surviving. We do what we can to survive.' Barrett rocked her in his arms.

'You meant to kill me, you witch.' The old man came to life and shook a fist in the air. 'You're taking my son. My fortune. The both of you. You pretend to care, but it's all a lie.'

Annie stared at the older man. Once her eyes were on him, he wailed. He groaned with so much effort it shook his hip and made the pain worse, but he didn't stop.

The strength that had naturally been in Barrett's body his whole life left him. He could feel the power draining from his body.

He'd brought Annie into a world and taught her to fight. A woman raised to believe in goodness and beauty, and now he'd taken that from her. As clearly as a child could be taught the alphabet, he'd taught her that the world was a cruel and evil place. And he couldn't take away what he'd done.

He'd thought it for the best, but before, Annie could believe in rainbows and halos and parents who always loved their children and now he'd introduced Annie into a world of madness around her. But she'd survived. She'd shown her true strength. The one he'd been too blinded to realise that she'd had all along.

His father writhed in pain. Gavin bent over him, completely dispassionate and humming. Annie stared at them, taking in the wailing and the humming. His family.

Carson stepped into the room. 'Barrett, the magistrate is at the door looking for you. He's distraught. He said he was ambushed from behind.'

The fates his father relished had conspired again.

'Annie, I can't risk him being near you.' Barrett stepped away, moving into a cloak of his aloneness.

The wailing stopped.

'I dare say it's not as much risk as you think,' Gavin

said. 'His hip will likely not mend properly.' He shook his head. 'He's older than we realised. Frail.'

Annie studied her fist. 'I can't believe it.' She looked at Barrett. 'It worked just like you said it would.' She looked at the Viscount. 'I didn't even know what was going on when he stepped behind me.'

'I was just going to befriend her.' His father stared at Barrett. 'And she tried to kill me. The witch tried to kill me...'

Annie's mouth opened, but it took a moment for her to speak. 'I wasn't. You came in to my room. You didn't knock.'

'You attacked me,' he screamed out. 'You attacked me.'

'Nonsense,' Barrett answered. 'You always blame everyone else but yourself. Even when you know it isn't true.'

'We'll get him back to his house,' Gavin said as he and Carson stood on each side of the Viscount, 'and as soon as we get him to bed, we'll be back for the wedding.'

'No,' Barrett raised a hand. 'We're marrying first. If you wish to attend, then Father can wait. He's now invited to the wedding.'

Annie stood by the fireplace of her father's home. Barrett's father quietened and he lay on the main sitting-room sofa, apparently interested in the marriage and curious about her family.

Her mother stood at the end of it and her father turned away, sniffling.

'So the special licence is to be utilised now?' the cleric asked, standing. 'In that case, I suppose we should get on with the formalities. This couple seems to be well suited to each other.'

He smiled at Annie and Barrett. 'Should we continue? With the actual marriage?'

'I would love to,' Barrett said.

Her father sniffled again. 'It is a shame Barrett and Annie will not be having children, unless it is a miracle,' her father said. 'Much like the epidemeosis miracle cure I am just finding out about.'

Barrett smiled. 'Miracles happen every day.'

Barrett took Annie's left hand, pleased to feel not just love inside himself, but happiness and contentment. With Annie at his side, he had more strength than he'd ever expected and the wonderful feeling that he'd never need all of it.

The bitterness he'd felt at the past, some he didn't even know he'd had, had faded, because it had worked to create this moment. Without the struggles, he might not have become a man Annie could love and he might not have her by his side.

'Let's get on with the formalities, Annie. I could never again find a woman with such a strong right arm and who knows how to bargain.'

'That's true,' Annie agreed. 'I even talked Father into giving us the perfect wedding present.'

Barrett examined her face, trying to imagine what she wanted for a gift.

She smiled. 'Father is keeping the sofa.'

Epilogue

A nnie watched from the upper window of the sitting room as the servant ran from the house to the coach in the rain. He lifted the umbrella high, shielding the drops, and opened the door as her mother stepped out.

After taking her mother inside, he returned for her father.

The scent of rosewater wafted in the air. Barrett had slipped behind her.

She bent her knee, dropped her hip, stiffened her elbow in an L shape and clasped her right arm. But instead of throwing the elbow into his midsection, she threw herself into his arms. She tumbled against his chest and he captured her.

'You could just say good morning.' His voice rumbled as he rested his face against her head. Her heart tightened and a flush of love warmed her from the inside out.

'Not until you kiss me.'

He clasped her more tightly, lifted her and swung her around, rotating a full turn, taking her feet off the ground with his movement, her skirts fluttering at her slippers. As he let her feet drop to the floor and before she fully caught her balance, he quickly kissed the top of her head several times. 'Satisfied?'

Letting out a deep sigh, she leaned against him. 'For this morning.'

She heard footsteps on the stair and the Barrett she knew slipped back inside himself. He stepped away from her.

He gave a small bow to her parents as they rushed into the doorway. 'Mrs Carson. Carson.'

Her mother held a letter in her gloved hand, the felted tassels from her coat sleeve almost obscuring the missive.

'Oh, Annie.' She looked around the house, her brows furrowed. 'I like what you've done with the house. It looks so…medieval.'

'I suspect the chainmail will be finding a home elsewhere in the house,' Barrett said. 'Annie's become friends with an archaeologist and he presented it to her as a token of his appreciation for her funding his next adventure.'

'I think he had it altered especially for me. Or pieced together. I'm not sure exactly how it was constructed.'

Her mother walked over and jabbed her index finger against the metal. 'Interesting.'

'Yes.' Barrett locked his hands behind his back and looked at the floor. 'And I am not opposed to it. I just think perhaps we have a few too many artillery pieces.'

'None are functional.' Annie pointed to the spears. 'Papier mâché.'

Her mother gazed around the room. 'I suppose a future viscountess will be allowed some leeway and archaeology is a bit of a fashion at the moment.' She looked at a glass vase. 'What's that?'

'Sand. From Egypt.'

Her mother nodded while her father absently shook his head and breathed out through his nose.

'That is fascinating, but not as happy as my news.' Her mother waved the letter high, the fringe on her coat sleeve falling away. 'Laura will be here in a few months. She is returning to London.'

Her father sniffled, keeping his head low. 'All my daughters will be together again. I can hardly believe it.' When he raised his face and looked at Barrett, tears glistened in his eyes. 'Thank you for seeing that Honour is back as well. You brought my whole family together.'

'It's nothing,' Barrett said. 'Much easier than sitting with my father every few days. I appreciate that, Carson. He is calmer after your visits.'

'I rather like the Viscount.' Carson regained his composure. 'Sad his mind has waned so. You would not believe the tales he fabricates. He claims to have switched you at birth with another baby.' Carson rolled his eyes. 'Said he had another son the same age as you. Said your grandmother took one look at the new baby and made him change them back. Said you wet on him on the way home.'

'Interesting,' Barrett said.

'He's told me that story fifteen times if he's told me it once.' Carson shrugged, leaning towards Barrett and lowering his voice. 'Always laughs. Said he knew from that moment on that you'd grow up to be a son he could be proud of.'

'You do well with him,' Barrett said.

'He thinks you're married to a sorceress, though,' Carson whispered. 'I remind him you're married to our Annie, but he claims you married an evil witch with blazing eyes. He's afraid to be alone.'

'But he's doing well,' Annie said.

'Yes,' her father agreed. 'And the man knows more about financial affairs than anyone I've ever listened to.' He looked at Barrett. 'He insists I take notes and I've now filled up my first notebook. And a second one with all the tall tales. He wants them written down for a grandchild. As if I would ever show such a book to a grandchild of mine.' He touched the side of his head. 'Poor man. He's so delusional.'

'It's wonderful that you're making him contented,' Annie said.

She viewed her mother. 'The maid will be bringing us...tea...in a moment. I so like your blend. And I have teacups for each day of the week, just like you do.'

Her mother raised her chin. 'I'm so happy you are keeping the family tradition.'

Then Annie went to the tiny gong and picked up the small mallet and hit it. The ring reverberated, summoning the maid.

Barrett stared at the floor.

Her father squinted and looked at Barrett. 'That's not a family tradition. She's not the girl I raised.'

Barrett didn't lift his eyes, but Annie saw the grin. 'But it's the woman I married.'

In a few moments Myrtle walked into the room.

'Tea, please,' Annie said.

Myrtle nodded, whispering, 'And I've hid the coffee so your family will not know you're drinking the swill.'

'Thank you.'

Myrtle bowed. 'Yes, Miss Annie.'

In a few moments, she returned with the tea and the hour passed quickly with Barrett relaxing back in his chair and adding little to the chatter but a smile here and there.

'Well, we must be going,' her mother said, after finishing the tea and moving to the doorway. 'We only stopped to tell you the news about Laura. I wanted to get a toy for Honour's little one. I've heard they have cute little silver rattles and I thought it would make a lovely keepsake for Honour.' She looked around the room again. 'Lovely, dearest. Definitely suitable for a future viscountess.'

Then she scurried out, Carson behind her.

After they left, Annie walked to Barrett, slipping her arm through his. 'I thought you liked the chainmail.'

'I do. But I don't think it's appropriate for the sitting room.' He touched his upper lip, tapping. 'I've never seen how it fits on you, either. I have some ideas about that.' He walked over to examine the garment, the links slipping through his fingertips.

'There's a little warning voice in my head right now,' Annie said. 'It's telling me that your thoughts are not exactly innocent.'

He smiled and stepped to put an arm around Annie's waist. 'As I said, you should always listen to your inner voice.'

* * * * *